Kelts

Barrett Ross Akam

To Andy and Dan

Acknowledgements

I had just started to write this in early 2020 when I was laid low by an unpleasant virus which damaged the electrics in my heart. I spent ten days in Peterborough Hospital and then another ten in Papworth undergoing various investigations. Eventually I was released having had a pacemaker fitted. During those three weeks I wrote the first section of this book in my hospital bed. My thanks go to all the NHS staff I encountered during my illness for their care and courtesy. They are truly extraordinary people; every single one of them.

Many thanks to my lovely wife Hilary for reading through it all and making encouraging noises.

I am most grateful to *The Ferret,* that platform for fearless investigative journalism from where I learned about the true extent of the escapes of farmed salmon and also to *Fly Fishing & Fly Tying* just for being such an excellent magazine and from where I've included a small rewritten section of my own story, *The State of the Art.*

To quote Paul Vale´ry: "A work is never completed-merely abandoned." and so it is with this work. Proof reading is not my forte´, so any typos are all my own.

Kelt: 1 A salmon that has spawned.

2 An alternative spelling of Celt.

Preface

If, like me, you do not live by a salmon river and have to travel long distances for a few days' fishing with all the arrangements that entails, plus that interminable drive up the A9, you will know how frustrating it is to meet upon arrival, a kindly local who says, 'You should have been here last week.' So this book is partly about that idea except it's more, 'You should have been here in the seventies or eighties, it was full of fish then.' And also, more pertinently, it's about how individuals seem to be powerless in the face of huge corporations that apparently are too big to challenge. Still there is hope, and the thing is we fishermen do get lucky on occasion and success, however you define it, tastes all the sweeter for being hard won.

Barry Akam. November 2020.

1

1976

In the August of that summer unusual patterns in the jetstream had resulted in the North East of Scotland enjoying the warm and dry weather most often reserved for more southerly climes. The purple hills shimmered in an unaccustomed heat haze and the birch leaves and bracken were browning prematurely. The burns had shrunk, their stones bleaching in the sun. Only the River Skean that flowed through the small town of Strathskean and thence to the North Sea had some water, but its flow was sluggish and its level low.

On that river a mile or so upstream from the town was a little sandy beach by a large pool. On the bank was a wooden fishing hut with a red corrugated iron roof, and about it several bikes had been casually abandoned. A group of teenagers had gathered there. Some were lying on thin towels sunbathing, one or two were digging in the sand and others had collected round a small fire and were sharing cigarettes. The air was still and scented with the smoke from the fire and the cigarettes, there was the sound of happy chatter and the odd guffaw of laughter. A transistor radio played tinny pop songs, the music barely audible.

Only three of the group were in the water. The first, a tall willowy girl, was standing up to her mid calves, jeans rolled up to her knees, hands on her hips, gazing intently at two boys who were now swimming out in the centre of the pool. The boy who was furthest out was a reasonably competent swimmer, but the second, a big raw-boned youth, was clearly struggling to keep up with his companion, his arms flailing and splashing in an ungainly parody of the front crawl and his feet only just touching the slimy stones on the bottom.

'Frazer, Frazer! y'd better come back in now,' she shouted, but Frazer was suddenly out of his depth and in a second his head had disappeared beneath the surface.

A look of panic spread across her face. In that sickening instant she could see the possibility of a terrible tragedy.

'Robbie, help!' she screamed and the first swimmer turned to look back. He could not see Frazer, he could only see Mhairi's wildly waving arms and some of the others who had now stopped what they were doing and had gathered at the edge of the beach.

Robbie started to swim back, looking for Frazer. There was no sign of him, he was only aware of the others on the shore some twenty five yards distant. He ducked his head under the water. It was the colour of weak tea and it was translucent, the sunlight passing through it and dappling the stones on the bottom. Then beneath him he saw the pale body of Frazer, the arms and legs waving slowly and limply as if in some swirly dream.

He took a deep breath, jack-knifed downwards and caught Frazer by the hair. Frazer's face was all screwed up, his eyes tightly shut. A few bubbles escaped from his mouth. They were now only in about five feet of water and so Robbie, with a huge effort, was able to lever

Frazer's gangling body up to the surface and push him towards the shore.

He was met by a few of the others who had waded into the shallows to help and between them they dragged the seemingly lifeless Frazer up the beach. Two of the lads turned Frazer face down on to his front and started beating him on the back.

Frazer started coughing and then tried to sit up. His body trembling with the shock of it all.

'Whu, Whut happened?' he said, looking up at Mhairi.

He was seemingly confused, his face covered by wet ginger hair and the coarse sand of the beach.

She looked at him, her anxiety now turned to anger. 'Y' went out too far, y' fool,' she shouted, her eyes flooding with tears, 'Y' would have drowned if Robbie had no been there tae drag ye oot.'

'Aye,' said one of the lads, 'the Englishman pulled y' oot.'

Frazer turned to look at Robbie, 'Aye thanks,' he said quietly but there was a look in his eyes that was more resentment than gratitude. He got up shakily and went over to his towel and heap of clothes. He dried himself, and watched by the others in near silence, awkwardly pulled on his jeans and T shirt.

And so, chastened by the near disaster and the Sunday afternoon having lost its magic, one by one they gathered their things and headed back to their small town. For them the summer was over. Robbie was left alone on the beach. Last to leave had been Mhairi. As she got on to her bike she slung her bag over her shoulder and gave him a long look. 'See y' next summer, mebbes.' She grinned at him, tossed her auburn hair back and peddled energetically after the rest without a backward glance.

He watched her retreating figure. He was just a holiday acquaintance, just someone to hang about with, just another tourist. He was not part of her world no matter how much he would have liked to have been.

2

1971

A large woman, red of face and dressed in a stained ex army combat jacket, flowery dress and wellington boots was standing at the door of a long low cottage with dirty white walls and a rusty red corrugated iron roof. At the front of the building amongst the nettles and dock leaves rotting farm machinery was scattered randomly about, along with the rusting carcasses of two ancient vans. To the rear a line of washing flapped noisily in the stiff breeze and a dozen or so scraggy hens were pecking at the ground near a grey wooden hen house. The wind whipped her long black hair over her face and she had to hold onto the door surround to steady herself. Behind the cottage the birch and scrub gave way to moorland which ran on for dozens miles until it became the foothills of the Cairngorms. Even though it was mid May there was still some snow on the distant tops. It had been a long, cold spring.

She looked down the track which led to the farm buildings half a mile away, 'Frazer! Frazer! where the hell are ye, y' wee ...' As usual, when he was needed Frazer was nowhere to be found. He was the youngest and most wayward of her five children. She stopped in mid shout. She could now see his unmistakable figure coming up the hill.

Even at eleven years Frazer was big for his age. He moved easily over the terrain despite his ungainly gait. He wore a jacket two sizes too big for him, a pair of old jeans and wellington boots. He was carrying a couple of hazel sticks to the end of which had been tied some fishing line. When he got near the house he broke into a run. He leant the sticks against the fence. In one hand he carried a canvas bag. He held it up for his mother to see, his weather beaten face looking up at her for approval.

'Look Ma, I've got y' some troots.' He opened the bag to show her two small trout and two salmon parr.

'Good boy, Frazer.' She said distractedly. 'Hev ye seen yir Da?'

'Aye, he's doon the ferm.'

'Well go and get him wid y'. We have a letter from the council. Ah hope it's whit w've bin waitin' for.'

Frazer left the bag and the sticks by the door and shambled off back down the track towards the farm.

Soon he found himself in the muddy farmyard which was noisy with the bellowing of cattle coming in from the fields for the morning milking. Directing operations was a tall man with a craggy scowl of a face and an angular bony figure. He was leaning on a stick and watching the cattle. Every now and then he would raise the stick and shoo a beast in the direction of the byre.

'Aye, son whit is it?' growled Frazer's dad as he turned towards his son.

'Ma wants yer,' Frazer said, looking up at his father, 'yon letter's come.'

'Tell yer ma I'll be up directly,' he said not taking his eyes off the beasts as they made their ponderous way into the dark building.

The Rosses had been waiting for years for a council house. All Frazer's life had been spent in the tied cottage at the top of Glen Caoraich. The cottage came with Jim Ross's job as the farm's cattle man. They had brought up their family there, now they had a chance of leaving it for a modern council house in the town, a few miles down the strath.

Up to then life had been difficult for the family; the cottage was in a remote location at the end of a rough farm track and in the long highland winter the house was cold, dark and damp. Downstairs there was a living room with an open hearth, a small kitchen and a recently added bathroom. Upstairs there were two small bedrooms, Frazer's two sisters had shared one and Frazer and his two older brothers had the other. Frazer's mother and father slept on the sofa bed downstairs. More recently, however, Frazer's brothers had left home and were working in the oil industry up the coast in Inverness and this had led to some easing of the accommodation problem but there was still a desperate need for a move.

Jim Ross arrived half an hour later, his big frame filling the doorway. He held out his hand. His wife handed him the letter, wordlessly he took it to the lamp, ripped open the envelope and with little expression studied its contents. His features relaxed, he turned and looked at his wife. It was great news, the family could move into a three bedroom council house at the end of the month.

'Are w' moving then Da?' Frazer asked, somewhat apprehensively. His whole life had been spent in that cottage and in that glen.

'Aye, w' are son,' he said moving towards the sideboard and removing a bottle of single malt and a couple of glasses. He half filled them and handed one to his wife.

'Slàinte, aboot bloody time too. Here's tae us!' Frazer left his parents to their celebration and went out into the bright light of the May morning. The air was alive with the sound of birdsong and the birch trees were just coming into leaf, their delicate green leaflets shivering in the stiff breeze. His mind was in a whirl, for he did not want to leave Glen Caoraich.

Outside the cottage and to the left of the farm track, a smaller trail led downwards through the birch and heather into the tiny and overgrown world of the Caoraich burn. And it was down here that he went now to consider recent events.

3

The Caoraich burn was a small tributary of the Skean and was only seven miles or so in length. It began life in a remote loch on the moor some way above the Ross's cottage and tumbled down the glen and past their cottage in a series of pools, rapids and small waterfalls until it met the Skean a couple of miles from the town.

Due to its remoteness and difficulty of access few ever walked its length, although the pool where it met the Skean was a famous salmon lie, especially later on in the season when a good number collected before running up the burn to spawn. To walk up the Caoraich burn was to enter a world largely unaltered by human touch, a pristine world of insects, plants, birds and of creatures unaffected by human intervention or influence. That was until the arrival of Frazer.

This secret place was Frazer's domain. It was here he spent countless hours, often missing primary school until some letter came to the cottage demanding his attendance. Unobserved and unsupervised by adults he was free to live a feral life. He had made small paths up and down the burn. Little trails through the birch and alder, trails that ended at deep and secretive pools, trails that ended at small rapids and beaches of orangey yellow coarse sand. Like the native he was he knew every inch of his territory. He knew the gravelly runs and glides where the big salmon spawned in November; he knew the pool with the ancient pine tree on the bank under whose roots the otters had a holt and brought up their kits; he knew which pools held the brown trout and which little beaches he could dig up with his hands and capture the tiny lampreys that lived in the sand. He knew the glade where the capercaillie had their leck in the spring and the rough clearings by the farm track where the rabbits were and the pheasants walked.

He had absorbed all this knowledge by first hand observation, sitting motionless by the burn and in the glen for hours on end, seemingly impervious to the hordes of midgies and birch flies. However, when he did attend the tiny primary school at the nearby village, mostly during the winter and late autumn terms it had to be said, he painstakingly worked his way through any natural history books and magazines available in the reading room, to where he was often sent for one transgression or another. As he read his face was furrowed in extreme concentration and his index finger traced out the letters and his lips silently sounded out the words.

Frazer was an ill-disciplined, difficult and disruptive pupil, his mother and father were difficult and disruptive also and so, Frazer's middle aged and middle class teacher, who had come off worst in several confrontations, was inclined to turn a blind eye to the frequent absences, apart from sending the occasional letter, certain in the knowledge that he would soon be the responsibility of the Strathskean Academy, and good luck to them!

And so, despite his intermittent schooling and borderline literacy, Frazer had an excellent and precocious understanding of the natural world in which he lived. However, he was no mere observer or nature lover. Frazer regarded the creatures and environment of Glen Caorich mostly as a resource to be exploited either for food or for pleasure.

When he was about eight years old a gamekeeper friend of his father had shown him how to snare rabbits. All that was needed was a simple piece of wire fashioned into a noose and attached to a peg which was driven into the ground at the edge of a rabbit hole.The noose was carefully positioned so when the rabbit dived back into its burrow it would be caught by the neck. It was then just a case of pulling the unfortunate creature out of its home and dispatching it with a heavy stick. Using this method he had, over time, snared a good number of rabbits which his mother skinned and made into stew. When he was a couple of years older his fingers were strong enough to prize open the jaws of the rusty old gin traps his father kept, and these he used to trap the foxes and pine martins that came at night to the hen house looking for a meal.

More recently he had been given his elder brother's BSA .22 air rifle and this acquisition allowed him to extend the number and variety of creatures he killed. In his young mind's eye he was a big game hunter and on his safaris through the glen or round the farm buildings he would shoot any unfortunate creature he came across no matter how small. He took a delight and pride in his marksmanship. He liked the thud the slug made when it hit its intended target, and he liked to hold and feel the warmth of the tiny broken feathery bodies and see their glazed eyes. In his short career had shot goldcrests, dippers, wagtails and the sand martins which nested in the sandy cliff near the farm, as well as a host of other common species. However, bigger game could be eaten and, over the course of the summer, he would regularly bring home pheasants, hares, rabbits and pigeons and what the Rosses couldn't eat Jim sold or traded for drinks in the public bar of the Strathskean Hotel.

4

And so, half way through the August of 1971, the Rosses moved into Number 9, Crathie Crescent in the council estate on the northern edge of the town. It was fairly large, white pebble-dashed semi detached house with a neat front driveway and reasonably sized rear garden complete with a wooden shed. Naturally the Rosses were thrilled with their new accommodation. Frazer's sisters shared a large bedroom and his parents were luxuriating in upstairs sleeping and their modern bathroom. Frazer himself had the little single room at the back which overlooked the garden and one or two other gardens as well. In the distance, past the roofs of other houses, Frazer could just make out the tops of the Cairngorms and he spent his first few days gazing wistfully into the distance and thinking with a distinct lack of enthusiasm about his imminent start at the Strathskean Academy.

However pleased the Rosses were at the move their pleasure was not entirely shared by most of the other residents of 'The Crathie' as the estate was known. The Rosses had long had a reputation in the town as the 'wild ones from the Braes' due mostly to the Friday night antics in town of Frazer's siblings, Jim Ross was also treated with caution, he was not a man to tangle with, especially after he had had a drink. It was also true to say that the Ross men were fully paid up members of the underclass in the strath: the semi employed , the poachers and the drunkards, all well known to the local constabulary. However, the good wages available in the oil industry had lured Frazer's brothers away up the coast and now their visits to the town were now mercifully infrequent.

Only a few weeks after their arrival, the Ross's house was instantly recognisable by the rusty blue Ford Transit propped up on blocks in their drive, the ancient muddy Land Rover parked on the pavement outside and the stack of pine logs and random bits of equipment piled haphazardly on the overgrown lawn, the whole assemblage guarded by Jim's viciously noisy terriers. It was as if they had subconsciously re-created their previous habitat in a more urban setting. It hadn't taken long for the neighbours to learn to cross over to the other side of the road to avoid setting off the dogs, or indeed in engaging any of the Rosses in conversation, although behind closed doors plenty was said about them.

5

One of the slightly unusual features of Crathie Crescent was that the houses on the opposite side to the Rosses had been built at a higher elevation due to the fact that the whole estate had been built horizontally across a sloping hillside. This meant that most of the even numbered houses seemed to look down at the odd numbered ones. Number 12 was such a house, and the family who lived there were called the Macdonalds. Bill Macdonald's living room was at the front and for many years he had looked out with pleasure down the crescent at the row of neatly kept houses with their immaculate front gardens. The frontage of his own house with its carefully manicured lawn, container plants and weed free driveway was a testament to his organised mind. He was the store manager at a local distillery, an elder of the Kirk and the secretary of the Strathskean Angling Association.

   The arrival of the Rosses had caused him major disquiet. Not only was his orderly and generally peaceful view ruined by their rusting blue van and other assorted rubbish, but the frequent noisy nightly comings and goings of the two Ross girls infuriated him. Both girls were now older teenagers and on many nights they would be collected by youths driving customised hatchbacks which screeched up complete with thudding music and snarling exhausts. On some occasions, especially weekends, one or either of the girls would arrive late at night or even in the wee small hours and the car would remain outside the Ross's house for some time, its exhaust gently burbling and music pounding while its occupants engaged in God only knew what. As an elder of the Kirk Mr Macdonald certainly did not approve.

   Over time, Bill and the rest of the mostly worthy folks on The Crathie, got used to the Rosses and largely ignored them, save to cite the family as prima facie evidence of a steep decline in current public morals.

Bill and Morag, his wife, had two daughters, Mhairi and Kirstie, and their upbringing had been austere and orderly in the highland Scottish tradition. In fairness to their parents the family's financial resources were limited, Bill's job being only modestly remunerated, but they made the best of it, and whatever spare cash they had went on music lessons and other cultural opportunities for the girls. It was generally a most happy and secure home.

Kirstie, several years older than Mhairi, had done well at the academy, could have gone on to university, but chose instead to have a career in the local bank. She had a steady boyfriend who she had met at the Kirk Sunday school, an equally serious minded youth of solid farming stock. Bill and Morag were entirely happy with the liaison and in their minds had already planned the future wedding and were looking forward to their future grandchildren.

Mhairi, the younger by seven years, was constructed of different material. While her sister was a solidly built individual with a conventional outlook on life, Mhairi was the opposite. Mhairi was slender and athletic of figure. At her primary school she had been, by some distance, top of the class and her teacher was often hard pressed to keep her occupied for she devoured material at an astonishing rate. She had a fast brain, a retentive memory and an enquiring mind. This latter ability got her into trouble at times because she would question the social orthodoxies of the time, wanting to play football with the boys, to not go to church and she disagreed volubly with her father's often stated, deeply held conservative views in general and especially those about the role of women, and always to his intense irritation.

Bill Macdonald worried about his daughter, he loved her beyond life itself but he did not know how to cope with her waywardness and independence of thought and action. She was constantly challenging, not in an aggressive or unpleasant way for she was a very loving girl, but just as he felt he had achieved a small amount of peace of mind and things were on an even keel she would want to do something or say something that met his disapproval. He hoped that her graduation to secondary school would calm her down. And it did. At the Strathskean Academy Mhairi flourished, her teachers recognising her ability, provided the intellectual challenge she craved and placed her with the few other individuals who were as equally motivated and as sharp.

For all her intellect and desire to shine academically, Mhairi was quite a social creature. As soon as school was finished she would dash home, complete whatever homework and chores she had to do, and then after tea in the spring and summer she would be out and about with the other young teenagers in the area.

They would generally meet at the nearby park and hang out, mess about on the swings, and play football, at which Mhairi excelled. Occasionally, they would go up to the quarry in the woods above the estate where there was a rusty wire swing attached to an ancient Scots pine, which whirled them, screaming with excited terror, out over the abyss. Sometimes, especially on warm summer weekends, they would go down to the Skean, to one of its little sandy beaches, and light fires, smoke cigarettes, paddle in the water and generally muck about in the way that healthy kids are supposed to do.

During the summer holidays this group was often joined by a regular visitor to The Crathie, a lad from Tyneside called Robbie. He stayed with his aunty Mary's family who were unfortunate enough to be Frazer Ross's immediate neighbours. Robbie was a bit of a novelty, with his strange way of talking and shy smile. He was not really "one of them" but he was tolerated in an easy kind of way. They referred to him as "The Englishman" and he had to endure their light hearted ribbing and attempts to imitate his accent.

Frazer was a part of this group too, although he did not spend all his time with them as he was still occupied with his own hunter-gatherer activities. At school with his peers he was fairly taciturn, often ill-tempered and inclined to throw his considerable weight about if he didn't get his own way. He was frequently in trouble with the school authorities. The other lads on The Crathie were wary of him, because he dominated the group, the girls a little uneasy in his presence and when he was missing the mood was always lighter and more relaxed.

Surprisingly, especially for the first three or four years of their holiday time acquaintance, Robbie and Frazer got on quite well, Frazer didn't regard Robbie as any sort of competition in the group pecking order and moreover, Robbie, coming from an industrial urban background, loved to roam about the woods and glens of Strathskean which were, of course, Frazer' s natural habitat. They would sometimes go off up the woods together, wandering about for hours with Frazer's air rifle, Frazer being the guide and leader, and shooting at whatever caught their eye.

Robbie's passion however, was fishing, and every summer and the odd Easter as well he bought a ticket for the water controlled by the Strathskean Angling Association. Due to their generosity It was incredibly cheap for youngsters to fish although the day and weekly tickets were quite expensive for visiting anglers. Frazer fished too, although only when the water was right. He was more interested in fishing for the pot or selling his catch on. Frazer, typically, fished without a ticket, believing that it was his right because as he said, 'troot fishing is free in Scotland. OK?' the fact that he was in fact trying to catch sea trout and possibly salmon an irrelevance.

6

The Association rented seven miles of the river Skean upstream of the town bridge. There was some good water, a score or so of named pools, and the visitors and locals caught between them several hundred salmon a year and a similar number of sea trout. Fishers came from all over Britain and indeed from further afield to fish the Skean, both the Association water and the private beats, their bookings in the local hotels and guest houses were an important part of the local tourist economy.

Below the town bridge the Skean plunged down through an impressive rack of rapids about half a mile in length before flattening out in a series of perfectly formed narrow and deep pools. After four or five miles or so the river spilled into a wide sandy estuary.

This exclusive few miles of river above the tide and below the town bridge was the jealously protected preserve of the Skean Castle Estate, and was divided into six beats, each beat being fished by two "rods" as the fishermen were called. Each beat had its own hut, complete with stove, veranda, car park, picnic table and ghillie, the professional whose responsibility it was to organise and help with the fishing. By each hut, bobbing gently at the edge of the stream, was a traditional clinker built wooden salmon boat, painted dark green, about sixteen feet in length with an elevated seat for the fisher at the stern. The ghillie did the rowing while the fisher cast his fly over otherwise unreachable salmon lies. These boats were also used to ferry the fishers from one side of the river to the other. The cost of a beat for a week, especially in August and September, was eye-watering, if indeed you could get on, for their beats were booked up years in advance.

During the summer days in the high season a Land Rover or two would arrive at each beat's hut about nine o' clock in the morning and decant the tweeded fishers, their wives, dogs, picnic hampers and other accoutrements. The fly rods would be assembled, the ghillie would advise on fly choice and show the fisher where the exact taking points were in the pool at that particular level of water. If the rod was not an experienced fly fisherman then the ghillie would have his work cut out, fortunately most were quite skilled and had their own ideas but consulted the ghillie anyway, just to preserve the status quo. Some ghillies were noted characters and became tetchy or downright rude if their advice was disregarded. Others were more diplomatic. All expected a considerable tip at the end of the week.

Upstream of the town bridge the Association water was no less attractive, it boasted several wonderful pools, and was set in the most picturesque Scottish highland scenery. There were even fishing huts, but no boats and no ghillies. The difference was, anyone with a ticket could fish, and if the water was above a certain height, fishers could use worm and spinner if they so wished. The main rule, usually, but not always observed, was that a fisherman had to start at the top of the pool and fish down it, taking a step downstream between each cast, a simple and effective way of making sure that more than one person could fish any pool and no one fisher could hog the best lies. Courtesy dictated that the angler fishing was given a few yards before the next entered the water upstream. There was usually a bench at the start of the run and often there was an old fisher or two patiently waiting their turn chatting about the current prospects and the state of the river.

To the salmon fishers the concept of 'water' was paramount. Too much water and the fishing was useless, too little and the fishing was hopeless. The Skean, all fifty odd miles of it, was a fast spate river, tumbling down through rapids and rocky pools. When the rain fell, especially up in the mountains where the river was fed by a thousand tiny burns, it rose quickly, its volume and pace increasing with each mile. At first the river was quite clear, albeit with a peaty tinge, but as the land became saturated the water in the muddy fields, tracks, hillsides and roads spilled over into the burns and the water then became quite thick, brown, and full of suspended sediment carrying with it all sorts of debris. After a while, depending on the extent of the rainfall, the river would slowly clear and return to its normal level, and it was this period, shortly after the flood, that was so eagerly awaited by the town fishers.

Any significant rise in water, especially in the summer months, would stimulate the salmon into running , those already in the system would maybe move further upstream and those in the estuary or lower pools would attempt the ascent of the half mile or so of rapids that separated the Skean Castle beats from the Association water. If the water was low, as it was generally for long periods in the summer, The Skean Castle pools would fill up with hundreds of fish waiting for sufficient volume of water to navigate the rapids. Then the fishing could be spectacular. Fishers on the Association water struggled in these conditions because their water did not hold the salmon for long periods of time, the fish passing fairly swiftly through on their upstream migration. There were one or two pools that did hold fish, especially later on in September, the mouth of the Caoraich burn being one. At the top of the flood and as the river slowly cleared the fishing on the Association water came into its own. Fresh fish temporarily populated the pools and the fishers appeared in numbers.

So, in the town, and indeed other parts of the country, a keen eye was kept on the weather forecast. For many visiting fishers luck played a big part, holiday bookings were arranged months in advance so they had to fish even when conditions were poor. Many locals, however, would fish only when there was a decent chance of a salmon. When conditions were really good, the river fining down from a big spate, the banks would be lined with folk, all spinning and worming away, fly fishing, in this case being ineffective at that height of water.

Most, but not all of the locals had tickets, and many were fishing for the pot rather than entirely for the sport of it. The ancient river watcher, Murdy, did his best to regulate this but his little red van was well known on the river and his arthritic knees meant his bailiffing was restricted to the pools near the car parks.

Sometimes small groups of unsavoury characters would drive up the A9 from the industrial south and spend a couple of days intensively worming or spinning a particularly productive run. Sometimes they were challenged and occasional prosecutions were made but, by and large, they got away with their poaching. Anyway, there were plenty of fish in the river, weren't there?

7

Late August 1975.

The house was quiet and still when Robbie slipped quietly out of his room at his Aunty Mary's and padded down the stairs to a kitchen still warm from the previous evening. He opened the fridge and took out a packet of sandwiches, filled his flask with boiling water and stuffed it and the sandwiches into a haversack. Pausing only to pull on his waterproof and wellingtons and pick up his fishing gear he slid out of the back door.

   Outside the neon street lights cast their orange glow, the air was cool and the scents of wet foliage strong. It was just before three o'clock in the morning and he was anxious to get to the river. The last two or three weeks had been fairly dry and a huge number of fish had stacked up in the estuary and in the Castle Skean pools downstream of the town. To his delight and excitement and, with only with four days left of his holiday, two days of torrential rain swept across the region and the river had risen by about three feet above the normal summer level.

Now the rain had stopped and the darkness was giving way to the greyest of dawns. Soon he had left the Crathie estate behind and was scrunching his way down the gravelly path by the wee burn and through the woods towards the Skean, Robbie was betting on getting to his favourite spot just as the flood water was beginning to drop.

The path ended at the point at which the burn joined the Skean. At normal levels of water there was a small beach of coarse sand and a lazy eddy caused by the burn mouth and some big rocks, but now the beach and rocks were mostly covered and the eddy was much larger. Robbie knew that at this height of water there was a great chance of sea trout and even a salmon or two resting there.

Upon arrival, and to his dismay, he saw that there was another fisher who had beaten him to the eddy. A large, dark, ungainly figure silhouetted against the silvery grey river: Frazer.

'Hae ye ony worrms English? Ah've run oot. Ah only had a couple,' Frazer growled without turning round.

Robbie delved in his bag and pulled out an old biscuit tin from which he removed a handful of black headed worms and some moss and put them in Frazer's tin which was balanced on an old bench by the path. Behind the bench Frazer's ancient canvas fishing bag lay in the grass and by the side of that a gleam of silver betrayed the presence of a freshly caught sea trout of about three pounds in weight.

'Ah see y've had one already,' said Robbie, with just a tinge of envy.

'Aye, y' need tae stop blethering and get yir line in the watter,' came the succinct rejoinder.

Robbie tackled up. He had a hollow glass spinning rod about nine feet in length and a Mitchell 300 fixed spool reel, a recent and fairly expensive birthday present. He threaded the 12 lb yellow Platil nylon line through the rings and, after a bit of a rummage in his bag brought out a small round lead weight, a split shot and a size eight hook. He pushed the line through the hole in the lead, put the split shot on the nylon about eighteen inches from the end and closed it with his teeth. He tied on the hook , and gave the whole a sharp tug or two to test its fastness. The lead was able to run freely up the line but was prevented from running down to the hook by the split shot.

Taking three of his now depleted stock of worms he began to thread them carefully up the hook, over the barb and up the first inch or so of line. When he was finished he examined the squirming mass and, satisfied that the hook was completely concealed, he joined Frazer at the river's edge.

Frazer grudgingly stepped down the bank a yard or two, moved the forked stick he was using as a rod rest and Robbie was able to cast out. The technique was as simple as it was effective at this height of water. What you did was cast your bait into the main flow, allow it to sink and the lead would bounce round over the stones until it and the worms came to a rest at that point where the strong current met the quieter water at the edge of the eddy. This was where the fish would rest on their journey upstream. If a fish took the worms the fisherman would feel its bite, the line running through the weight straight to the hook.

The exact place that Frazer and Robbie were fishing was the first piece of calm water that running fish would encounter after battling up through the rapids below the town bridge.

Frazer pointed at a stick that, on arrival, he had pushed in the sand at the edge of the water. It was now clearly two inches from the edge.

'Look at yon stick, the watter's drapping aff. W' should get some fish soon.'

By now the light was stronger, and a stiff breeze blew up the river, on the town bridge a car or two crossed, their engine sounds muffled by the dull roar of the rapids downstream.

None of this impinged on Robbie's consciousness. His mind was concentrating on the yellow nylon line in his hand, he was waiting for that electric tug, tug, that would signify that in the swirly opaque water something was eating his worms.

He did not have to wait long. A kind of grating pull signified that something indeed was at his bait. However, he did not feel that vibrant tugging that would have signified a sea trout, or perhaps a salmon so, with his suspicions confirmed, he wound in sixteen inches of muscular, writhing, slimy eel, the bane of the worm fisher's life. Removing the eel from the water was the easy part, on the bank, and in the wet grass, an eel was a nightmare to unhook. Invariably the creature would have swallowed the hook and when you grasped it, it would wrap its mucous covered body around your wrist and slither backwards through your fingers. Usually the only option was to cut the line and re-tackle.

'Fuck, fuck,' mumbled Robbie as he eventually cut the line and tied on a new hook. He wiped the slime off his hands in the wet grass.

Frazer thought this was hilarious, 'A sea troot for me and a fuckin' eel for the Englishman,' he laughed.

Robbie re-cast. He placed his rod in a forked stick as was the local custom and stood back to await developments.

Frazer didn't have to wait long for another bite. His rod bent over and about twenty yards downstream a sea trout whirled out of the water, falling back with a splash. A minute or two later Frazer was unceremoniously dragging the unfortunate fish up the beach. He smashed it on the head with a thick stick and threw it behind the bench to join the other.

'That's two nil to me,' he said, quite unnecessarily in Robbie's opinion. Frazer turned most of their exploits into a competition: fish caught, birds shot. He was happy so long as he was ahead.

Now the grey early gloom had given way to a brighter morning light and the stiff upstream wind had softened. The roar of the rapids downstream was less noticeable. The river was slowly fining down. Frazer's stick was now a few more inches from the water's edge.

Frazer had another bite, this time a bigger sea tout. It, too, was dragged up the beach and dispatched in the same brutal way. Robbie reeled in, checked his worms, and re-cast into the slightly stronger water at the head of the eddy. This time, instead of putting the rod in the forked stick he held it at an angle of about forty five degrees from his body, the index finger of his right hand curled round the line so he could feel the lead bounce round the stones with the current.

After a further hour with no results for him but yet another sea trout for Frazer, Robbie was beginning to think that this might not be his morning after all. Upstream on the opposite side two other fishers had appeared, spinning their way down towards the bridge.

Suddenly, he felt a slight tug on his line. Another tug, this time a little stronger. He resisted the temptation to strike. Another tug and then another, more insistent this time. Now. He lowered the rod tip and wound in hard.

Immediately his rod bent over into a hoop shape and the taught yellow line was torn from his reel with alarming speed and power. Before he even realised what was happening at least half of the line on his reel had disappeared upstream. Robbie adjusted the clutch so that he could begin to bring the fish under control but it was far too heavy. It had now stopped running and seemed to have fixed itself solidly to the bottom in the powerful water at the head of the pool. Reeling in and keeping his line taught he moved up the bank to a position parallel to the fish. He put as much pressure on it as he dared, he was attached to an immoveable force by a singing yellow thread. He was unable to make any impression on it.

By now the other fishers on the far bank had stopped fishing and were looking at the contest.

Frazer too, was on hand to offer helpful advice, 'Y' want to pull it oot as hard as y' can.' but Robbie did not want to risk a break and he was worried that the line had somehow become snagged around a rock. Every few seconds the fish would shake its head, otherwise everything was solid.

One of the fishers on the far bank, no doubt bored by the seeming inactivity of both Robbie and the fish shouted across the river to him, his voice barely audible above the water and the wind. He told Robbie to move downstream and change the angle of attack so that the fish might be pulled off balance in the strong water. Robbie took his advice moved about twenty yards downstream still keeping as much pressure as he dared on the line.

Suddenly, in a shower of spray, a large salmon erupted from the water at the head of the pool and crashed back with a massive splash. Robbie gasped for he had not had a glimpse of his fish until that point. He could hardly believe his eyes.

Now the salmon ran downstream close to the far bank and Robbie struggled to keep in contact with it, then it turned in towards Robbie and swam into the eddy close to where it had been originally hooked. Robbie raised his rod and pulled the salmon closer to him. It seemed to tire at this point, turning on its side, silvery golden gleams beneath the surface betraying its distress. Thinking he might be able to pull it onto the small beach by the eddy Robbie moved down towards the water's edge and applied as much pressure as he dared, the line cutting through the water as the fish rolled and plunged.

Slowly, slowly, it came in towards the bank, it was on its side, its pectoral fin waving in the air like a miniature sail. Robbie was just believing it might beach itself when, suddenly, it twisted round in a silver arc and shot off back into the main stream, line again leaving Robbie's reel at an unbelievable rate.

This time the salmon headed down towards the tail of the pool. Here the water quickened its pace as it shallowed up underneath the bridge before thundering away downstream through the rapids.

'Aye, it's got its second wind,' remarked Frazer, in a smirky way.

Robbie was speechless, the now exhausted salmon, the magnificent prize that had been so nearly his, was now wallowing in the flat water above the rapids twenty yards away, its big tail occasionally slapping the surface. Little by little, helped by the strong current, it was heading inexorably downstream towards the white water and its freedom.

And so, caught in that moment as if in a photograph, two early strollers on the bridge looking down at the boy on the bank, his rod bent over at an alarming angle, the line taught and whining in the wind attached to a plunging and splashing salmon, the boy's companion, arms folded, with a grin on his face and the other two fishers on the opposite bank who had stopped to watch the drama.

Robbie had no choice, he just had to hang on. The rod bent over at an even more alarming angle, the line seemingly stretched way beyond its breaking point. But it did not snap, and neither did the hook pull out. And the salmon, helped by the current, now kited back towards Robbie across the tail of the pool, almost underneath the bridge, until it was directly downstream of him in some slack water near the side.

Fortunately, for Robbie, if not for the fish, help was at hand. One of the fishers from the other bank had seen what was happening and had crossed the bridge and was now wading into the water slightly below the fish. He had a large gye landing net, and carefully positioning it underneath the fish, he lifted upwards with a smooth stroke.

The salmon was in the net and it thrashed and writhed about sending spray everywhere. Robbie's saviour, an elderly local fisherman, waded to the shore and with a smile and a 'well done laddie,' handed the net and its contents to Robbie who spluttered his thanks.

'Aye, it's a bonnie fish right enough,' remarked the old fisher who had now climbed out of the river, 'it must be getting oan for aboot fifteen.'

The salmon was duly dispatched with a stick the old man found on the bank and together they laid it out on the wet grass. It was still quite silver but not fresh run. It was a good yard in length and had the pronounced jaw of a male fish.

Robbie gave his thanks again to the old man who picked up his net, gave it a shake, and with a wave of his hand went back across the bridge to rejoin his friend on the other bank.

Robbie was too excited to fish on, and in any case his supply of worms was almost exhausted. He looked around for Frazer to tell him he was away home but of Frazer there was no sign except for the twig he had stuck in the sand in order to gauge the water level. The fish was too big to fit into Robbie's haversack so he put the fingers of his right hand into its gills and holding its body off the ground and with his rod in his left hand he slowly made his way back to the Crathie.

After weighing it on his uncle's spring balance [14 lbs 10 oz] and a photograph or two in the back garden Robbie laid the salmon out on his aunty Mary's draining board and enjoyed the gasps of amazement and congratulations from his cousins as they came in from work. The salmon was cut up into steaks, some eaten that very night and the rest put in the freezer for future consumption.

Next day, the last of his holiday, Robbie went to Cattenach's the wee fishing tackle cum newsagent's shop in the town and proudly recorded his catch in the Association's returns book, as the regulations demanded. Several other salmon and sea trout had been caught that week, but Robbie's was the largest.

On the train home Robbie reflected on his holiday. He was still excited by his fish, replaying its capture over and over in his mind, and although he had caught several sea trout and even two small salmon in the past this had been an experience beyond his young imagination and one that would shape his future thoughts. He loved the summers in Strathskean, the fishing, the freedom and the whole unspoilt beauty of the highlands and he wasn't overly keen on returning to his school and life in an industrial Tyneside.

At the same time that Robbie was heading southwards Frazer too, was thinking about Robbie's salmon. He was sitting in the dusty cluttered gloom of the tiny shed at the bottom of their small garden. He was annoyed that he, the local, the expert, had been upstaged. It was true he had four sea trout for the morning and had managed to sell them to some neighbours but it still rankled that the Englishman had landed such a substantial fish. He didn't like to think of how much one of his Dad's mates could have got for it at one of the local hotels. He was glad that Robbie was on his way home, the novelty of their association had waned and now they hardly spent any time in each other's company. The door of the shed was slightly ajar. From his seat on an old crate Frazer had a good view of the lawn on to which he had thrown some bits of bread. A starling flew down from the house roof for the free meal. Frazer raised his air rifle.

8

1976

Frazer effectively had left Strathskean Academy in the February of 1976 it being felt by all parties that a period of extended work experience was the best option. He had been allowed to return to take his exams but he had never had any intention of doing so. He was working as a farm labourer up at the ramshackle Caoraich farm, effectively replacing his father who was now only occasionally present, now that he was living in the town and earning some cash by doing shifts in the Strathy Bar. The farm manager, an elderly chap, was happy enough to employ Frazer who knew exactly what was what seeing as how he had been brought up there.

Caoraich cottage, that draughty home to the Ross family for all those years, had now fallen into disrepair. When the Rosses left in 1971 it had needed much attention to bring it up to modern standards and the estate had had neither the money nor the inclination nor any reason to refurbish it. The track up to the cottage was mostly overgrown, and all around the cottage the rusting bones of abandoned agricultural machinery stuck out of the nettles and dock leaves like the carcasses of prehistoric beasts. The once red corrugated roof was now corroded and holed and grasses grew out of the guttering. In the back garden, the wooden hen house was partially collapsed and a small birch tree grew out of the doorway.

Frazer had found a key, and was quick to realise the potential of the cottage as a convenient and secluded centre for his other operations. There was no power now, but there was still running water from a stand pipe outside and in the kitchen there was an ancient calor gas stove and a table, chairs and a broken sideboard. In the living room the paper was peeling from the walls and there was still, and now covered with plaster which had fallen from the low ceiling, the damp and mouldering sofa bed on which he himself had probably been conceived some seventeen years ago. An eerie stillness gripped the room and the dank darkness was only just alleviated by the shafts of dusty light from the small windows. In the kitchen, in wooden crates stacked against the wall, Frazer had stored his traps, snares and nets, the tools of his other, more lucrative trade.

At that time Frazer's source of income was the pittance he received for his work on the farm and whatever cash he could get by selling game in season and out. Just as he ignored the need for licences and permissions to fish so he ignored the official seasons for game. He just took what he could when he could. There was always somebody in the strath who would take some rabbits, a brace of pheasants, or a salmon or two for cash, no questions asked. It had been this way for centuries, the fishing and shooting owned and enjoyed almost exclusively by the estate owners and their guests, and guarded by and large, and with varying degrees of enthusiasm, by ghillies and game keepers. The money he received for this enterprise Frazer had saved, and by that autumn he had enough to buy an oldish, but still serviceable trail bike. It was a smoky and noisy BSA Bantam, 175cc two stroke, it had been owned by a mechanic from up the strath who had now bought himself a hatchback and was keen to get rid. It was ideal for the rough off-road riding Frazer wanted to do. More importantly, he could now get from The Crathie to the farm in just ten minutes or so and as he was mostly riding on forest trails and tracks he didn't need insurance or, indeed, a licence did he?

9

1977

In the Easter of that year Robbie and Mhairi had had a brief encounter, not exactly a romance but a definite whirl. They had gone out for a couple of walks, just to give her a wee break from her revision she said, and then, on the last Saturday of his stay, they had gone, by bus, into a rainy Inverness where they had walked about hand in hand, had something to eat, gone to the cinema, smooched in the back row, got the last bus back to Strathskean and walked back up to The Crathie arm in arm, disengaging only at the exact point where they could be observed by her father from his front window. Robbie had been keen to prolong the romance but as he was about to head back to Tyneside and she was committed to getting her grades it was not a practical proposition. She kissed him goodnight and said she'd see him in the summer if he was up.

Although Bill Macdonald might have missed the goodnight kiss it was witnessed by Frazer, who, as ever, had been lurking in the shadows. The previous year Frazer had had quite a thing for Mhairi but when he had asked her out she had told him that she regarded him as a good mate and not a romantic partner. He was still quite aggrieved by her rejection of him, however he was now seeing some wild eyed lassie from up the strath. He'd tried not to think about Robbie since the incident in the river, but here he was again turning up like the proverbial bad penny in Frazer's domain.

10

June 1977

It was a warm early June afternoon in Dock Street, South Shields. Sheila, Robbie's mother, opened the door to their narrow kitchen. A blast of hot air hit her. The sun was streaming in through the side windows and the heat in the room was oppressive. Three or four bluebottles were frantically buzzing away on the glass trying to escape. Sheila opened the cupboard under the worktop and brought out an aerosol of fly spray. "Guaranteed 100% Knockdown" it said on the side, "Kills all Flying Insects Dead." She gave the can a shake, and moving around the kitchen gave the whole area a good blast. Coughing slightly with the fumes she retreated back to the lounge. In the kitchen, one by one, the blue bottles fell onto the windowsill and after a few seconds of twitching were still.

At the back of the kitchen on a shelf by the door was a large fish tank. A small electric aerator sent a stream of bubbles up from the gravel on the bottom and some strands of elodea pondweed reached the surface. Small dace and roach drifted gently about and on the gravel three or four loach were feeding. These were fish that Robbie had brought back from the Tyne on his excursions up river. He was particularly proud of his collection.

Within a few minutes of Sheila spraying the kitchen with the insecticide all were showing signs of distress and by the time Robbie got back home from school not one was alive.

11

Late August 1977

Cattenach's Newsagents and Fishing Tackle shop on Main Street was the first stop for any self respecting angler visiting Strathskean. Alan Cattenach, the shop's ancient owner and fount of all knowledge piscatorial, sold the tickets for the Association and each sale was accompanied by a resume' of current prospects and advice as to what fly or which pool would lead to certain success. The front of the shop was that of a conventional newsagent's: racks of magazines, daily newspapers on the counter, confectionary and cigarettes on the shelves behind. However, the back of the shop was an Aladdin's cave, seemingly stretching on forever into a tobacco scented gloom, and was overstuffed with all sorts of rods, nets and display cases of salmon flies both ancient and modern. Robbie was a frequent customer, buying bits of tackle and soaking up the great man's wisdom, which was always freely given. In fact it was Alan who had taught

Robbie to cast a fly and had since encouraged him to make the fly his preferred method.

This summer, although not quite as warm as last year's, was still pretty dry by Highland standards and the river was low, and Robbie's only hope was to use the fly, worming and spinning being prohibited during low summer levels.

Robbie pushed open the shop door, a bell tinkled in the distance, and Alan Cattenach emerged from the gloom of the back shop in a cloud of smoke. He waved his cigarette theatrically by way of greeting, 'Aye yir back again, a bit later this year,' he observed , immediately dissolving into a paroxysm of coughing. He leant against the glass counter for support.

'Yes, I am, I'm not over hopeful , it's been very low hasn't it? and ah've only got a few days.'

'Aye, it has, but there's a few aboot, The grilse is still coming through right enough.'

Detailed instructions and directions followed and Robbie left the shop with a weekly ticket and a few flies in a little packet and, at Alan Cattenach's insistence, the loan of an ancient but entirely serviceable fifteen foot double-handed salmon fly rod and reel. He had been ordered to fish early and late, and as his ticket started at midnight he resolved to be on the water at first light. He was not overly optimistic, but being on the river at dawn in summer was a very special, almost spiritual experience, or so he believed.

He hadn't got more than a few yards up the street when there was a sharp whistle and a 'Hey English.' He turned round and saw it was the slender figure of Mhairi with a huge grin on her face. She was dressed in the uniform of the local supermarket, her hair was scraped back severely under a cap and she wore a maroon tabard with the name of the company prominently displayed.

'Hey,' he said grinning back, his heart missing a beat, 'how's things? long time no see.'

'Absolutely excellento,' aim off to Edinburgh,' she said in a mock posh Morningside voice.

'Well done yersel,' so yir aff to Embra.' he replied mimicking the local accent. 'Whit grades did ye get?'

It transpired that she, of course, had got straight A's in her highers, and would be off to Edinburgh University to study Economics in a mere four weeks' time. Meantime she was working on the checkouts and trying to save some money. Robbie, himself, had hopes of going to uni, but in England you had to wait until you were eighteen, unlike Scotland where you did your exams at seventeen and got to go a year earlier.

'Mebbes I'll see y' later,' he said, a tad nervously.

'Aye, Ok, later, after tea, call on me,' she replied, striding away up the street in the direction of her work. He watched her retreating figure until she disappeared into the supermarket by the crossroads. As usual with her he felt a mixture of emotions, it was like she was real, but somehow unobtainable, as if she had moved into a different world and he had been left behind.

Later that evening he walked up the Macdonald's path past the immaculate front garden, and before he could knock on the door it swung open and Mhairi stepped out, simultaneously giving him a peck on the cheek and linking his arm with hers.

'Quick, away down the road,' she said with a snort and propelling him quickly along the pavement, 'I don't want any o' they busybodies gossiping,' and soon they were out of The Crathie and walking down towards the river. However, their departure had not gone unobserved by Frazer who had been cleaning his newly acquired transport: the Bantam. As he wiped the mud from the frame his lips were set in a tight grimace.

Down by the river, they sat on a hardwood bench which overlooked the bridge pool, site of Robbie's previous salmon triumph, the air was soft and a few sand martins were hawking over the water, soon they too would be heading south as the summer slid slowly into autumn. There was a faded brass plaque on the bench which bore the legend: "In memory of James Grant 1910-1970. He loved this place."

They sat and chatted quietly as the light slowly ebbed away, mostly about her future plans for Edinburgh, she was going into a hall of residence with two friends from the Strathskean Academy, and she had already begun her packing. She was excited, a whole new world was about to open up for her, Robbie had tried to put his arm around her, but she skilfully evaded his manoeuvre and was content just to remain with arms linked, and he realised that whatever romantic attachment he might have wished for, or dreamt about since their Easter dates, was now just that: a dream. She had moved on, she was now no longer a schoolgirl, she was now an independent young woman, and he was still the schoolboy.

Now as the night approached they decided to head back to The Crathie. She had a full day's work ahead of her the next day, and he was now determined to go fishing at first light so they couldn't stay too late could they? At her door, in the dark, he put his arm round her lithe frame, hugged her tight and breathed in her perfume as she kissed him on the cheek, and said she'd see him around, and wished him good luck with his fishing. It was "Ae Fond Kiss" right enough.

12

And so, after a handful of hours of fitful, dreamy sleep, and having quietly exited the house, Robbie propped his uncle's bike on the fence by the layby at the top end of the Association's water. A liquid and dull light was gradually bringing colour to the birch leaves stirring gently in the light breeze. The air was cool and scented. He untied Cattenach's rod bag from the crossbar and with that and his old canvas rucksack headed off down the path by the burn through the trees to the river. Presently he arrived at an ancient fishing hut with faded timbers and a rusting red tin roof.

Sitting on the steps of the hut he extracted from his rucksack a pair of waders, an old weighty salmon fly reel, a box of flies and a spool of twelve pound nylon. He pulled on the waders, took the three sections of the split cane rod from their bag, pushed them together and squinted along their length to align them. Then he fixed the reel to the rod and noisily pulled off a few yards of flyline which he threaded through the rings. At the end of the flyline there was a loop to which he attached about ten feet of the nylon and to this he carefully knotted on a small, dull reddish-brown shrimpy looking fly which had been tied on a double hook. As Cattenach had remarked amid his coughing: 'Yir bound to get a fish on this wee devil, ye cannot fail.'

Thus equipped he walked to the head of the run. A narrow neck of fast water gushed noisily and untidily into a larger glide which, in turn, slowed into a pool of perhaps fifty yards or so in length. At the far side of the pool there was a steep sandy cliff which had been colonised by hundreds of sand martins which were now wheeling and soaring over the river bank. Beyond this the birch and whin scrub gave way to a majestic Caledonian pine forest and the purple foothills of the Cairngorms. As he looked, a large salmon leapt out of the water and fell back with a crash. Over the next couple of minutes several others splashed about. The pool was full of fish.

Gingerly he waded out into the fast water at the head of the run. Although the water was brown in colour it was translucent and he could see the boots of his waders quite clearly. Behind each stone there was a little triangle of coarse orangey yellow sand. If he stood on this his footing was more secure. The current pressed against his thighs pushing him downstream, and he stumbled slightly remembering that he only had thigh waders and he shouldn't go out too far.

Robbie was on the right hand bank, facing downstream, and for this, as Cattenach had patiently explained, you needed to be able to perform the mystical double speycast which involved bringing the rod right across your body to the left and then making a big roll cast with your right hand. In this way none of the fly line went behind and so you were able to fish with trees and bushes close, where conventional fly casting was impossible. Robbie only just understood this concept, but the rod, all fifteen feet of it, was quite supple, if somewhat heavy, and lent itself to the easy rhythm of the cast.

So, after a few entanglements and only a minor loss of temper, he was shuffling his way down the run, casting with a kind of rhythm, the fly landing about fifteen yards diagonally downstream.

Salmon continued to crash about in the run making his heart thud. If only... Most were quite red now, they had been in the river for some time and were in their spawning livery. His line went out once again, this time a slightly longer cast. It swung round and just as he was about to draw it in there was an electrifying tug, tug on his line. The ancient reel screeched and he was playing his first salmon on the fly. A few minutes later he drew it up to a pebbly beach at the tail of the pool. It was a cock fish of about ten pounds.

As it lay on its side in the shallows he extracted the wee double hook from the corner of its mouth. The jaw, or kype, was well developed, and the once silver flanks had turned a reddish brown. He thought momentarily about killing it and taking it back, but common sense prevailed, and he turned the fish around in the shallows so it was facing upstream and held it in the current until it slowly swam off.

Nevertheless, it had been a thrilling experience, anyone's first salmon on fly was a considerable achievement he thought and this had mostly, but not entirely, offset his earlier emotional distress about Mhairi. And pondering upon these matters he peddled slowly back to The Crathie.

13

That evening the weather broke and heavy rain and wind swept down the strath with more deluges forecast. The river was bound to flood and fishing would be out of the question for at least a few days. Robbie cursed his luck. He spent his time lounging around, bored and ill tempered, reading and wandering aimlessly along the banks of the now flooded river watching the brown water thunder its way towards the sea. He only caught the occasional glimpse of Mhairi through the rain streaked front window as she headed down the road to work.

On the last afternoon of his stay, the rain having temporarily stopped and the river still too high to fish, Robbie decided to go for a walk up through the woods at the east end of the town. The way there took him through the town park which had all the usual arrangements of ornamental flower beds, grassed areas and a kiddies' playground. Next to the playground was an open-sided shelter and leaning against this was a muddy BSA Bantam trail bike. On the ground beside the shelter a couple of chopper bicycles had been carelessly abandoned. There was a smell of cigarette smoke and some raucous laughter. As Robbie walked past he saw that it was Frazer and a couple of younger lads, both of whom should have been in school, the autumn term having started earlier that month. All of them were smoking and Frazer was drinking from a can of lager. Other empty cans lay in the detritus under the bench.

He hurried on by, not wishing to engage with Frazer. He had had little or nothing to do with him since the previous summer's incident in the river and he had become conscious of a certain animosity that Frazer held towards him. In fact, as he had only been up briefly at Easter and, just for a few days now with Frazer being at work, or riding around on his trail bike their paths had not crossed and so he was slightly surprised when Frazer called after him.

'Hey English, is it no aboot time ye fucked aff back tae Geordieland?' Frazer's words were slightly slurred, it was obvious he'd had a can or two. Frazer's two wee mates were guffawing at the jibe.

Robbie turned round and looked at Frazer who was sprawled over the bench in the shelter, a fag in one hand and a can in the other. He held Frazer's gaze for a moment or so. 'What's that to you Frazer, it's none of your business, is it?'

'Aye well, we don't want ye here, do we lads?' Frazer got to his feet and, looking back at his companions with a grin, took a few steps towards Robbie who held his ground.

Frazer was taller and bigger than Robbie, but Robbie was quick and agile and could look after himself as he had had to do on more than one occasion back on Tyneside. He had no fear of Frazer, but he recognised that the situation was getting difficult. Frazer's friends had now stood up and were standing a few feet behind him, expecting action. Without warning Frazer swung his large boot in the direction of Robbie's groin, and Robbie was only just able to deflect the kick, which left a muddy smear across the top of his jeans.

'Haway, what the fuck do y' think yer doing, you stupid bastard!' shouted Robbie more in surprise than alarm. He circled away and to the right of Frazer who continued to lurch towards him.

'Who are y' callin' a bastard,' replied Frazer, unsteady on his feet and slipping on the wet grass as he continued his pursuit. 'Y' can just fuck aff away home, and don't bother coming back, naebody wants y' here!'

Frazer's two wee mates were now standing alongside of him.

'Aye,' said one, 'y' heard what the man said. Fuck aff.'

And so Robbie, angry and puzzled by Frazer's overt aggression, turned and walked off slowly, their laughter in his ears. He knew they wouldn't follow. They would be content with their little victory.

He was quite angered by the incident mostly because it was unfair, he hadn't sought the confrontation, and it was so, well, mindless. He thought the best course of action was to head back to his Aunty's house and get packed for his morning train to Newcastle.

As he approached the top of The Crathie the rain started up again, blown in by a stiff breeze. By now a few houses had their lights on and as he passed by the Macdonald's house he stole a glance up at Mhairi's window. It was in darkness. It would be quite some time before he saw her again.

In fact, Mhairi was in her room, but had not yet turned on the light. She was watching the rain barrelling in from up the strath and clattering against the glass. She was thinking about her imminent move to Edinburgh. She was sure she would miss her friends and home comforts but, being the adventurous soul she was, she was more than ready to spread her wings. Going to Edinburgh University was a big deal. As she looked out she saw the solitary figure of Robbie walking past her house, all hunched up against the rain and wind, saw him glance up at her window and she wondered a little about him and his obvious fondness for her. She really liked him, he was different with his easy manner and good humour but, being the practical girl she was, she felt that she had been right not to let the relationship, if there even ever had been one, develop, given the imminent change in her circumstances. She pulled the curtains, switched on the light and turned to her packing.

The next morning, Robbie had plenty of time on the six hour train journey to Newcastle to gather his thoughts. As the train sped southwards the highland scenery was replaced by a gentler green coastal landscape. His dark mood lifted slightly as he considered the occurrences of the last few days. The incident with Frazer had angered him, but on reflection, it was understandable. Frazer was now, according to his Aunty Mary, someone to stay well clear of. Up to goodness knows what, she said, and where had all that spare cash come from she had wondered, casting a disparaging look in the direction of her neighbours' house.

Frazer was apparently earning some money as a farm worker, money that had been spent on "that bike." On fine summer evenings the sound of this inadequately silenced transport disturbed the silence as he hammered noisily along paths in the woods and then later up and down The Crathie, much to everyone's annoyance.

As to Mhairi, well, he was really smitten, he loved her lithe figure, her sharpness of mind and that infectious laugh, and he had dreamed about her and thought about her often, but he realised that, for him, she was unobtainable, a kind of romantic ideal against which all others were to be compared.

He thought, too, about his fishing, which gave him so much pleasure, and his recent successes. He enjoyed everything about Strathskean, the freedom it gave him to explore and wander up and down the river which was to him always interesting and ever changing. He truly felt at peace when he was there. As the train rattled over the Tweed viaduct at Berwick and on through Northumberland he dozed off. In his mind's eye, he was wading down the Manse Pool, the water a perfect height and just tinged with brown, a salmon splashed noisily downstream of him, he executed a perfect double spey cast, pitching his fly about four feet above and to the right of the fish. The line swung round... He was roughly jolted of his reverie by a loud Geordie voice telling him that the train would be shortly arriving at Central Station Newcastle.

He retrieved his case from the rack, got off the train, and walked out of the station to his bus stop. The rain beat down, almost drowning out the noise of the traffic, there was an acrid smell of diesel and the orange streetlights were reflected in the black wet mirror like surface of the road. His bus shuddered up he hopped on and, leaving his case downstairs, he went up to the top deck and hunched down in a seat near the front.

The bus passed over the Tyne Bridge and swung left on the A184 towards South Shields, Robbie's home town. Through the rain spattered window Robbie could see the orange blurry street lights of the interconnected industrial towns of the South Tyneside conurbation stretching as far as he could see. Felling, Hebburn, Jarrow were all subconsciously ticked off until he got off the bus at Tyne Dock. He walked up TempleTown Road and then up the dimly lit Dock Street. Taking out his key he climbed up the steps of the end terrace house that was his home. He opened the door and chucked his case and rucksack on the parquet floor of the narrow hall. There was a light on in the kitchen, the sound of the TV in the front room and the smell of fried food. Shouting to his Ma that he was back he clattered up the stairs and went straight to his bedroom which was at the rear of the house. He took off his jacket, draped it over the back of his chair and looked out of his window at the dark outline of the terraced houses and beyond them, the huge angular shapes of dockyard cranes silhouetted against a sulphurous sky. Truly it was another world.

Back in Strathskean Frazer was feeling quite pleased with himself. His two wee mates had been very complimentary: 'Aye Big Man, y' certainly told the English tae fuck aff, so ye did,' was what they said. He had developed quite a dislike of Robbie. It was a seasonal thing, a summer irritation like the midgies. At first, in the August holidays when Robbie was up, when they had been young teenagers, he had quite enjoyed spending a bit of time showing him his world, stravaging about the woods and river banks and Robbie had been an interested companion and appreciative of Frazer's teaching. He, Frazer, had been in charge. However, as they became older, Robbie had become a little bit of an irritation, less interested Frazer's shooting and trapping, and more interested in the fishing. And then there had been that salmon, the indignity of the river rescue and the subsequent merciless ribbing he'd endured about him having been 'landed by an English fisher.' But it was the friendship with Mhairi that had really got to him, seeing how he'd had a crush on her for ages and she'd rejected his overtures. He had been mad with jealousy when he had seen them together.

Now he felt he had re-established the status quo. Robbie wouldn't be back. He'd been told.

14

January 1978

Because Westoe RFC shared their ground with the cricket club there was only one pitch actually at the clubhouse and so the third and fourth teams played on alternate weeks at Oakleigh Gardens some two miles to the south of the town. Here there were a couple of sports pitches of undulating grassland adjacent to a small residential area at the edge of the low lying Cleadon Hills. Two sets of stunted white rugby posts a hundred yards apart delineated the rugby pitch. At some point in the pre-season the appropriate lines had been marked out by the council but after several months' exposure to the elements some, if not all, were indistinct.

There being no changing rooms or other facilities up there both teams had to change at the clubhouse in town, and then, in their playing kit, get into the opposition's coach or their own cars and drive up to the pitch, bringing with them the flags, oranges and suchlike. Sometimes the referee was provided by the county society , but often it was an elderly committee member called Stan and it was his happy job also to inspect the pitch prior to kick off, and remove any dog mess, cans, bottles or other detritus.

Usually, the elevation of the playing field at the foot of the hills afforded an excellent panorama of Tyneside with its dockyard cranes and the high rise buildings of Newcastle in the far distance, however, when the teams arrived on this January afternoon, a fine, cold, wind driven rain obscured the view. At half past two the light values were apocalyptic, and it was with a distinct lack of enthusiasm that Westoe Fourths levered themselves from their warm cars, warmed up by jogging and stretching and then arranged themselves in some sort of order under the direction of their solid, eighteen stone skipper Wes, a forty seven year old ship yard welder. Westoe were at the uphill half of the slanting pitch. The opposition, Percy Park, from north of the river, waited for the kick off in the mud at the lower end. They had won the toss and everyone knew it was better to play uphill in the first half, rather than have to force tired unfit bodies up the slope in the second.

Robbie, along with his mate, Gaz, being the youngest by far in the Westoe team had to put out the flags of which there should have been fourteen, but in fact they only had been given eleven. They had been drafted in to the team owing to the fact that Sunday's colts game had been cancelled. Robbie was keen to have a 'run oot' as it was called with the Fourths who were always short of a player or two. Since the summer he'd thrown himself into his rugby with renewed enthusiasm and he was playing for his school first team on Wednesday afternoons and also on Saturday mornings. On Sundays he played for Westoe Colts, the club's under 19 side. Mostly he played open side flanker, being quite big, but as he was quick as well he was quite comfortable playing in the backs, he and Gaz were playing outside centre and winger respectively. Westoe Fourths liked to have a couple of kids in the outfield, they could run swiftly, and chase balls which were punted randomly and speculatively down the pitch by the ageing fly half, an ex Norwegian international, whose once brilliant running and passing game was now but a fond memory.

At that level of rugby the game was fairly static affair with a large number of scrums and line outs. What both sets of forwards lacked in athleticism they made up for in bulk and by the time the game was nearing the half time mark both packs were blowing hard after thirty minutes of trundling around and they were literally steaming from their exertions. The pitch was very wet and with such little grass that both sets of forwards were completely covered in mud. Stan, the ref, was struggling to tell them apart. In contrast, both sets of backs had mostly clean kit, the ball having hardly ever come their way.

By the time the half way stage was nearing Robbie had yet to make a tackle, his opposing centre never having received a pass. However, there had been much fruitless chasing of long kicks down the pitch, one of which had resulted in a try for Gaz. The score at this point was nine nil to Westoe, one converted try and a penalty. Percy Park had defended stoically and when the half time whistle was blown the general feeling was that a nine point lead would be difficult to defend given the slope of the pitch and the general knackeredness of Westoe's pack.

The kick off was delayed for a few moments to let an old lady and her little dog cross the pitch and, then, predictably, the Percy Park fly half kicked the ball long and high down into the bottom corner just where Robbie was positioned. He caught the looping ball cleanly and then, side stepping his opposite number who had rushed up quickly from an offside position, punted it into touch close to the halfway line. There was a few mumbled compliments of 'well played son' from the forwards, relieved that they didn't have to defend a lineout near their own try line.

The game lurched back and forth in the gathering gloom, it was mostly played in Westoe's half. Robbie and Gaz had their work cut out and each had to make several crucial tackles. After fifteen minutes or so Percy Park were awarded a penalty under the posts which they successfully kicked and then, only a couple of minutes later they managed a barged over try which they duly converted. Nine points all.

Now in the last fifteen minutes of the game the cold rain was turning to sleet and that, along with the strengthening wind blowing right into the Percy Park lads' faces, negated the advantage they had had from the slope, and so the game slowly lost its intensity rather like an old clockwork toy winding down. Stan blew for full time. Nobody minded that he had cut a few minutes off the second half. The battle was over, the honours shared, the opposition cheered through two lines of players, backs slapped, hands shaken, the ref thanked and the balls, eleven flags, etc. collected by Gaz and Robbie. Time for a hot shower and a pint or two.

By quarter to five the bar at Westoe Rugby Club was noisily starting to fill up. Today it was mostly the players from the second and fourth teams emerging freshly showered from the changing rooms, also there was a handful of spectators and some club members who had been in the bar most of the afternoon. On days when the first team were at home there would usually be a good number of spectators filling the clubhouse from the final whistle onwards , but today they and the thirds were away over the river at Percy Park.

Robbie loved the atmosphere, the good humour, the loudness, the camaraderie, the fun of it all. He and Gaz had been thanked personally for their contributions by Wes and Gaz was made to down a pint of Exhibition in 'one' as he had scored the team's only try. Now at six thirty the clubhouse was rammed, the first team having returned with a famous victory. Jugs of beer were passed round, songs were sung, the atmosphere vibrant.

Robbie and Gaz were now sitting in the Colts corner along with a handful of the other younger players. Soon, as per usual, the talk turned to what was happening that Saturday evening. Since the summer Robbie had made a conscious decision to socialise with his peers, something he'd not always done before and now he was 'one of the crowd' and always included in what was going on.

'Aye,' said Jacko who was the Colts' scrum half, 'Bill Clarkson's folks are away for the weekend, and w' can gyan roond there, if w' want. Bill says it's fine as long as w' don't make a mess.'

That suggestion met with general mirth, Bill's parents wouldn't normally welcome a bunch of eighteen year olds into their immaculate house. In fact, they had specifically prohibited it, but Bill wouldn't want to admit that to his mates. Of course they all thought it was a great idea.

For Robbie's contemporaries , most of whom were in their last year in the sixth form or had apprenticeships, going down town to a night club or even having a few beers in a pub was usually only an occasional treat. To get some cash Robbie sometimes did casual labouring on his father's building sites and odd jobs for an elderly neighbour, but that income was sporadic, so going round to folks houses with a bottle or two was an affordable way of socialising.

Besides there were compensations. Recently Robbie had been seeing a girl called Val who was, like himself, in the upper sixth and was hoping to go off to uni in a few months. She was a bright spark, very focussed on her ambition to study Dentistry, and some of her drive had rubbed off on Robbie. He was now, much to his parents' delight, committed to getting decent 'A' level grades and going to uni to read English.

So, having played an enjoyable, if not exactly demanding, game of rugby that afternoon, and now surrounded by his mates in the warmth and bonhomie of the club and, with an evening prospect of drinking a couple of beers and smooching with the highly attractive Val on Mr and Mrs Clarkson's shiny leather sofa, life was temporarily on an upward trajectory. He felt great. He had not had a single thought about Strathskean for months now.

15

1980

At five o' clock the October light was draining away and the lights of The Strathy Bar shimmered in the puddles of its car park. A battered, mud spattered Land Rover Series 111 swung in off the road, and came to an abrupt halt near to the hotel wall. Its driver, Angus, a big grey bear of a man, slammed shut the door without locking it and, shielding his face with his arm against the wet, ran the few steps to the hotel entrance and pushed his way through the bar door into the noise and warmth of the smoke filled room. It had been raining steadily for a few days and the deer stalking on the estate had been called off yet again due to the persistent downpour and poor visibility. No stalking meant unhappy guests and no tips for Angus, one of the estate's two gamekeepers.

'Aye aye, Angus,' said the barman, 'weather's nae better eh?' and without being asked handed him a pint of Deucher's and turned to the optics to give him a large dram of Grouse.

Shaking his grey head Angus slid a ten pound note to the barman who tilled it and left the change on the counter by the dram. Soon Angus was deep in serious conversation with two or three other estate workers and the bar slowly filled up with the usual after work Friday crowd all wanting a drink and an unwind before they went home to face their families.

Out in the darkening car park a large figure detached itself from the shadows and moving swiftly, using the other cars as cover, went to the rear of Angus's Land Rover. Pausing only to check that he was unobserved, he opened the tailgate and removed a long canvas bag and a holdall before disappearing into the woods at the rear of the hotel.

A few hours later Angus, now in a much happier mood than when he arrived, left the Strathy and got back into his Land Rover. After a couple of attempts he managed to locate reverse and, without hitting any of the other parked cars during his complicated exit manoeuvrings, drove slowly to his home, a cottage on the estate. At no point had he thought to look into the back of the Land Rover, nor did he check it or lock it upon his arrival some fifteen minutes later.

It was well past eleven o' clock when Angus climbed out of his bed on the Saturday morning. He had a bit of a headache, a dry mouth and felt a little queasy, but not too bad considering, he thought. He was still wearing yesterday's vest and underpants it having been as much as he could do to get his trousers and socks off given the circumstances. He pulled on a pair of tweed breeks and a thick jumper and gingerly went down the narrow staircase.

The kitchen was dark and the stone flags cold on his bare feet. He lit the gas and banged the kettle down on the hob. His wife Susan, had left earlier for her work up at the big house and he dimly remembered her saying something about needing to 'talk about this' when she got home. He was pretty sure he knew what 'this' was. He spooned four lots of sugar and some instant coffee into his mug and filled it with the boiling water. Alternately blowing and sipping he looked around the kitchen. His coat had been thrown over one of the chairs and his boots lay where he had discarded them, by the door.

He looked through the small window. Outside the rain had ceased and a thin sun was breaking through the clouds. For the first time he noticed his Land Rover. It was parked untidily, its bonnet stuck in the hedge at the side of the cottage. A strange and awful feeling ran through his body. Hastily he pulled on his boots, threw open the door and in three or four strides reached the vehicle. He swung the tailgate open. His hunting rifle, a Remington .308, complete with scope and suppressor and the holdall containing dozens of rounds was missing.

He retired to the kitchen to think. He was the senior gamekeeper on the estate. He was responsible for the considerable collection of shotguns and rifles kept in locked steel cabinets in the gun room in the castle, as required by law. Having a rifle stolen from a locked car was bad enough, but having one taken from an unlocked vehicle whilst its keeper was in a bar having a few drinks was the very definition of criminal negligence. If news of this got out, not only would he be a laughing stock locally, but he would almost certainly lose his job and the tied cottage that went with it. His lordship was not known for his leniency. Far better to keep silent and see if he could cover up the loss somehow. There was another Remington in the collection wasn't there? As to who might have taken it, well there were several likely suspects in the strath.

A couple of days later, there having been no gossip in the town about the missing rifle, Frazer judged it timely to have a look at his latest acquisition. Frazer reverentially placed the long canvas bag and holdall on the rickety table in the kitchen of Caoraich Cottage. He unzipped the bag, withdrew the Remington and, admiring its sleekness and balance, squinted through the telescopic sight. There was a little pocket in the bag and from this he took out the cylindrical silencer and screwed it into the muzzle. He carefully checked the four shot magazine, it was empty, as he thought, Angus would never leave a loaded rifle in his Land Rover.

16

Frazer pushed open the door of Caoraich Cottage and stepped out into the grey pre dawn light. There had been a slight frost and the puddles crackled under his boots as he walked down the track that led past the farm to the main road. Under his arm he carried a large bulky canvas holdall, and checking carefully that there were no cars in earshot, he loped across the tarmac, hopped over the crash barrier and disappeared through the browning bracken and birch scrub that led to some large farm fields by way of an overgrown path. This path was in a gully a few feet lower than the fields. Frazer stopped, looked carefully around, and withdrew the Remington from the holdall. Holding the rifle in front of him he quietly and slowly crawled up the bank. At the top of the bank there was a three strand wire fence which served as a notional boundary to one of the fields. Pushing the rifle in front of him through the vegetation he ever so gently and slowly raised his head and peered through the grass and bracken. It was brighter now, a wind was blowing into his face and the grasses at the edge of the field were swaying. One hundred yards away, directly opposite Frazer, at the edge of a wood and by a track three red deer grazed, pausing every few moments to look up for danger.

Frazer lined up the biggest of the deer, a hind, in the crosshairs of his telescopic sight and, controlling his breathing, gently squeezed the trigger.

The wind carried away the boof of the silenced rifle shot and the deer collapsed instantly, and after a few twitchings was still.

Frazer stood up, and quickly skirted round the edge of the field towards his prize. He looked at it briefly as it lay awkwardly sprawled in the grasses, its eye already glazed. He felt no emotion. Taking hold of its still warm rear legs, and with some considerable physical effort, he managed to drag the carcass through a gap in the fence and into the wood near the track. There he concealed it behind a large Scots pine. A few hours later he returned with his Transit, loaded the deer and, with the whole operation unobserved, returned to Caoraich Cottage just as the last of the day's light was sliding away.

17

July 1981

It was well after eleven o' clock on a Friday night early in July in Strathskean and Bill Macdonald was comfortably ensconced in his favourite armchair, looking out of his living room window down The Crathie. The summer light had only just started to dim and he thought he should be out fishing the Caoraich pool for sea trout but here he was in a sentimental and emotional mood, partly brought on by the three large glasses of Glen Livet he had consumed. On his lap were the photographs he'd taken of Mhairi's graduation ceremony and the programme with her name in it. The Strathskean Herald had written a nice little piece about her and included a photograph. She was the first in their family to graduate. He couldn't have been more proud. He was even almost reconciled to the strong possibly of her working abroad.

Ten days earlier Bill, Morag and their other daughter, Kirstie, now pregnant, together with her husband Hamish, had all driven down the A9 to Edinburgh for Mhairi's graduation. They had taken their seats in the Great Hall along with dozens of other proud parents , watched in awe as the begowned procession of professors and academics took its place on the stage, and clapped enthusiastically as the name of each graduate was read out and presented with the degree scroll by the Vice Chancellor. Of course Mhairi had got the First she was hoping for, she had worked hard for it, but being herself, she had also taken full advantage of the student social scene.

Later that day, at a celebratory meal in a posh restaurant, Mhairi enlightened her folks about her future plans. She was staying in Edinburgh and sharing a flat in Morningside with some friends. She was going into hotel management, she had a job lined up already as a trainee manager with a large international hotel group. It was a profession which offered excellent financial rewards and amazing travel opportunities she said.

Bill looked across the table at the slender, poised young woman that was his younger daughter, and, almost as if he were seeing her for the first time, he realised that her life would be totally different to anything he himself had experienced. It was as if she had stepped into a different reality a million miles from Strathskean.

At around about the same time, give or take a day or two, Robbie was in a curry house in Levenshulme. He was with his parents, Dennis and Shiela and they, too, were celebrating his graduation. He had read English and, much to his surprise given the amount of time he had spent socialising and playing rugby, he had got a respectable degree.

Like the Macdonalds Dennis and Sheila were equally proud. Dennis held down a foreman's job at a local building firm and was not one to mince his words.

'So, what are y' thinkin' o' doing noo? Y'll need to get some coin in yer pocket fairly soon.'

'Aye Dad, I know, I thought I'd come back home and get my usual summer job job with you lot on the sites, save a bit of cash and then ah'm thinkin' of doing a teaching qualification at up at NCC, there's a couple of me mates up there already.'

'Aye, well son, that's a decent plan, we'll only charge you a few hundred a week for yer scran!' his dad said with a laugh, 'won't we Sheila?' Robbie's dad was quite pleased with his son's choice of profession. To him it represented security and respectability, and, since the recent review, the pay, if not generous, was at least reasonable.

Sheila smiled, 'Aye that's fine son, it'll be nice to have y' at hame wi' us for a bit.' Thirty years on Tyneside had not altered her northern Scots accent.

She had missed her son when he'd been at Manchester and was glad of his news. Sheila and Dennis were elderly parents, Dennis had been over forty and Sheila late thirties when Robbie came along. He was their only child.

In fact Robbie been thinking of doing this for some time and had actually applied. Northern Counties was a teacher training college about forty five minutes away or so away from Tyne Dock, on the other side of the river, you had to go through the Tyne Tunnel to get to it. His mates, both ex Westoe Colts, were in the last year of their teaching degrees, and had spoken enthusiastically about the vibrant social scene and the favourable ratio of women to men.

18

1981

A. Chisholm and Son, the butcher's shop on the main street of the Bridge of Skean, a small town some twenty five miles up the strath, was run by a cheerful and ambitious twenty something who was known to one and all as Andra. His real name was James Andrew Chisholm, but when he took over the business from his father, Andrew, the original Andra, he found that the name somehow came with the shop. Not that he minded. His friendliness and affability concealed a sharp business brain and an eye for the main chance.

In past years the shop had catered for all the traditional butchery needs of 'The Brig' as the town was known. In addition, every Friday for decades, regular as clockwork, Andra's father had loaded up his van and driven round the remote farms and villages of Strath Skean where he delivered telephoned orders and sold directly at the door. Now, the demand for that kind of local service had declined, partly due to most folks now having cars, and the arrival of a big supermarket in the town. The traditional butchery business was struggling, new initiatives and new markets were needed.

Tourism in the strath was on the up and the number of small hotels, guesthouses, bed and breakfasts and rental cottages were increasing in number. Even in winter folks were driving up the A9 for the skiing and walking. Andra's shop window was always crammed with beautiful displays of mouth-watering meats and pies. Locals and visitors alike stepped inside to purchase his locally sourced and reared produce, after all it was cheaper and far, far better than that on offer in the supermarket at the other end of the town.

The young Andra had made sure that he was on personal terms with the vast majority of hotel managers, B and B owners and chefs up and down Strath Skean. In addition to the successful shop he had developed a substantial business in selling direct, much as his father had done in the old days, but now on a more ambitious scale. He had a unit on the tiny industrial estate at the back of the Brig and it was here he and his three staff prepared the meats, pies and game for sale and distribution around the strath. Of course, most of the meats came from the nearest abattoir in Inverness, and very good they were too, but Andra also had another supply chain: very local, and much, much, cheaper.

On a wet evening in November a dark blue Transit van squelched into the dark yard behind Chisholm Meats in the Bridge of Skean industrial estate. It scrunched to a halt on the wet gravel, reversed swiftly up to the back doors of the unit, and its large angular driver jumped out and shambled to the rear of the van. The unit doors opened, bathing the rear of the Transit in a white light.

Andra emerged from the glare, 'Aye aye, Frazer, whit have you got for me?'   Wordlessly, Frazer opened the back of his van. Inside were three deer carcasses and a couple of sacks of pheasants.

'Ah great, that's jist whit ah need, let's get them in here.' And so the two of them pulled the deer one by one out of the van and carried them into the unit, leaving them in a corner, a stiff pile of legs and antlers. Frazer went back and retrieved the two hessian sacks containing the pheasants. Flinging them onto the floor, he turned to look at Andra who was extracting some banknotes from his wallet.

'Right Fraz, I'll see ye in a week or so, I can tek a couple mair deers, and if ye can manage some mutton that would be great too.' He handed Frazer the notes.

'Ok Andra, I'm nae so sure about the sheeps, naebody minds aboot the deer, but I might have to get the sheeps from over the hill.'

'Aye, well, see what ye can do, Fraz, catch ye soon,' and with that he closed the doors, plunging Frazer into the early evening darkness.

19

Spring 1982

Robbie looked out of his steamed up classroom window. Outside the cold March wind chased whirling tornadoes of rubbish around a tarmac playground. Beyond the playground the school playing fields with their bent metal goalposts gave way to a saggy chain link boundary fence which had netted a huge quantity of wind-blown litter, behind that there were rows of red brick council houses and then in the far distance the cranes on the river stood like angular trees on the horizon.

Well, it wasn't actually his classroom window, it belonged to a Mr Ord. Mr Ord had not only generously allowed Robbie the full use of the classroom, but also his two year eleven sets and as many of the lower year ten and nine sets as he thought he could dump on Robbie who was on his second, and final, PGCE teaching practice.

Mr Ord was a small wizened man in his late fifties or early sixties. He smelled of stale cigarette smoke, moved slowly like an aged tortoise and had a hacking emphysemic cough. He didn't say much, but one look from his gimlet eyes would silence the entire class. He was the only teacher left in the school who had qualified under the emergency teacher training scheme after the war. He did not rate the new fangled post graduate course, but was pleased to take a student or two because it meant that he could spend half the working day in the staff room reading the Daily Mail and smoking his bloody roll ups.

Mr Ord was known to one and all as 'The Count' because a former student had once broken into the school and painted the legend: 'Ord is a Count' right across his classroom door.

As Mr Ord himself remarked: 'The poor bastard couldn't even spell that properly!'

As part of the arrangement the school had with Northern Counties College Mr Ord was required to 'tutor' Robbie in the finer aspects of English teaching. Mr Ord used an ancient text book with the younger kids, working his way through methodically, chapter by chapter, page by page. The CSE exam course was mostly delivered in the same way, apart from the coursework element, which was now apparently Robbie's special assignment.

'Right Robbie,' wheezed Mr Ord , who, coincidentally, knew Robbie's dad quite well, 'classroom management:

divven't give the little bastards an inch. Get in there and dominate right from the very start.'

When Robbie protested that that approach flew in the face of what he had been taught at N.C.C. which was all to do with producing stimulating and differentiated lesson plans that would fascinate and engage even the most unruly of pupils. Mr Ord was scathing, 'Them lecturers couldn't teach their way out of a bliddy paper bag. Go in hard.'

Twenty minutes into his year 9 lesson [assessed] Robbie had not 'given the little bastards an inch' as per instructions. His heavily brutalised lesson plan involved the kids writing copious amounts and then reading silently. One or two of the boys had tried to talk but Robbie had aggressively shouted them down. Mr Ord, who was listening to Robbie's teaching performance from behind the stockroom door, nodded in silent approval.

The lesson ground on. With ten minutes or so to go a small girl at the front of the class put up her hand. 'Please sir, ah need the lavvy.' There were a few muffled giggles which Robbie shushed immediately.

Robbie ignored her.

Three minutes later, 'Please sir, ah really need the lavvy.'

'Shut up, and get on with your work, you should have gone at break, and there's only ten minutes or so left till the end of the lesson.' was Robbie's curt reply. He stood behind her as if to emphasise the point. The girl began to sob silently, her shoulders shaking. After a minute or so a small puddle of urine formed under her desk as the girl continued to weep. The rest of the class laboured on in an unpleasant silence.

In the lesson evaluation conducted in the smoke filled staffroom, Mr Ord was effusive in his praise: 'That was aal reet,' he wheezed in a detailed summation, 'y'll probably survive.' The incident with the girl was dismissed as an occupational hazard, 'It was her own stupid fault.'

Although Robbie had been extremely disconcerted by that event, and Mr Ord's preferred teaching style was clearly neanderthal, Robbie, however, did take one important lesson from Mr Ord's philosophy, and that was without control of the class, teaching was impossible. You might as well go home. That priceless piece of knowledge, not actually grasped by all teachers, in Robbie's future opinion, was to serve him well over the coming decades.

Dennis, Robbie's dad, was in the snug at The Ship Inn, Cleadon, later on that evening. Through the cigarette smoke he spotted Jack Ord who was hunched over an empty glass at the end of the bar, his usual place on a Friday.

Dennis ordered a couple of pints of Ex and slid one down to Jack, he took a deep slurp of beer, wiped the foam from his whiskers and asked how his lad was getting on.

'Yer lad's fine,' came the reply, 'he'll make a decent teacher, when he's had a bit more experience.' That was praise indeed from the ancient educator.

Dennis was pleased at Jack Ord's words, he'd always thought that Robbie would be do well, after all the lad did have a bit of personality for God's sake.

20

Robbie often thought that it was easier to get to most holiday destinations in Europe than to Uisken, that tiny piece of heaven near the end of The Ross of Mull. That's what made it so attractive in his opinion. He had first discovered it when he was touring round the West Coast with Elaine, his girlfriend at the time. They were looking for somewhere to camp before visiting Iona and, looking at their OS map, had decided to take a left at Bunessan and drive over the hill to see what they could find.

A couple of miles on the single track road took them the top of the hill and an amazing view. It was a clear afternoon and the sea was a glittering mirror. As they looked to the right they could see Ardalanish Point and beyond that the wide vastness of the Atlantic. Straight ahead Colonsay, and behind and to the left, Isla and Jura were clearly etched into the sparkling waters. Downhill the road led to a scatter of four or five cottages and then the beach. There were one or two tents and a couple of caravans on the machair above the high water mark and Robbie's courteous enquiry at the croft confirmed that they were welcome to camp for as long as they wished, but a donation to the RNLI would be welcome. Washing was in the wee burn that spilled onto the beach, and fresh water etc. was to be found in the public conveniences back in the car park opposite the Argyll Arms in Bunessan.

It wasn't too long before they had pulled all their kit out of the van, pitched the tent on a flat bit of machair at the end of the beach and had got the evening meal sizzling away on the barbeque. Later the small breeze dropped and they went for a walk along the kelp covered sand and then up and over the heather brae on the myrtle scented headland toward Malcolm's Point and Carsaig beyond. They never saw a soul, and were overwhelmed with the solitude and timeless beauty of the place.

In the morning they woke up to the sound of the waves breaking gently on the beach and the cries of the seagulls. After breakfast Robbie went to his van and with some effort pulled out the canvas holdalls that contained the Avon Inflatable Sportboat and fifteen horsepower Johnson he'd acquired a couple of years ago from his mate Mack, of Macintosh Chandlery, a lad with whom he played rugby at Westoe.

He pulled the deflated boat down to the high water mark on the beach in front of his tent, inserted the floorboards and pumped up the neoprene tubes. A few minutes later he attached the motor and stowed the oars, petrol and his fishing gear. As soon as the tide reached the boat he would be ready to launch.

He and Elaine had changed into wetsuits and, donning their lifejackets, they pulled the boat between them through the slight breaking surf until they were waist deep and then they jumped in, Elaine paddling away to keep the bows facing the waves while Robbie started the motor.

At first the boat moved slowly through the clear shallows, Robbie being careful not to hit any of the kelp covered rocks, but as soon as they reached the clear blue of the bay proper he opened up the throttle and the boat surged exhilaratingly away on a fast plane, bumping over the short chop. As soon they were clear they headed right, along the coast to Ardalanish Bay which was about a mile or so west of Uisken.

The entrance to Ardalanish Bay was guarded by some small rocky islets and Robbie, recognising a fishy place when he saw one, cut the engine and assembled his two spinning rods. On Elaine's he tied a heavy Toby, and on his own he put up a set of three pollack feathers and a two ounce lead.

It wasn't long, in fact her first cast, and Elaine was shouting excitedly, 'Haway Robbie, I'm in,' her rod bending over at an alarming angle. A few shrieks and gasps later and Robbie had lifted out a beautiful golden olive pollack about four or five pounds in weight. He unhooked it and hit it on the head. It would make a delicious meal.

There followed a couple of hours' excellent sport. The whole area was productive, and as long as they fished close to the kelp fringes and outcrops they caught and returned pollack after pollack as well the occasional coalfish. Elaine caught a couple of mackerel too, which they kept for future bait.

After a while they decided to move into Ardalanish Bay itself, and were just motoring slowly towards the point when Elaine shouted, 'Hey Robbie, what's those buoys for over there?' she was pointing to an arrangement of a dozen or so large fluorescent buoys apparently holding up some poles and a kind of large netting structure. There was another similar arrangement about half a mile away along the point.

At first Robbie, was nonplussed, but then he remembered that there had been a couple of fast skiffs with massive outboards pulled up at the top end of Uisken beach. They were salmon boats and what he was looking at was a large salmon bag net permanently moored in the bay with a leader net stretching at right angles to the shore.

So, he thought, what must happen is that the returning salmon would be swimming along the shoreline until they encountered the lead net which stretched at right angles to the shore, then, not being able to swim through the obstruction they would turn and follow the line of the net which led them inevitably to the bag at the end. Here they were trapped until removed by the fishermen. It was not a long season, but the huge numbers of salmon caught made it a lucrative one for those who owned the netting rights.

Thoughtful about what he and Elaine had seen, they returned to Uisken and their own fresh fish supper and an evening walk. He didn't think there were many salmon rivers on Mull, certainly none on its south coast and he wondered where the fish had been headed.

Chatting about these nets with a couple of local lads in the Argyll Arms later on that holiday, he discovered that the Ardalanish netting station had not been used for many years but then had been re-commissioned by some mainlanders who had seen the potential. And now that the question of nets had been raised in his mind he was surprised to see just how many he noticed as he and Elaine drove about the island. They were ubiquitous, leading out from the shore, or near the mouths of small burns, or in inlets, and he reflected on the vast number of salmon that would never complete their journey.

They spent quite a few more days in Uisken, the weather being so nice, much of it on the water. Robbie had discovered that towards evening it seemed that the pollack or saithe as they were called in Scotland, moved up in the water column and so it was possible to catch them on a fly rod. He had with him his reservoir rod and a fast sinking shooting head and that, coupled with a big white lure, provided amazing sport.

When they were not fishing they took the boat down past Malcolm's Point and on to Carsaig where they drifted under the towering cliffs watching the wild goats and eagles. On the way there and back they frequently saw dolphins, porpoise, minke whales and even the odd otter on the bladderwrack at the edge of the tideline.

The other Uisken campers were really friendly too, and it transpired that most of them came back year after year with their families. Robbie felt really welcome and was quite happy mooching around chatting, or going for long walks. In the evenings he and Elaine would barbeque fish, drink whisky and sit looking out of their tent at the ever changing ocean as the evening light leached away.

At the end August most of the Scottish campers had headed south like sand martins at the end of summer and so as the weather changed and the rains swept in Robbie and Elaine broke camp and headed to Fishnish and the ferry to the mainland at Lochaline. Two days later they were back in the industrial bleakness of Tyneside.

Robbie was to return to Uisken on several more times over the years as a regular summer visitor but not with Elaine, who had decided that she was going to break with the Tyneside rut she was in, which also included Robbie, who was showing little signs of wanting to move away. She wanted to do some serious travelling. Partially as a result of her decision, and partly because he belatedly, at the age of twenty seven, had realised that he probably needed to move on with his at life and career he started looking around for other jobs.

21

In the new year, a few months after Elaine had gone to New Zealand Robbie left Tyneside to take up a teaching post in Manchester. He'd initially got a house share in Didsbury with a couple of other guys his age, and he reverted to, or more precisely, recommenced his bachelor lifestyle. During the week there would be a few drinks late on at his local, or after training twice a week at Burnage Rugby Club, and then, Friday out with the other young staff, Saturday, school rugby in the mornings and then his own game in the afternoon. Most Saturday nights in the season he would be out with the team, or at a party somewhere. Sundays were a recovery day, with some marking and a snoozy evening in front of the TV.

In the summer, he would go fly fishing with a couple of mates across to Ladybower, or Tittesworth, both less than an hour's drive away. Sometimes they went and fished the Dove near Ashbourne, if they could get on. Occasionally he would go coarse fishing during the autumn months when he had some time. From time to time he would visit his folks back in Tyneside and catch up with the lads at Westoe.

However, it was Scotland that drew him back summer after summer. He would load his van with his boat, camping equipment, and fishing tackle and head off to the Western Isles, nearly always ending up on Mull. Sometimes he had a companion, sometimes he was alone. At Uisken however, he met up with the other regular temporary residents and enjoyed his annual fix of life on the beach.

22

Robbie was alone in the Upper School staffroom at Southern High. He was 'on call' ready to rescue any colleague who was being overwhelmed by the challenges of teaching inner city teenagers. Southern, as it was known, was a huge comprehensive of approximately seventeen hundred male students which had been formed in the late sixties by the amalgamation of a secondary modern school and a famous grammar school. Consequently it was on two different sites, a mile or so apart, the grammar school buildings being the "Upper School" with the fourteen to eighteen year olds, and the old secondary modern, the "Lower School" containing the rest.

The Upper School staff room was oak panelled, with several large tables and various comfy chairs scattered about. Its smell was unique: of leather chairs, of tobacco, academia and of random games equipment. The older members of staff, and there were still a few of those dinosaurs left, had their special chairs, woe betide anybody who inadvertently sat on them. Broadsheet news papers lay open on one or two tables, their cryptic crosswords ostentatiously filled in. At lunch there were usually two bridge schools on the go. In one corner there was a sink, kettle and cups.

Robbie made himself a cup of coffee, and silently bet on who he would be called to rescue first. Period seven on a Friday usually meant Simon Smithson, a middle aged Religious Studies teacher and Oxford graduate, who was reasonably effective with his 'A' level classes but was completely useless with the viciously feral mixed ability groups. Most subjects were taught in sets, however, Religious Studies along with PHSE, was taught in mixed ability groups. Robbie thanked the God he didn't believe in for being spared that particular purgatory. He had just taken a sip from his mug when, sure enough, the phone went.

Picking up the clipboard which, he often thought, legitimised his authority as the deus ex machina who arrived to sort out any given problem, he exited the staffroom, bounded down the stairs and proceeded in the general direction of mobile classroom 4c.

The Upper School was a nineteen thirties brick building of two storeys with the offices and such in the middle and, either side, two rectangles of classrooms on the ground floor. The classrooms were connected by a glass covered walkway, and in the centre of each rectangle Portakabins had been placed to give extra accommodation for the previous raising of the school leaving age. At the front of the school there was a cricket square and two football pitches, a rugby pitch at the side, and behind, the sportshall and PE department.

From the walkway Robbie was able to observe classroom 4c. A hulking youth, known as Maurice, had been sent out and was in the process of tearing up his exercise books and making a pile of them against the class room door. As Robbie looked on Maurice took out a cigarette lighter and was just about to set fire to the pile when Robbie shouted and hammered on the glass. When Robbie returned, having escorted the would be pyromaniac to the "Pupil Support Unit," he knocked on the door and entered the chaos within.

Mr Smithson was looking a bit frazzled to say the least, he had a sheen of perspiration on his bald pate, and there a was a wall of noise. A group had been playing cards in the back corner and they sheepishly put them away when

Robbie stared at them. At the front of the class a small bespectacled youth was valiantly trying to complete a worksheet, his desk surrounded by bits of soggy paper thrown at him from those behind. None of the windows was open and the room stank of sweat and cheap deodorant. Robbie's practised technique in these situations was to stand in a corner, say nothing but make pretend notes on his clipboard. This nearly always worked.

After a while and some uneasy shuffling the class settled down to a worksheet about the caste system, a topic Robbie thought both irrelevant and apt given that one or two of the examples of humanity displayed before him were from the arse end of the social spectrum. And that was comprehensive education in a nutshell he thought, in any moment you would be teaching highly motivated groups of A level students who were trying to get into the top universities, and then the very next you could be dealing with the feral underclass. At least two of the lads there were on the books of famous football clubs, and were just marking time. Some of the others were destined for university, professions, business or trades and the rest, well, one could only hazard a guess.

Jack Ord's early advice to Robbie about class control had really served him well and he had rapidly established himself as a teacher who was easy to get on with, but could sort things out should need arise, which it sometimes did. Being a youngish, fit rugby player had helped as well. His greatest strength was probably that he actually liked most of the students he taught, and they liked him.

His arrival and his first few years there had coincided with a period of massive staff change, the old and tired had shuffled off to an index linked retirement and there were promotion opportunities for the likes of Robbie, who found himself Head of the English and Drama Faculty, simply by being in the right place at the right time. Actually he quite liked the job, he found it was easier to be in charge rather than working for someone else. And of course the pay was better than that of an assistant teacher.

23

Wee Jimmy was sitting in an armchair in his "office," a steel shipping container with the words "Nordstar

Freight" on the side. It was quite homely and the "scaffies" as they were called in the Doric had furnished it with a bit of carpet, a table, chairs, a gas stove and a radio. It was sitting in a commanding position at the entrance to what had once been the Strathskean Municipal Householders' Waste Disposal Facility but had now been rebranded and modernised, and called Strathskean Recycling Centre.

Originally the site had been a huge gravel quarry and for a long time the bin lorries came and tipped out the refuse for the two bulldozers to pile up in great mounds. Hundreds of wheeling and screaming black headed gulls fought over semi-edible gobbets. The periphery of the site had been guarded by netting strung upon long poles which caught some of the wind-blown litter, the rest escaping into the scrubby birch hinterland.

Now, as Wee Jimmy could see from the open doors of his container, a large part of the site was still landfill and barred to the public, but a special section right at the front of the tip close to the entrance had had been cleared to form the new public recycling centre. There was a one way system and as you drove through it you passed various yellow skips, each one specifically labelled as to what you could put in it. At the end of the line, bell shaped containers took different colours of glass bottles and cans. All in all there were about fourteen different categories: electricals, cardboard, metal, and so forth. Wee Jimmy and his co-workers were on hand to help householders with their recycling and also to check that the right stuff went into the right skip. For most individual householders organising the recycling was a pain, but do-able, and to be fair, most tried to comply, but for small tradesmen it was a nightmare. Under the old system they had just taken their unsorted waste to the tip and left it in a pile to be bulldozed away. Now, not only were they expected to sort it but, as traders, they also had to pay for the privilege. However, for some, there was cheaper solution: Frazer.

As soon as the new regulations came into play and when the local decorators, one man builders, plumbers and such started moaning in the bars about the inconvenience and the fucking cost of it all, Frazer, always a snapper up of illegal opportunities, realised there might be some easy money to be made.

He claimed, not that many believed him, that he had access to a disused pit up behind the farm at Caoraich and that, for a consideration, he would pick-up and dispose of waste that would otherwise be too costly, too unpleasant or too difficult to dispose of legally: asbestos roofing panels, old paint and oil for example.

And so, from time to time, he might get a telephone call from a mate who had had been installing a new kitchen somewhere and had the old sink, units, tiles and rubble to get rid of.

Frazer would appear at the site with his Transit van, between them they would load it up, cash would exchange hands and Frazer would ostensibly drive off to his pit. Actually there was a pit behind Caoraich Farm but Frazer had never dumped anything there.

Frazer's waste disposal technique was simple. He would drive out to the coast road and after a few miles turn off on one of the minor roads that took him up over the moor. He did this at night, there was never anyone around, and, because the roads were high up, he could see the lights of approaching cars long before they got near to him. He usually looked for a lay by or field gate to park in and then he would open the back doors and, in a matter of minutes clear his van.

24

Jack MacGregor opened the back door of his croft and took a deep breath of "sweet heilan' air" as he put it. His croft was high up on "The Braes," the hilly moorland between the coast and the mountains. His eyes took in the sweeping panorama of the undulating moorland as it ran down to the pine forest. The air was still, for it was early yet and over the silver mirrored waters of the Firth of Skean, and way beyond over the Moray Firth he could make out the misty blue shape of the Black Isle. It was a constantly varying view of shifting clouds, light and colour of which he never tired. And now, since his beloved wife had passed on, it gave him great solace.

He let his two collies out of their kennel next to the byre, started up his ancient Land Rover, opened the back door for them to jump in and, in a cloud of blue smoke, bumped and jolted his way along the rutted cart track that led to the road. He was going to check on his sheep which were in a field less than a minute away.

As soon as he got near to the field he realised with a sinking feeling that it had happened again. An substantial pile of rubble and broken kitchen units topped by a steel sink complete with its taps prevented him from opening the gate. As if that were not bad enough, bits of tiles, plasterboard and wood were scattered over the road and in the verge. It had taken him the best part of a whole morning to clear the last lot. He sighed in despair. It was happening too often. There was also the matter of the missing sheep. He looked at the passenger side of his Land Rover where he kept his shot gun. He knew what he'd do to the bastards if he ever caught them.

25

1999

It was a warm early summer evening in Timperley, South Manchester, and Robbie was sitting at the patio table overlooking his back garden. The sun was just starting to dip behind the trees and the shadows were lengthening. He'd had a couple of beers, well more than two actually, and he was in a vacant and pensive mood. Some soul music drifted out from the open door to the extension and inside he could hear Kim, his partner, clattering about in the kitchen and telling her daughter it was time she went upstairs and sorted out the mess that was her bedroom.

So, he was sitting there and what was flashing upon his inward eye, again, was his job as a Senior Teacher and Head of the English and Drama Faculty at Southern High, his fairly recently acquired Ph.D., his well maintained and extended four bedroom 1930's semi, its long garden [properly landscaped by a previous owner] not to mention his stunning partner of the past few years and her lovely daughter. Everyone he knew, he admitted, would have said that if anyone had it made it was him. And he had accumulated all this when he'd not really planned any of it, and he didn't actually really want any of it but he had got it anyway almost by accident. And he would be a fool to throw it all away wouldn't he?

Except it wasn't him, what he really wanted, now more than ever, was to live a life less urban and more rural. Specifically, Scottish rural. To quote his namesake: "My heart's in the Highlands, my heart is not here." How, or even if, he was going to accomplish that was at that point completely beyond him.

He'd met Kim at a primary school liaison evening. She was chair of the PTA, and he was doing the publicity bit for Southern High School. She was a single mum and manageress of a local building society. He thought she was lovely and used all his Geordie charm to chat her up. They dated, got on really well, moved in together, life was fine. After a while they got a mortgage and bought the Timperley house. She wanted stability for herself and her daughter and he wanted someone nice to live with and he wanted to feel as if he was moving forward with things.

They had settled into an easy pattern of existence. He worked really hard during term time but he was usually around when Kim's daughter, Carrie, came home from her school. Kim sometimes had to work on Saturday mornings so Robbie was around then too. During the winter months on Saturday afternoons he went up to Burnage Rugby Club where he still had a run out with the vets, and during the spring and early summer he managed the odd day's fly fishing with some mates at Tittesworth or Ladybower.

Kim was definitely a city girl, she liked dressing fashionably and she certainly had the figure for it. As for holidays, a few days in the sun somewhere in a posh hotel was her thing, and Robbie was happy to acquiesce, because that meant that from time to time he could escape to the West Coast of Scotland for his fix of wilderness camping and fishing. Kim had made it abundantly clear, in her usual humorous and forthright way, that she had absolutely no intention of joining him, besides which, she had a proper job, didn't she, and only had limited holidays where as he, Robbie, had weeks and weeks of paid leave so he might as well bugger off to the wilds and leave the worker in peace.

So that was how it had been for quite a few years, but by the time that Carrie was ready to leave home and go to uni, Robbie and Kim, over the course of a year or two, were drawing apart in a slow and vaguely amicable way. Partly it was circumstance, Robbie's job had changed for the worse and partly whatever joint needs had kept them together before had faded away. Kim loved her job, she was now the area manager of her building society, and was travelling the length and breadth of the North of England having important meetings, frequently staying in hotels for extended periods. Home life was not the same any more.

Latterly, in the wonderful world of education, exam results and percentage pass rates had become all important, the be all and end all in fact. Initially, this was no problem for Robbie, whose English and Drama faculty was blessed with excellent teachers who got great results. However, in a drive to improve the school's overall performance, the new Head, not a mate of Robbie's by any means, had decided to restructure the school and its faculties to pair the weak with the successful in the hope that the former would benefit from close alignment with the latter.

Suddenly, despite all his vehemently voiced protests, Robbie found himself responsible for Modern Foreign Languages as well as English, Media Studies, Music and Drama in the sparkling new "Faculty of Communications," a poisoned chalice if ever there was one, given that the MFL results, according to a recent Ofsted, were, "significantly below national standards," or, in Robbie speak: "a crock of shit."

Also, the head of MFL was universally referred to, although not to his face, as Le Coq, he was well known to be difficult and had weeks of time off sick when things got challenging. Robbie's hitherto easy and effortless glide through his professional life suddenly became stressful and problematic, seeing as what he knew about MFL teaching was fairly limited and that department had major issues with staffing. Some of the MFL staff were competent, but in all honesty, teaching bloody French and German was a nightmare in Southern and needed the kind of committed leadership and dedication that Le Coq was unable and unwilling to provide.

He was considering his options. At exam board meetings he had met a couple of teachers who had "sold out" to the private sector, and very nice their lives seemed too, what with their eight week summer break, small classes and country house environments. Working in an international school was another option, five years of toil in the sun and sand and then set up financially for an easy retirement.

In the end he and Kim came to a friendly agreement about the house: she kept it and then remortgaged it. Luckily, for Robbie it had increased considerably in value so, after all the financial dust had settled, he had a lump sum to invest. As to all his stuff, he put all that in storage. And then it was off to the UAE and a three year contract as Head of English at The Queen Eleanor International School.

26

2010

Frazer Ross, his partner, Elsie, and their two youngest offspring had eventually managed to move into the more spacious farmhouse at Caoraich. The two older kids had left the strath and were working away, one of the lads had joined the police force much to Frazer's disgust. Caoraich Cottage had been finally reclaimed by the estate and it, along with one or two other cottages near the farm, was in the process of being turned into holiday accommodation. That seemed to be the way of things these days.

Frazer rented the farm, well large croft actually, as it was, from the estate. He had some sheep, cattle and a few fields with potatoes. Frazer was still running his alternative business, but he was finding it more difficult now. He was very well known in the strath and the new generation of police was much cuter than the old. There was actually less need for him to operate far afield as there were always a fair few deer wandering into his land, along with pheasants and other game. So his only problem was their illegal dispatch, butchery and supply.

Alec Monroe switched off the engine on his quad bike, hopped off and strode across to the corner of his field where a ewe was entangled in some loose fence wire. He was a small energetic man with a neat ginger beard and balding pate, quick to anger and aggressive of mien. Muttering obscenities under his breath he set about extricating the ewe from the fence. The corner of his field was neat and precise and over the fence was an untamed mini forest of bracken and small birch trees. It was Frazer's fence, the corner of his field abutted Frazer's croft.

Alec Monroe was Frazer's neighbour and tenant of the next farm down the strath. It was called The Mains of Skean, and it was a huge farm, an amalgamation of three others. Monroe ran it with ruthless efficiency, completely the opposite of Frazer who ran his croft with ruthless inefficiency. Monroe was absolutely no friend of Frazer's. In fact they had had a fair few run ins. These had mostly been about the poor state of Frazer's fencing, the occasional disappearance of cattle and the fact that Frazer was sometimes to be seen skulking about Monroe's land with a shotgun.

Monroe's farm was a mixture of cereal and livestock. He had two hundred acres of barley which he grew for the whisky industry and animal feed, a few sheep and also a large head of beef cattle. There were also some holiday chalets, or lodges, "nestling in the age old Caledonian pine wood" as the advertising on his brochure went.

At the heart of Monroe's operation was the scientific application of all available fertilizers, pesticides and chemicals. All his land had been vigorously and regularly sprayed and also heavily fertilised with nitrates. This allowed him to get two crops a year as well as plenty of silage. His livestock too had all been thoroughly treated with all sorts of chemicals and antibiotics.

This resulted in a green monoculture on which his antibiotically infused cattle grazed. The excess chemicals washed off the land and trickled into the wee burns and ultimately into the Skean itself, where downstream from his farm, lush waterweeds grew during the summer months, fertilised by the run off from his fields. Farmland birds and other wildlife were no more, and as for insects, well, they were few. Fortunately not every farm in the strath was so controlled, in fact there were one or two making an enlightened and successful effort to redress the relentless downward trend in bio diversity.

Had there been a league table for the aforementioned bio diversity, Frazer's croft would have been near the top, not by any conscious effort on his part, but by the fact that he did nothing in the way of artificial fertilisation, nor insect control. In the spring and summer, his fields were a riot of wild flowers, insects swarmed, birds nested, and, in the gloaming, bats hawked around his buildings and owls hunted mice around the farmyard. It was his very own shambolic biosphere.

27

2014

Colin Prince settled his considerable girth into a business class seat on the British Airways flight BA 225 to Nassau. Next to him, Gloria his wife of some twenty five years had already made herself comfortable and was reading the in-flight magazine in the hope of purchasing some goodies later on. He didn't mind, he earned a small fortune as an financial analyst in the city, working long hours, with an additional hefty commute at either end of each day, so they deserved their annual fortnight of luxury didn't they?

As the 747 levelled out at its cruising height of thirty three thousand feet over The Scillies, Colin opened the first of several miniature bottles of wine he and Gloria would consume over the next few hours. They had pre-ordered their food and as they ate, drank and snoozed the night away, the 747, burning aviation fuel at the rate of eleven tonnes per hour, and with hardly a shudder of turbulence to vibrate the drink in their glasses, took them ever closer to their holiday destination.

Upon arrival at Nassau International Airport the Princes transferred to a Flamingo Air flight to one of the Out Islands on which was situated their accommodation for the next twelve days, a private island retreat: The MacLune Blue.

This was the very latest in the MacLune chain of luxury retreats and consisted of a series of wooden bungalows scattered round a meticulously groomed white sand, palm fringed beach, each with its dedicated butler and maid service. The central area boasted more sumptuous accommodation, an infinity pool, three intimate gourmet restaurants and a couple of bars as well as a gym and a spa. The whole complex wound in and out of the palm trees and shore line giving the impression of naturalness and space, a oneness with the environment. And so it should, it had cost many millions to design and construct.

From the time they woke up in the late morning to the time they sank contentedly into their king sized bed at night, the guests' daily meanderings between lounger, beach, pool and bar were punctuated by plentiful opportunities to consume the very finest in food and drink. The waiter service from immaculately attired staff was one of world class deference and attentiveness.

It was a truly unbelievable luxury experience and it came at a truly unbelievable weekly tariff.

On their first morning in the resort the slightly jet lagged Princes were sitting in the Caribbean sunlight enjoying a post-breakfast cocktail at the pool bar when they were approached by a slim, elegantly dressed lady. 'You must be Mr and Mrs Prince,' she said in a gentle Scottish accent. 'I'm Mhairi MacLune, one of the resort directors. Welcome to MacLune Blue, I'm sorry that I wasn't here to greet you personally last night, but I was at our other resort on the other side of the island.'

'That's perfectly OK,' said Colin, 'we're just relaxing after the flight, it'll take us a day or two to acclimatise. What a fantastic place you have here, it's amazing!'

'Absolutely stunning!' agreed Gloria as she took a sip of her second margarita. It was nearly lunchtime after all.

As Mhairi went through the well rehearsed welcome speech, her eyes took in the Princes, so typical of the resort's bloated clients, many of whom had made their money in finance, property or sales. Some had made their money in other ways. One didn't ask. They were used to spending huge amounts to get what they thought was an exclusive experience, but the exclusivity resided in the amount they were prepared to pay rather than in genuine quality.

As a business concept, she had many a time thought, MacLune Blue and the hundreds, if not thousands, of other luxury resort hotels just like it was a winner. Having saturated winter advertising slots in the first world countries with seductive pictures of white sands, blue seas, palm trees and unlimited food and drink, hundreds of thousands of wealthy western folks bought into the dream and were prepared to spend their good or bad money to be flown half way around the world to sit by a pool in the heat in a third world country and eat and drink to excess. True, the resorts did offer 'daily excursions' but these were often highly organised visits to landmarks or tourist markets. There was little or no engagement with local culture, probably just as well given the level of local poverty. The guests were in an hermetically sealed bubble, Their actual location almost an irrelevance as long as it appeared "exotic" on the photos they sent home.

Mhairi excused herself from the Princes who were now engaged in animated conversation with another couple, and, nodding to the barman, took up her usual seat at a small table in a shady corner by the pool. The barman brought over a coffee and she opened her document case, took out some papers and photographs and prepared to make her big decision. The last twenty odd years or so had been quite a journey she thought, it was time to make a significant change to her direction of travel.

28

1989

They had left her in an adjacent office sitting at a shining walnut table with a huge cup of coffee in front of her. She wasn't nervous at all, she had been on top of her game: poised, articulate, authoritative. All the qualities one would expect from a potential assistant general manager of a large luxury international hotel. The last few years working for a budget hotel chain had served her well, she had experience of every department, and general management was where she wanted to be.

After fifteen minutes or so she was called back into the board room and invited to retake her interview seat. In front of her, arranged in a semicircle round a conference table with a backdrop of a foggy River Clyde were the seven members of the MacLune family, the sole proprietors of MacLune Luxury Hotels.

Sir James spoke, his voice educated, patrician, 'Well, Miss Macdonald, you have made a big impression on us. It's our unanimous decision to offer you the post of

Assistant General Manager of the MacLune Beach Hotel in Mombasa! What do you say?'

There followed the congratulations, the signing of the contract, the champagne and the dinner later that evening where she found herself sitting next to Donald, Sir James' youngest son. And that was where it had all started really.

29

George Jameson, the portly general manager of the MacLune Beach, Mombasa, buzzed his PA and asked to see Mhairi, his deputy. As he waited he looked out of his office window at the busy hotel reception where he could see that she was engaged in conversation with a guest. She had settled down to her new post with considerable aplomb, he thought, and he found her really easy to work with. She just had a natural touch with staff and guests alike. Her effortless efficiency had made his own job so much less stressful.

There was a knock on his door, 'Hi, Mhairi, I've some news for you. We are being honoured by a visit from one of the MacLunes, Donald, to be exact. He's coming to spend a few days wi' us to see how we're daeing I guess.'

Like many of the MacLune hotel chain's senior employees he was of Scottish extraction.

George went on to explain that the huge MacLune business empire of which hotels were only a part was run centrally by Sir James and his eldest son, daughter and daughter in law. In his opinion the youngest son, Don, had not shown the same kind of family aptitude for, or dedication to business, having spent his formative years as a semi-professional skier and socialite sliding about the resorts of Europe until injury had forced an early change of career.

Now, armed with a degree from a Swiss university in Hotel Management one of his jobs in the organisation was to visit the MacLune hotels about the globe and report back to base on their general health and wellbeing. A sort of benign trouble shooter. The sort of job that required smooth social skills rather than hard analysis, the sort of job that would keep him usefully occupied but was not critical to the overall success or otherwise of the enterprise. He was the public face of the MacLune chain, athletic, charming, affable. Nice work if you could get it, opined George who would have loved that kind of employment himself. In fairness, Mhairi already knew quite a lot about her employers, she had done due diligence on them before she applied for the job, and she thought that she understood the kind of people they were. Sharp business people, but ethical too.

She had chatted to Don at the dinner the MacLunes had arranged for her in Glasgow at time of her appointment, and she had to admit that she had found him very attractive. She was certainly looking forward to his visit.

And had she understood just a little more about Don, she would never have married him.

The next couple of weeks passed in a kind of surreal state for Mhairi. From the moment he slid his rangy frame into the passenger seat of the Landcruiser, turned on the easy charm, and hit her with his wide grin she was smitten. As was he. Perhaps for the first time in her adult life she had let her guard down, deviated from her career driven path, let someone else in. They spent large amounts of time together, ostensibly checking the hotel systems and accounts, but finding the time for walking along the beach hand in hand, long lunches and intimate dinners. George observed all this with a kind of benevolent cynicism. Don was effectively his boss so he made sure they had the time together, and, of course he said nothing, but he was just a wee bit concerned, he knew what Don was like.

Their wedding just a few months later, took place at the Kirk in Strathskean and then moved on for the grand reception to a MacLune hotel near Inverness. Bill and Morag were the epitome of proud parents, Mhairi had married into the wealthy business class, Sir James and Lady Susan were very nice and said lovely complimentary things about Mhairi and how lucky Don was to have found her.

Privately, Sir James and Lady Susan were pleased that Don had chosen someone so clear headed, intelligent and capable for his wife and hoped and prayed that she would be strong enough to make him settle down to a life of stability, but they knew their youngest son.

The couple eventually based themselves in the Bahamas where Mhairi was able to continue her career in management at one of the MacLune hotels and Don was able to occupy himself with his inspection trips abroad, and at home playing golf and bone fishing on the world famous Nonya flats. Their daughter, Seonaid, was born in the summer of 1990. Life was for the early years of Their marriage, busy and rewarding. Don seemed happy enough and he certainly tried to be a hands on dad, to start with at any rate.

Gradually, and so slowly over a number of years as to be hardly noticeable, for Mhairi and Don family life became more and more fragmented. As Seonaid grew into a teenager and needed less parental input so Mhairi was called upon to occupy herself more and more with the running of the MacLune business. Don was spending ever increasing time 'on the road' as he called it. In reality on extended jollies around the globe, just making sure all the systems were in place and that the various managers were behaving themselves as he said.

Don enjoyed this "work" if you could call it that. He had always been a rolling stone and the life itinerant suited him. A few weeks in one location was as much as he could bear. The constants in his life were his sporting interests, his international playboy mates and being able to relocate to another reality when he felt he'd had enough of the present. At the beginning, his commitment to his marriage with Mhairi, his parenting of his daughter, Seonaid, had existed as a serious concept in his head much longer than he could have or would have predicted, but inevitably, over a decade or so, he had reverted to his true self.

Typically, after one of his trips, he would arrive back like a sailor home from an arduous voyage, bringing his stories, his presents, his charm and his affability, and then, after a week or three, the inevitable restlessness and ennui would overcome him and he would have to make his exit.

As for Mhairi, she was determined that Seonaid would be brought up with some kind of work ethic. She did not want her daughter to be another socialite, another useless, if decorative, appendage on the international circuit. Luckily Seonaid had inherited her mother's steely intellect and sense of purpose. Medicine seemed a good direction of travel: ethical, demanding and useful. She was working hard towards this goal.

Now, whilst Mhairi had been able to rationalise Don's slow disengagement from a shared family life, believing he needed space for his sporting and leisure activities and not wishing to alienate him, and in doing so, affect negatively his relationship with Seonaid, however, as time went by and with things deteriorating, there was a definite limit as to what she would or could condone.

Don was away so much now that Mhairi had got used to his absence, but she felt that she was no longer in any sort of a viable marriage. Frankly, as she admitted to herself, she just did not love him anymore. She had no concrete evidence , but she was sure he had been unfaithful to her. There was no physical intimacy between them, and there hadn't been for far too long. He was detached and cold towards her. Now, on the ever decreasing occasions when he was with her, he would drink far more than was good for him and retire to a separate bedroom.

When she had tried to talk about their situation and their marriage he was reluctant to engage in any sort of discussion about it. He was apparently happy with the status quo. Married, but not married. Beneath the affability was a kind of petulance, he was a spoilt boy who wanted his own way all the time.

30

By six o' clock the bar at the MacLune Cayo Largo was full, and in one corner around a table, amongst the regular hotel guests, a small group of fly fishermen was celebrating a successful day on the flats. Holding court, a big affable guy in his early fifties beckoned to the waitress for another round of beers.

'Hey, Don,' said one of the company, 'here's to us, and let's hope we have as good a day tomorrow.'

'Aye, well the forecast is great, with light winds, we should be lucky, I'm off for a shower and a snooze now, and see you at dinner, cheers everyone!'

And with that he stood up and, holding his beer high in one hand, made his way through the noisy throng to the door where he was met by a tall, dark haired lady. A couple of his companions smiled knowingly at each other, but made no comment, the whole episode unrecorded and unremarked upon save for the waitress who had taken out her phone.

Sitting in the shade at the table in the pool bar area at MacLune Blue Mhairi checked through the papers and photographs. Highly uncomfortable though it was for her to look at them they showed in graphic detail over the last few years Don's descent into infidelity and a wild party lifestyle. She gathered them up, placed them back in the folder and, decision made, returned to her office.

31

2014

The ancient Tomnahurich Graveyard occupied a position close to the northern outskirts of Inverness quite close to the Caledonian Canal. Unusually for such a place it had a strangely shaped, tree covered hill as its central feature and this had long been associated with the supernatural. And, in truth, it did have its own distinctive atmosphere. Gravelled roads wound round its different sections and gravestones, both ancient and modern, leaning and upright indicated the last resting places of decent highland folk.

Here on a Thursday in early May a group of mourners huddled round an open grave. The unseasonably cold wind whipped at their coats and one or two of the more elderly had to cling on to their companions for support. When the minister had said the age old words, and the coffin had been lowered into the grave he turned to those gathered.

Fixing a slightly startled Robbie with his beady eye he said, 'Aye, an open grave is an invitation for us all to put oor ain hoose in order,' and went on to make more points about living a life free of sin and loving the creator. Mary Mackenzie, Robbie's aunt, had died after a few months illness and was now being interred in the same grave as her husband who had pre-deceased her by six years.

The address did not last too much longer and it was with some relief the mourners returned to the warmth of their cars to reconvene an hour or so later in one of the reception rooms of the Strathskean Hotel. A finger buffet had been laid out on white linen covered trestle tables along with some bottles of wine and fruit juice.

There was much shaking of hands and the room was filled with the low murmur of muted conversation. Robbie's mother Sheila was doing the rounds of the relatives. Since Robbie's dad had died a few years previously she had been a fairly frequent visitor at Strathskean and Mary had also been down to Tyneside a few times. When Robbie was younger there were quite few aunts and uncles from the Scottish side of his family scattered through the glens. The family referred to them as "The Ancient Ruins." Now, however, most of them had passed on, and so of those present most were cousins of his or friends of Mary's.

He moved round the room, introducing himself and shaking hands. He noticed an elderly couple at a table near the door. At first he did not recognise them but then he realised it was Bill and Morag MacDonald. The last time he had seen them was way back. Naturally they had aged somewhat.

Robbie made his way over to their table. Bill was in a wheelchair and so they had not attended either the church service or the interment. Bill had a large dram of the Strathskean in front of him. Robbie shook both of their hands, pulled up a chair and sat down.

His voice was soft and Robbie had to lean nearer to hear. 'Well Robbie, sorry for yer loss, yer Aunty Mary was a lovely soul and she wull be sorely missed, aye she wull.'

'Yes, she will, but according to my ma she'd been suffering for some time and mebbes it's a blessing. So, it was a cold send off up at Tomnahurich.'

Aye well, we couldna' make it, ah'm no as fit as a was and it's too far for Morag to push me. I was at yer uncle's, but that's a few year ago now.' He took a sip of whisky and sighed.

'I wasn't able to come to Brian's funeral, I was working in an international school in the UAE at the time, I'd just started and I couldn't get back, and speaking of expats how's Mhairi doing, the last I heard she was running an hotel in the Bahamas. How is she?'

'Aye she was, right enough, but things have no worked out as well since then. She and Don have split up and she's getting a divorce. It's just very, very sad but that's the way of the world these days.' Bill shook his head, took another sip from his dram and wiped a tear or two from his eye. He was visibly upset. Morag put a hand on his arm, 'Wheesht, Bill, it's OK, it's time w' were off home now.'

'I'm really, really sorry to hear that, Bill, I suppose these things happen.' Robbie couldn't say anything but platitudes, his own private life was a mess too. He was disconcerted by the old man's grief so he didn't really process the news. He made his farewells and left, heading for the public bar, he needed a beer.

It being the middle of the afternoon, there were only three or four locals in there and they were mostly sitting at tables with their pints and reading papers. Only one person was at the bar and he was sitting on a stool at the far end hunched over a pint, his immobility suggested he'd been there for some time. Robbie went up to the bar and asked the barman for a pint of lager and a small Grouse, he was staying in hotel that night and he didn't need to drive anywhere.

He put the tab on his room and took a long swig at the lager. Sighing he looked around, it was a nice bright room with the obligatory tartan carpet and lovat green curtains, on the walls hung pictures of salmon fishing in days gone by and gaudy salmon flies in display cabinets. Above the fireplace there was a plaster cast of a huge salmon, the legend on the brass plaque said: "Salmon 37lbs, caught 17th March 1953 from the Caoraich Pool by Major Ronald Stewart." Robbie wondered what the chances were nowadays of catching any salmon at all in March let alone one of that size.

He took another sip from his lager and glanced at the figure at the end of the bar who was now sitting up straight on his stool and was looking directly at him. He was a ginger haired and bearded individual with piercing pale blue eyes and a tall angular figure. He had the ruddy complexion of the outdoorsman and as if to confirm that he was wearing khaki ex-army trousers, a green sweater and hunting boots.

'Aye, English, ah thought y'd be up fer yer Aunty's wake,' said the figure in that rough voice that Robbie instantly recognised, 'ah'm sorry fer yir loss.' And he extended his huge rough hand for Robbie to shake.

Robbie held out his hand and the two shook. Well, it wasn't as if everything was forgotten was it? But it was a start.

So, a couple more drinks and a brief catch up, Frazer made his apologies and slid away, Robbie decided to go for a walk round Strathskean. Actually this was the first time he'd been back in three decades. Of course he'd seen his Aunty Mary and Uncle Brian a few times over the years, but that had mainly been when they'd been down visiting his mother in the North East.

He left the hotel and walked down the main street. It had changed considerably since he had last been there. Cattenach's was still a newsagents, but it was now called National News. There was still the co-op and hotels, but many of the smaller shops were now estate agents, coffee houses or fast food outlets. Parking along the road was problematical, every space taken, filled with smart looking cars, many with European plates, and, indeed he remembered how the population of the town trebled in size during the tourist season. Not that there was a defined season these days what with the "grey pound" meaning that a steady stream of visitors would be trickling through the town for much of the year. A bit like a run of salmon thought. However, a glance upwards to the tops of the granite buildings told a different story, with missing tiles, flaking paint on window frames and grass sprouting from rusty gutters.

He took a left at the park and walked down the wide path through the ancient Caledonian woods to the river. The scent of the pine, the myrtle, the tiny chirpings of small bids brought a thousand memories whirling back, and suddenly he was a young teenager again, at home in a place he loved.

Soon he came to the bridge over the River Skean. Below, was the half mile or so of rapids that separated the Castle water from the town water. Above was the pool where he had hooked and, with the help of a local fisherman, landed his fourteen pounder. He continued upstream. By the Caoraich pool there was a hut and a lichen covered bench, he sat down. The wind had dropped and the late afternoon sun was warm on his face.

There was the silhouette of a fisherman on the lower half of the shimmering water. He was pretty good as far as Robbie could see; his relaxed spey castingsending the line out right across the river at an angle of forty five degrees. With every cast he moved slightly further downstream. Soon he reached the flat water at the tail. A few casts more and he made his way slowly out of the pool and, using his wading stick as a prop, levered himself manfully up the bank and came and sat down with a sigh next to Robbie, the water dripping off his chest waders.

He was an old chap with a short well trimmed beard, and twinkly blue eyes.

Robbie said, 'Are you having any luck?'

'Not as yet, there's jist the odd fish in the river at this time of the year noo. It's early. We usually get a few in towards the end o' the month and then it slowly builds up through the summer. Mind you we get a great run o' sea troot in June, some o' they fish are crackers. I had wan aboot twelve poonds last year.'

As he spoke, some trout started to rise to a hatch of wee olives along the deep eddy on the far bank. Robbie pointed them out.

'Aye the river's full of troot, nae body fishes for them.'

Robbie thought that he would, given that some of the rises he saw were from quite hefty fish.

The aged fisher stood up, adjusted his wading stick, lifejacket and net and clumped his way down the steps to the entry point at the top of the pool.

'Cheers noo,' he shouted, and within a minute was up to his waist in the river and lost again in his rhythmic casting.

This short encounter had set off all the old familiar yearnings and cravings in Robbie. He had no time now to stay and fish, he had to get back to the madness of Warden Hall School, but he knew, sooner or later he would reacquaint himself with the River Skean.

32

Robbie had endured a few completely forgettable years in the UAE, save that he had taken full advantage of the opportunities to travel, especially to Southern Asia. He had enjoyed that, but he was a northern lad at heart and of course he longed for cooler climes. The upside of sticking it out meant that he had amassed a decent sum of money to fund his emerging long term plan and that was how he came to be Head of English at Warden Hall School, an independent school a few miles west of Newcastle up the Tyne valley.

The pay had been reasonable, and they had thrown in accommodation on the premises, and Robbie, having read the shiny brochure and having looked at their superb website could see himself spending the twilight years of his teaching career with small classes and well motivated students in pleasant and relaxed surroundings. However, Robbie's background of teaching in professionally run, well resourced big state schools, and then in the highly pressurised international school system had not prepared him in any way for the reality of working at Warden Hall.

Warden Hall did one thing superbly well, and that was the marketing of itself. The image the school presented to the parents, and the outside world was one of a traditional and ivy clad ancient English public school, albeit a very small one. The students ate in 'The Refectory', they went to see matron in 'The San' if they were ill, they did their 'Prep' in the evening. The academic staff were expected to wear gowns and each had his or her own entry in the school brochure detailing their, occasionally fictional, former glittering career and qualifications.

When visitors and parents arrived they were ushered in to an oak panelled study with a huge polished walnut table, on which were copies of magazines such as "The Field" and "Country Life." The school magazine was there too with articles about gymkhanas, fox hunting, and the local pheasant shoots. The secretary would bring in a silver tray with coffee and biscuits while they waited for their appointment. About the walls were photographs of past sporting teams and under decorated plaques the names of past house captains and suchlike.

Many of the students came from either farming or business backgrounds, and generally they were a nice enough lot to get along with, except they had little drive for academic success, having lived cosseted, wealthy lives. More than a few had been sent to Warden Hall because they were thought to be a little sensitive or too precious to withstand the hurly-burly of larger schools. Many were waiting to slide seamlessly into the family business. The problem was not the students, but rather some of their wealthy self-made parents whose own education had been limited, but who also had expectations for their offspring that were unrealistically high, and, also, their attitude towards the staff, who they treated more like lowly employees rather than respected professionals.

As Robbie was to find out, the management of the school was unlike anything he had experienced before. In all of his previous positions the school had been run efficiently by the management team: the head, deputies and senior teachers and they were supported by the governors who were to act as a kind of higher authority should issues arise. At Warden Hall there was a headteacher who was nominally in charge of all the day to day stuff, but all the decisions of any import were made by the owners, a doddery couple in their eighties, and their difficult and only son, Charles, who was the self styled Principal of Warden Hall.

In the early days of the school Charles's parents had run it with some degree of competence, there was obviously a market for what they were offering, and it was a going concern with enough students in each year to make it economically viable. However, latterly, things had been a little tighter financially and so various savings had been introduced. The quality of food served was one, and the distinctive aroma of chef's economy fish pie was one Robbie would take with him to the end of his days.

More significantly, there was no finance available to purchase extra texts and resources so what was taught was dictated by what had been purchased in days gone by. Robbie, who had been accustomed to working with state of the art computer kit, and being able to source whatever set texts he deemed were the most appropriate for his students, found this frustrating. His requests for extra funding were always gracelessly rejected.

There was a small boarding section housed in the east wing of Warden Hall and this was presided over by Matron, an ex army nurse, definitely one of the "don't mess with me" brigade. She was of stocky build, with a huge chest and short cropped dark hair. Thick framed glasses and a small mouth topped by a faint dark moustache completed the image. Robbie thought the kids must be really genuinely at death's door if they asked to go to the San. Matron was helped out by two other care assistants, known as Matron's Minnows, small timid women much given to scurrying about in a perpetual state of panic.

Robbie's apartment was quite close to the boarding section, and he was, as part of his contract, required to do the occasional week end duty which he didn't mind too much, given that his accommodation was virtually free. And on this memorable Saturday night, having just completed his rounds, and all being quiet, he was just about to enter his apartment for a well deserved beer when he heard the most earth shattering, banshee like screaming emanating from the staff bathroom a few doors along the corridor.

Before he could reach the bathroom door it burst open in a cloud of bath salt scented vapour and the rotund, semi naked pinkness of matron wobbled out. She was obviously in a state of complete agitation and distress. 'S, s, someone's looking in through the window,' she sobbed, simultaneously pointing into the room and trying to hold the bath towel over her breasts.

Robbie dived into the steamy room. The window was mostly misted up but he could see a small terrified face with two owl like eyes staring through. He recognised them instantly, they belonged to Little Leon, a tiny weird kid who was one of the boarders. There was no easy explanation for his presence because the staff bathroom was on the top floor of the three storey building.

It being impossible to open the bathroom window Robbie shot next door where there was a separate toilet. This was locked but he kicked it open and, sure enough, the window above the toilet pan was open. Standing on the seat he poked his head out into the darkness . It was a warm and humid night dimly illuminated by the orangey glow of the street lights by the road junction at the end of the drive. To his right Little Leon was perched on the bathroom window sill, one hand locked round a handle and the other round the pebbledashed corner, gripping it fast, his knuckles white. An unfriendly breeze ruffled his pyjamas, he was barefoot, and he had a small camera slung round his back.

Momentarily Robbie was lost for words and action too. He could only get his head and half a shoulder out of the window, he was too bulky. Leon was obviously "gripped", unable to move one way or the other. He had got on to the bathroom window ledge by swinging round on the big down pipe immediately outside the toilet, however the reverse operation was much trickier if not impossible. Shouting to Leon to hold on for God's sake, he beat a frantic retreat and phoned the fire brigade.

The Fire Brigade arrived and duly prized Little Leon off the ledge, and because it was a school incident, three appliances had turned up, plus North East Television, and a fair few tabloid journalists. They had a field day or night actually, the resulting headlines were hilarious. Charles, The Principal, was incandescent, it was not the kind of publicity he needed.

According to Charles it was, of course, all Robbie's fault. In a heated, and largely one sided exchange, Robbie told Charles exactly how things stood, and pointed out that the school's safeguarding policy was illegal, the quality of food fed to the students was third world, the internal organisation was shambolic, what the parents got for their many thousands of pounds a year was a travesty, and if he, Robbie, was blamed in any way for "Matrongate" then he, Robbie, would go to the press and talk about the school's multiple failings and wilful public misrepresentations, starting with how a school could have a Principal who had absolutely no qualifications whatsoever, not to mention a covered up alleged attempted rape and the paedophile music teacher at present awaiting trial at Newcastle Crown Court.

Actually, Robbie had been quick to uncover the truth behind Leon's evening bathroom antics. He got hold of Leon's mate, a devious, shifty looking bookmaker's lad from Alnwick who eventually admitted to betting Leon

140

that he couldn't get a photo of matron in the bath. And so the scheme had been hatched. This was not the first time that Leon had been in trouble. On an earlier school trip to Rome he had deliberately gone missing from the hotel, later to be found wandering in a local park by the polizia. On another occasion he had let himself out of the boarding house in the middle of the night and, "looking for moths," he was discovered by a disconcerted homeowner in a the conservatory of a nearby private house.

Robbie was not quite ready to resign after this incident, largely because his plans to move to Strathskean to start a life more Scottishly rural were not yet fully in place. However, his mind was made up, he would be heading north at some point in the next year or so.

33

Somewhere between the town of Strathskean and The Bridge of Skean twenty five miles up the river there was a magnificent Victorian hunting lodge with spectacular views over the river and surrounding countryside. It had been built in the late nineteenth century by one of

Scotland's leading industrialists as his summer retreat, and, upon his passing, had been owned his family until the Second World War when it had been requisitioned as training base for special operations, and thereafter it had been purchased by a medical society for use as a sanatorium for members who had overindulged on their own medication. In recent years, the upkeep of such an establishment was proving to be prohibitively expensive and so the decision was made to close and put whole estate on the market.

Now Glen Sionnach Lodge had been bought for a song, and a comprehensive programme of renovation was well under way. The new owner was going to turn it into an exclusive and luxurious country retreat, with over three miles of salmon fishing and also shooting and stalking available within its own extensive grounds. For those guests who were neither hunters nor fishers there were all the usual country house attractions: fine dining, guided trips to local distilleries, and walks in the spectacular unspoilt Caledonian pine forest.

Inside the lodge no expense had been spared and the sumptuous luxury of times gone by had been lovingly recreated. Each suite of rooms was individually themed, beautifully appointed, and with the most up to date facilities, tastefully installed. Outside, the gardens, once terribly overgrown, had been similarly made over and were a now beautiful and peaceful place in which to spend an hour or two.

The opening was scheduled for early June. Extensive and targeted advertising, especially in America, had been undertaken and initial bookings were excellent. The new owner really knew what she was about, after all she had had many years as a successful hotelier behind her and, thanks to her recent divorce settlement, she had a substantial amount of cash as well

34

2014

Dr. Gunnar Klas Hendriksson the CEO of Silver Salmon Ocean Farms, one of Norway's medium sized salmon farming businesses, looked out of the boardroom window at the rain and sleet slashing down and obscuring the view of the harbour in the fishing port of Allesund. Winter had come early that year, in more ways than one. There was a scowl on his big face, the meeting had not been a very positive one. A few years earlier the company had moved most of its farming operations to the West Coast of Scotland because of the well documented environmental problems at home, and now they were discussing some expensively catastrophic lice infestations and fish mortality in some of their newer farms in the Hebrides. They had lost many thousands of salmon to a virus, and that, plus frequent escapes and a damaging local campaign by local shellfish fishermen had meant profits tumbling.

'Of course, we know that one of the major factors is that on the West of Scotland much of the inland water is shallow and confined, and so there is naturally the problem with sea lice and the dispersal of wastes. We've all seen the graphs and stats.' A few round the table put their heads in their hands, they had heard this many times before. 'However, if we were to site a large open net farm in deeper water, further off shore, in a stronger tidal stream we might be able to harvest a bigger percentage, and attract less negative publicity.' The company's chief scientist, Dr. Nils Eriksson sat down.

'Ok, but on most of the North East coast there is a presumption against granting planning permission isn't there?' asked one of the board members.

'Yes, that's so, but just at the edge of the zone there is an existing licensed site in the Firth of Skean which is not currently in operation, and I have it on good authority that, for the right considerations, we could restart operations there, especially if the new farm was to be three or so nautical miles off shore and have a new plastic design with enhanced bio security features.'

And so the decision was made to proceed with the planning application. The company needed to keep expanding, and their smooth publicity machine swung into action with authoritative newspaper articles and television reports all extolling the new "clean, bio secure, environmentally friendly" deepwater farm, and the "naturally healthy, responsibly farmed" wonder fish it produced. The Scottish government were desperate to increase the production of farmed salmon too and so, the construction of Port Skean Salmon Farm went ahead, despite "consultation" meetings where environmental considerations were aired but ultimately downplayed or ignored, and several heated local protests.

Statistically, it was impressive. There were twelve cages each of ten thousand cubic metres capacity, each with an astonishing potential capacity of up to eighteen kilos of salmon per cubic metre, and this meant a huge biomass in excess of a thousand tonnes. This enormous amount of fish was kept alive and growing by a vast daily supply of feed pellets, antibiotics and pesticides while the metric tonnes of excreta and excess chemicals produced collected on the sea floor beneath the cages or was carried away by the tide and re-circulated around the Firth.

The physical security of the farm and the on shore site was carried out by a handful of employees, none of whom were from from Port Skean, and also an Inverness based security firm, but all the feed and suchlike was brought in directly by sea to the farm by a support barge. The salmon, when ready for harvesting, were hoovered out of the cages by a monster suction pipe on the barge and then anaesthetised and kept in oxygenated tanks before being taken for dispatch and preparation back on the mainland. The operation ran smoothly for some time, but locally some disquiet was growing. Then came the storm and the escapes.

35

It was officially called Storm Karin, but that's not what the inhabitants of the small coastal fishing village of Port Skean called it. It had screamed in from the North North East and its full fury of gale force winds and torrential rain had overwhelmed that part of the East Coast and the village had taken the brunt of it. All the residents were evacuated by the police and had been uncomfortably housed in the Strathskean Academy sportshall for the best part of three days while the huge waves abated and the floodwater from the Dubh Burn subsided.

When they returned it was to a village that needed a considerable amount of repair. Some of the houses near the burn had been flooded and their owners paddled disconsolately about retrieving stuff from within, and making sad muddy piles of household items outside their doors. A couple of cars had been swept along the road and had been upended against the wall of the kirk. Fortunately none of the houses on the higher ground had suffered other than minor wind damage such broken tiles and flattened fences.

Down on the front it was a different matter, the road was covered in pebbles, stones and drifts of sand all blown and washed from the shore. One or two kiosks had been crushed as if by a giant boot, their smashed wooden sides trapped against the link fencing and vibrating in the wind. Seagulls wheeled and swooped over the scattered rubbish.

In the harbour one or two of the smaller boats had been sunk, and an ancient rusty beam trawler whose moorings had failed was stranded along with piles of other wreckage at the high tide point on beach. Fortunately, with prior warning most of the local fishermen had either removed their craft from the water or made sure that their moorings were secure.

A quarter of a mile along the coast the wooden pier that belonged to Port Skean Salmon Farm had been reduced to an untidy jumble of timbers and their two Portakabin offices had had their windows broken and doors smashed in. Around the site was scattered netting, broken equipment and a small workboat was upside down on the grass at the other side of the road. Twisted bits of wire netting trembled in the stiff breeze.

Out in the bay, in the deeper waters of the Firth of Skean, viewed from the shore with binoculars, the salmon farm itself seemed to have survived the storm, after all, they had said that it was "virtually indestructible," but no workers from the land based team had been able to get out to it yet and neither had the supply barges that provided the tens of thousands of salmon with their daily quota of pellets, antibiotics and pesticide.

A Toyota Landcruiser pulled up at the wrecked site, the bulky figure of Anders, the Norwegian manager of Port Skean Salmon Farm, a subsidiary company of Silver Salmon, jumped out. Pausing to look round and shaking his great head in disbelief at the destruction, as if the ongoing vandalism to the site wasn't enough to cope with he thought. He gestured to the others in the Toyota. Two of the shore workers plus another two guys from Macbeath Security, the firm that Silver Salmon had hired to look after the site, emerged reluctantly into the fresh air, their yellow waterproofs and life jackets making them seem even bulkier than they already were.

Together the five of them unhitched the RIB on the trailer and manually pushed it around the wreckage and down to the slipway. Since the vandalism and the unwelcome media attention, both the farm and the on shore buildings had been protected by CCTV but as the cameras were located about the site Anders assumed that they had been completely destroyed by the storm. In any case, Anders was keen to get out to the twelve huge floating sea cages to check for damage and now that the swell had calmed down enough for him and his team to access them from the shore, there was no time to waste. Had he paused for a moment to look inside the Portakabins he might have asked himself why the monitors and their night vision recorders were missing and, indeed, if all the damage around the site had been done by the weather.

The journey out to the farm was very uncomfortable, the RIB was tossed about and sheets of water crashed over the bows. The sea was rough and lumpy still with haystacking waves where the wind hit the tidal current. Eventually they arrived in the lee of the farm and managed to tie up on one of the floating walkways that connected the cages. The floating office and store had been partially destroyed, and there was also quite a bit of superficial damage too, with lots of torn safety netting with the sea having even bent the metal safety railings in some places. Seals, always a nuisance, had obviously capitalised on the absence of human presence, but the majority of the cages seemed intact, their occupants leaping about as usual, but the plastic tubes on three of the outer cages, those bearing the brunt of the massive waves and hurricane force wind, had semi deformed and a big percentage of their salmon had escaped.

Anders stood on the pitching walkway and, turning his back to the spray, took out his mobile phone and shouted into it, 'Hey Boss, it's Anders, looks like we have three badly damaged cages, that's at least fifty thousand big fish away.'

'Aw fuck, that's a lot of cash not to mention that the environmentalists will have a field day.' Hendriksson, the CEO of Silver Salmon Ocean Farms, the Norwegian parent company, was not a happy man. The Port Skean operation had had more than its fair share of troubles.

'Well, I'll down play the numbers, no one will actually know how many have escaped, some must have been eaten by seals. I'll sort it.'

'Bloody hell, just send me the damage report, and I'll get the support boat over as soon as possible.' The line went dead. With the concentration of fish in each cage

running at about 16 kg per cubic metre at the moment
the financial loss was eyewatering and the environmental
cost incalculable.

36

A few days after the storm had passed, Alasdair Machrie,
or Lord Inverskean to give him his correct title, had waited
impatiently for the Skean to become fishable and as soon
as it was he was on the phone to James, the head ghillie
on the Castle Skean waters, 'Get yourself down to the
bottom pools and see if there are any fresh fish about, the
bookings are way down,' was the curt command.

Truly, it had been an appalling season so far, just a
tiny number of fish coming into the system, well down
even on last season's poor numbers.

The bookings, once so prized that they were
automatically renewed year on year were catastrophically

low. Even advertising on the phenomenally successful Fishpal website had made little difference. The Castle Water desperately needed to record some fish caught to resuscitate their flagging season.

James always liked to fish the Sea Pool, the first on their beat. It was slightly tidal, and fished really well until about a half an hour before high tide when the current reversed itself, before becoming completely still and then flowing downstream again as the tide ebbed. James especially liked the fact that the salmon were fresh off the tide, back in their river of birth after a few years at sea and they were at their athletic silvery best. The pool was long too, with a kind of open aspect as the inland Caledonian pine forest had given way to a low lying coastal scrub with yellow whin bushes and gravelly banks.

On that morning James started at the head of the pool, the wading was easy, the bottom being made up of gravel, most of the large stones and rocks having been removed by the netsmen in the bad old days. A gentle downstream breeze aided his casting and there was a good level of cloud cover: perfect conditions. To add to his sense of anticipation, a fish splashed downstream, at least there was one in he thought.

He had only made half a dozen casts when his line stopped and there was that electric tug tug, he lifted into the fish and it kind of plunged and writhed around on the

152

surface without making any kind of sustained long run. Most of the fish he'd hooked in the past usually headed off towards the far bank or indeed back to sea, often stripping dozens and dozens of yards off the reel. This one felt different, mebbes it wasn't a salmon at all but a bass, he'd caught a few of those before thanks to global warming, but always at night when he was fishing for sea trout.

Whatever it was it wasn't huge, about five or six pounds, and it did make a couple of short runs, but he was fishing with a powerful fifteen foot scandi style rod and it was soon in the shallows and ready to beach. It was a salmon, but as it lay passively on its side on the gravel, he saw that its tail was deformed as was the dorsal fin, all the classic signs of a farmed fish. Cursing, he knocked it on the head and continued fishing. Over the next couple of hours he caught several more farmed salmon all exactly the same size, the pool was full of them.

He gathered up the carcases and putting them in a couple of black bags, threw them unceremoniously into the back of his pick-up. He wondered how many had run further upstream, and what diseases they might have carried with them.

Back at the castle, He knocked on His Lordship's office door.

'You're back early, hope it's good news James,' said His Lordship.

Having debriefed his increasingly incensed boss, James left to fish some of the pools at the top end of their water, hoping not to find more evidence of farmed salmon. Meanwhile his boss was engaged, not for the first time, in a heated phone call with one Gunnar Klas Hendriksson.

37

Initially Robbie had, upon his relocation to Strathskean in the summer of 2016, rented one of the static caravans in the town's caravan park, which was up at the north of the town at the edge of the forest. However, he almost immediately found a small cottage that was entirely suitable for his needs. It was on one of the back roads out of the town and down towards the river. The cottage was not overlooked but he did have a couple of neighbours either side, who were glad to welcome a permanent resident, one or two of the other cottages in the locality having been turned into "mair bloody holiday homes."

The cottage did need quite a bit of work doing on it but he had plenty of time and at least the place was habitable in the short term. He'd got a local firm to sort the kitchen and he was doing quite a bit of redecorating himself. The living room had bi-folding doors which led out onto a south facing patio and garden with its view of the Cairngorms. All in all, it was a nice place to sit of an evening and enjoy a wee dram.

So, his early days as a Strathskean resident were filled with sorting out the garden and house, keeping up with his jogging, and visits to the gym. He had started to write as well, a memoir or two from his decades of teaching in the state sector. He'd decided to wait until the next year to get a season ticket for the Association water, but he was going to get a weekly ticket so he could fish out the last few days of the season. He visited The Strathy Bar as well and was now on nodding terms with a few of the regulars. Of Frazer there was no sign, except he'd seen him driving about in his pick-up from time to time.

Three weeks or so after he'd moved into his cottage, he was about to paint the skirting boards in the hall and needed an old newspaper or two to mask the floor. He'd found some last year's copies of the Strathskean Herald left in the woodshed by the previous owner and was just laying them out when his eye was drawn to an article about the refurbishing and grand opening of Glen

Sionnach Lodge. There was quite a spread with pictures, and an interview with the new owner, originally from Strathskean, one Mhairi MacLune. There was a picture of her standing in front of the impressive front entrance and a short piece detailing her career and her early life in Strathskean.

All thoughts of painting skirting boards temporarily abandoned, Robbie made himself a cup of coffee and took the paper to his kitchen table to read it more carefully. Even though the picture was faded and a bit blurry she was instantly recognisable to him, still the same slimness, self assurance and poise. He sat in the September sunlight in a kind of reverie, thinking back to the last time he'd seen her and remembering across all the long years the last time he had been with her, their evening together and that parting kiss.

Usually, at about eleven o clock, the housekeeping staff of Sionnach Lodge, having finished their morning work, would gather in the scullery for a well deserved cup of coffee and piece of cake. There they were often joined by Mhairi, who liked to catch up with all the local gossip and also it gave her a good opportunity to keep her ears open for potential problems, housekeeperrs always having sharp eyes and an interesting take on things.

Actually, Mhairi had been good friends at school with Moira, the senior housekeeper. Moira had left school before Mhairi, and had married a local lad, who worked as a mechanic at a Grant's Garage in Strathskean. Now they were trying to start up their own business.

On this Friday morning, the rest having gone home, Moira and Mhairi were left by themselves in the scullery. Moira had been asking for some advice about book keeping. Suddenly she said, apropos of nothing, 'Hey you know that wee cottage that's down on the Dulnain road, the one that Murdy Maclennan used to live in?'

'Aye, well?'

'It's got a new owner, an "English" guy... guess who?' She had heavily stressed the word "English."

'For God's sake how would I know Moira, there must be hundreds of English folk buying up houses here.'

'Ah well, y' once knew this one,' teased her friend, ' y' once were a wee bitty sweet on him, if ah recall.'

Mhairi coloured up slightly, putting her hand to her mouth she said, 'Y' don't mean...'

'Aye, the clue is that he is "English!"' laughed Moira, enjoying her friend's embarrassment, 'It's been bought by that Robbie Ingram. Seemingly, he's semi retired noo and he's come up here to write and fish. Aye he looks just the same, a really fit guy, he does a lot o' running and stuff.

He has wan or two relatives in the strath and since his ma died last year he's nothing to keep him on Tyneside.'

Moira, still chuckling, thanked her friend for the advice about book keeping, and with an arch wink and a, 'Yis'll mebbes have to gie him a call, I'm sure he's single, just like yersel.' She stood up and went out, her laughter echoing down the corridor.

Lost in thought Mhairi retired with a fresh cup of coffee to the sun lounge. She settled herself in one of the plush chairs. The view from the lounge was spectacular, on a clear day you could see the breeze playing on the forest trees and watch the shadows of the clouds chasing across the Cairngorms. She didn't notice any of that however, because she was thinking about Robbie, as she had done from time to time over the years. That summer just before she'd left for uni she had been fonder of him than she'd been prepared to admit to herself.

And now it was at least four decades since she'd seen him, she knew he was a teacher of course, her parents and Robbie's aunt and uncle had been friends and so some of the gossip had filtered through. She knew that he'd mainly lived and worked in Manchester, and had then moved to the Gulf but that was about it. She knew she had to meet him, just out of curiosity even, and wondered if she would be disappointed. Consciously disentangling herself from her line of self indulgent thought she finished her coffee, stood up and went to find the keys to her Land Rover. She had promised the chef that she would pick-up a couple of boxes of veg. from the greengrocers in Strathskean.

At the lodge entrance she paused, if she turned left rather than right she could go to Strathskean along the back road, a longer and more scenic trip, and, if she remembered correctly, one that would take her past Maclennan's Cottage. Just for a wee look so to speak. She felt childishly excited and couldn't understand why. The back road was the original drovers' road that wound its way along the south bank of the river, passing by a few remote cottages deep in the original forest before it straightened out in the wide farmland a handful of miles west of Strathskean.

As she drove out of the forest into the broad strath there was a straight stretch of road ahead and she noticed a jogger on the other side coming towards her. The road being quite narrow at that point she slowed down to a crawl so that he could pass easily. He was a middle aged guy, obviously one of the serial keep fit types that were often to be seen running about these days, and as he passed her he gave her a cheery wave and a big thank you smile, and then kind of did a double take as he spotted the Glen Sionnach Lodge logo on the Land Rover. Mhairi had recognised him instantly.

She pulled over into a field entrance, switched off the engine, and got out. 'Hey English,' she said, 'Yir still mobile then.'

'Aye, jist aboot!' he replied. He was standing by the gate with one hand on the gate post as he recovered his breath.

He was taller and chunkier than she remembered but in really good shape. Still the same smile. There were a few beads of sweat on his forehead which he brushed away.

'And yourself,' he asked, reverting to his normal accent, 'how have you been? all these years, my God, it's been about four decades!'

'Well, you know,' she paused, not really knowing what to say. Her mind was a whirl, she was somewhat disconcerted by the intensity of her feelings towards him. 'Why don't you come up to the Lodge later, we can have some tea and a bit of a catch up.'

'Ok, excellent, see you about three ish then.' With that, and a cheery wave he was off up the road at a steady lope.

At about three o' clock that very afternoon Robbie parked in the large gravelled car park to the side of Sionnach Lodge. Mhairi was waiting for him on the granite steps to the main entrance. 'Welcome to Sionnach' she said, taking him by the arm, 'I'll gie y' the grand tour.' So they walked round the beautiful gardens and admired the views, and looked at each other, and grinned and laughed and, still arm in arm, went inside for tea.

Later that week they had dinner together, then, at the weekend, a longish walk followed by a leisurely meal in a hotel further down the strath. Soon they were seeing each other most days and a few weeks later they went off to Edinburgh for 'a wee city break' .

They were sitting in Le Bistrot on the Royal Mile late on the Sunday morning enjoying a very non French all day breakfast. Robbie looked at Mhairi, she was eating toast, and had some marmalade on her chin, he reached over and wiped it off with the corner of his napkin. 'You know,' he said, 'this, us, is really good, I don't want it to end, I mean, I hope we've got a future together.' He was struggling to articulate his feelings, was it all too soon to mention?

She looked at him with her serious face, 'Robbie, I feel exactly the same, I don't want this to end, I want a future with you too, and we have one, but there's no rush, we're together now, we're a couple, aren't we? and we have all the time we need.'

They finished up, Robbie paid the bill and, holding hands they stepped out into the sunshine of the Royal Mile, and were soon lost amongst the other tourists, just another couple in love in Edinburgh on a Sunday.

By the early winter Robbie was spending about half the week in Strathskean improving his cottage and doing his writing and the other half at Glen Sionnach. He enjoyed doing the physical work in the gardens where he helped the ancient gardener, and he just generally made himself useful about the place. For both Robbie and Mhairi life had become remarkably good.

38

In the Fishers' Bar of the Inverskean Arms Hotel on a Friday, a handful of local fishermen were gathered for their evening beer. There were two or three lobster and crab men and two scallop divers, brothers Craig and Allan. Both brothers were ex navy, and had also worked on the rigs before returning to Port Skean to set up their scallop business. Craig, a large muscular individual, who was the elder, was talking about the condition of the seabed, and he was not using scientific terms, 'Aye, the hale fuckin' seabed near the Eilean Dubh is aw covered in shite. The fishing is ruined, and the viz is crap noo as weel.'

The Eilean Dubh was a large rock in the Firth a couple of miles down the coast, and the seabed around it for several miles was a mixture of rocky outcrops and sandy gullies. It was impossible to trawl, but excellent and productive ground for the creel fishermen and scallop divers. Now its sustainability as a fishery was being compromised by the effluent from the salmon farm.

'Aye, ah'm no surprised, oor catches have been way doon too,' agreed one of the crabbers, 'ah've nae doot it's that fuckin' ferm,' and with that he directed a filthy look at the two Port Skean Fish Farm workers who had hitherto been enjoying a quiet pint before leaving for their homes a few miles down the coast. They quickly finished their beers and left.

'Aye, yer right enough, Wullie, but there's fuck all we can dae aboot it, they hev CCTV noo, and they gentlemen lookin' efter it twenty four seven.' The increased security was due, in no small part, to some expensive damage that had been done to the on-shore operation, with various bits of kit stolen, and such like. "They gentlemen" referred to the shore based fish farm employees and the guys from the security firm who were quick enough to intercept in their RIB any local boat that they thought was

163

getting a bit too close to the cages. Much as they hated to admit it there wasn't a whole lot the local fishermen could do about the situation at the moment, so they ordered more pints of Deuchars and settled in for the evening.

39

Frazer was in the bar of the Cairngorm Hotel, he'd just delivered some organically produced beef to the chef. The transaction was almost entirely legal, the bull had been killed in a registered slaughter house, and the dressed meat returned to Frazer who was able to sell it on to those establishments which were running entirely law abiding operations. In the last few years Frazer had found there was a considerable, and growing, market for legal organic, as opposed to the mostly illegal meat and game he had hitherto supplied.

As he sipped his pint he was lugging in to a conversation of a small group of English birdwatchers. Judging by their accents they were from the London area. They were talking about all the birds they'd seen up by the RSPB reserve in the hills above Strathskean.

'I'll tell you what,' said one of the party, swilling his pint around his glass in a philosophical way, 'I would give my eye teeth to see a capercaillie, I've never ever seen one, and I would love to, but the guy up at the RSPB reserve said they were almost impossible to see at this time of the year.'

'I'm with you there,' said another, 'Mebbes we'll have to come back in the early spring.'

At this point Frazer politely interjected, 'Excuse me interrupting, but if it's capercaillie yir wantin' to see there's a couple up at the back of my ferm. Aye, and there's a load of other stuff as well, like pine martins and w' hev otters in the burn.'

And so, as easily as that, Frazer's wildlife guiding business was born. The next morning at about eight o' clock Frazer turned up outside their hotel in his Land Rover and they set off for Caoraich Farm, or 'Caoraich Organics' as it would shortly appear on the website designed by one of Frazer's daughters.

Frazer turned off the A95 and drove up the rough track that took them to Caoraich. He explained that to start with, a visit to the loch on the moors above his land might be profitable, as there were a pair of slavonian grebes nesting there. The track wound past his farm and past the fairly newly refurbished Caoraich Cottage which

Frazer pointed out as the place, 'Where ah grew up.' Another fifteen minutes of steep rocky track brought them to Loch Caoraich, a fairly large expanse of peaty hill loch glittering in the sun. It was so remote, few people visited it.

Frazer pulled the Land Rover off the track onto a relatively flat piece of ground. The birdwatchers got out, shouldered their tripods with cameras and telescopic lenses and the whole tiny expedition with Frazer in the van traipsed across the heather to the edge of the water. Frazer led them to a wee gravelly beach which had a view of a small island in the marshy shallows fifty or so metres away. On the island, in the reeds at the edge of the water, was a nest and there a pair of slavonian grebes and three chicks went about their daily business unaware that their domestic life was about to be observed and photographed.

After a couple of hours of blissful observations, the party headed back to Glen Caoraich and the promised capercaillies. These proved more difficult to find, but after an hour or two of battling through the birch wood scrub in the glen these, too, were located, observed and photographed.

Back at the hotel that evening the Luton birdwatchers were fulsome in their praise for Frazer. Not only had they all seen the elusive capercaillie, but they had some great photos of slavonian grebes. Subsequently, one of their number wrote an article about their experience in "Ornithology Today" and this did Frazer no harm at all.

Frazer turned out to be an absolute natural at guiding birdwatchers and other naturalists, not only did he know every inch of the terrain, but he also had an encyclopaedic knowledge of every creature that lived there. Additionally, that whole Caoraich Glen area had remained largely untouched by modern farming practices, and the bio-diversity, compared to other sites, was astounding. Frazer was no academic, but his natural understanding was unparalleled, his large, man of the woods, wild haired appearance and gruffness added to his authenticity and authority, after all he was one of the glen's natural inhabitants. As a guide Frazer was the real deal.

In some kind of extreme Damascene conversion, Frazer, the erstwhile plunderer of all things natural, became an avid conservationist. The Strathskean Herald ran an article about his conservation guiding, which caused a few of the local underclass to snigger into their pints as they recalled some of his previous activities, but they wouldn't dare to laugh in his face. He was happy in his new persona, and, with the aid of his partner, Elsie, and their two daughters had even tidied up the farmhouse environs so they looked less like a nettle infested graveyard of rusting agricultural equipment and more like an eco farm.

40

2018

A muddy Land Rover Defender drew up in the forecourt of Sionnach Lodge, it bore the logo "Caoraich Organics" on the door. Frazer jumped out, he looked like an extra for a modern version of "Braveheart" his large frame dressed in camouflaged trousers and jacket, with a peaked cap and wild gingery hair and beard.

Robbie, jogged down the steps to meet him, they shook hands. 'Morning, Fraz, your clients are inside, I'll just get them for you.' He turned round and went back up the steps and emerged with a couple of American birdwatchers who were hoping to see osprey, great northern divers and goldcrests. He introduced them to Frazer and, placing their packed lunches and waterproofs in the boot, helped them into the Land Rover.

Since Frazer had become mostly legitimate, in addition to the supply of organic meat to Sionnach Lodge, he had picked up a fair number of clients for guiding from there as well. It was lucrative for him, because they paid a fair whack to start with and they were often generous with their tips. Frazer had also come to terms with the fact that Mhairi and Robbie were living together, not that that had been an issue for him at all, in the embracing of his new persona he had forgotten some, but not all, of his former jealousies and prejudices.

41

The fishing on the Sionnach Lodge water was expensive, and had traditionally provided the Lodge with a significant part of its income. From late June onwards until the end of the season in September, the beats were usually fully booked by folk who stayed at the Lodge. Lately, in common with all the other salmon rivers in Scotland, catches had been dwindling, and so bookings were down. The Sionnach Lodge water had some good holding pools, especially at the top and the bottom end, but there were some long, deep tree lined stretches in the middle which had little current and were not so productive. The fishing was managed by two truly ancient ghillies, Davy and Tam who knew every stone in the river and where and what the salmon would take depending on water height and other mystical factors.

Although Robbie was now a fully paid up member of The Strathskean Angling Association, and he also got to fish the Sionnach Lodge water from time to time. He had to be diplomatic here because the last thing he wanted to do was to tread on venerable toes and Robbie always made a point of consulting Tam or Davy or both of them before he went down. Actually, the way the fishing was, there was little chance of a salmon before June, when the first runs came in, the famous Skean spring run having been non-existent for several decades. However, Robbie liked fishing for trout, the forgotten species on the Skean, and the Lodge Water contained some fine specimens.

In April and May there were usually good hatches of olives, with impressive rises of decent trout. Hardly anyone fished for them though, certainly not on the Lodge beat. When Robbie had been down he had caught some excellent trout on dry olives, and also on Czech nymphs, he had written a couple of articles about this untapped resource which had been published in the angling press. On the back of this Sionnach Lodge had some early bookings from anglers who specifically wished to fish for trout. Davy and Tam were pleased about this because it meant an extra tip or two for themselves at a time of the season when bookings were usually non-existent.

On a morning in late April Robbie was sitting in the fishing hut at the top beat on the Sionnach water. He had brought some elevenses for Tam and Davy and they were comfortably munching their way through iced buns and drinking tea. The water was at a good height and already a few olives were starting to come off. Robbie was intending to have a couple of goes down the pool with his Czech nymphs before putting up a CDC olive, his very favourite dry fly. The conversation turned to sea trout, or to be more accurate, the absence thereof.

'W' always used to hev a great run o' sea trootl here, starting late May, but the last two or three years they've drapped right aff,' observed Tam.

Davy agreed, 'Aye, and ye ken why, it's that fuckin' salmon ferm in the firth. Ivry sea trootl an' ivry salmon that comes through here has to swim by those fuckin' cages. They get covered in lice, and if it's no the lice then they get some sort of disease. W' never had ony sick fish in this river until they started. The fishing's fucked, an' it's all they bastards' fault.'

Davy was absolutely right thought Robbie, the fishing in the Skean had been in a slow decline for years but, since the opening of the huge salmon farm in the firth, it had crashed. Last year they had pulled out several dead salmon from the lower beat, and they'd sent one off for analysis, apparently it had died of salmon gill pox virus. It was shocking enough for millions of farmed salmon to die in cages out at sea but transferred infection was the last thing that an already struggling population of wild fish needed.

'I'm just off to give my wee flies a swim,' said Robbie pulling on his waders, 'mebbes I'll get one of your sea trout Tam!'

'Y've nae fuckin' chance o' that,' came the good natured rejoinder, ' Gud luck anyway.'

Robbie started in the faster water at the head of the pool even though Tam had said "the troots wull nae be in the streams yet." As he worked his way down he reflected on the quality of the trout in the river. There were some really big specimens, and he had heard it said that maybe these bigger browns had been sea trout once and then had reverted to their natural state. This might account for their size. Just at that point his line drew taught and he was into a solid trout, it held in the strong water for quite a time before kiting round into the slacker current near the bank. He netted it, slipped the hook out and tipped it back into the water. He looked back at the hut. Tam gave him a cheery thumbs up, apparently there were "some troot in the streams" after all.

42It was a brilliant morning in early June, and the strath was at its finest, the sky clear blue, the birch trees in their newest green and the just arrived sand martins hawking over the fields near the burn. The rough track up to Caoraich Cottage and the loch went through the farmyard at Frazer's and on that Saturday morning the farmyard was full of noisy cattle. Now that the cottage was a holiday rent Frazer was used to cars stopping in the farmyard and asking for directions. However, this was a black pick-up and on the side was written the unwelcome logo: Silver Salmon Ocean Farms.

Two large individuals got out. The driver smiled at Frazer and said in heavily accented English, 'Hi, can you help us, we are looking for Loch Caoraich.'

Frazer shooed some of the cattle away, 'Aye, ah can, is it some birdwatchin' yir efter? There's some quite rare stuff up there at the mo'.' Frazer, of course, knew that these two were not interested in the slightest about ornithology. The rumours were true, Silver Salmon were looking for a site for a smolt farm.

'No, we are just doing a little feasibility study for the Estate,' replied the second man. He did not specify what exactly would be feasible, and his body language suggested that there would be no further communication.

Frazer thought it would be pointless to delay them. 'Well y' jist continue up this track fer aboot four miles and the loch's on the moor at the top. Y' cannae miss it. I'll jist move the beasts fer ye. ' Frazer shooed some of his cattle out of the way. The two got back into the pick-up and drove slowly through the yard.

In the pick-up Anders turned to his companion, 'So that's the famous Frazer, do you think he will cause us any problems?'

'Well I'm sure he's not going to be very happy about all the construction traffic coming through his farm. It is going to be difficult if he chooses to be obstructive.'

'Well, apparently, he has become very eco, look at his fucking farm, "Caoraich Organics," what's that all about? Anyway once our smolt nets are up and running there won't be much in the way of heavy traffic.' Anders laughed. 'Not too heavy anyway.'

Frazer looked up the track, a thin cloud of dust hung in the air like a harbinger of doom marking the passage of the pick-up. He was not happy, he was the natural inhabitant of Glen Caoraich and his territory was being invaded.

42

In the couple of years since they had met up again on the back road to Strathskean, Robbie and Mhairi had become inseparable. Robbie had spent ever increasing amounts of his time up at the lodge until he was actually living there. He was still renovating his own cottage, and occasionally some friends or family would stay in it for a few days, but mostly it was empty. He was considering letting it out as a holiday cottage, but he was half kind of conscious of his neighbours' feelings. In the meantime he kept its interior and the gardens in tip top shape.

Mhairi had streamlined the operation at Sionnach to some extent. Initially, the bookings had been good but recently things had tailed off slightly. A significant factor in this was the way the salmon fishing was deteriorating. Fishermen were becoming increasingly reluctant to spend large amounts of cash on fishing that was mediocre. And the numbers of salmon in the river had significantly declined, although that was not the exact phrase Lord Inverskean had used in a recent phone call to her.

It was generally agreed that most, if not all of the decline, was to do with the salmon farms, and one in particular. Fortunately, the two Sionnach ghillies, Tam and Davy were a decade or so past retirement age and were now only employed as needed, with Robbie filling in from time to time. He really enjoyed this work. His own spey castinghad come on in leaps and bounds, until he was good enough to instruct, and, thanks to Tam, he had a reasonable knowledge of the best lies on the beats. The trout fishing too, was developing if somewhat slowly, with a few anglers now coming up in the spring to target some of the specimen brownies that were in the Lodge Water. The rest of the time Robbie made himself useful about the place, doing all sorts of jobs. He thrived on the variety and the physical effort involved and he felt content. Really, for the first time in his life he didn't feel that there was something missing.

It was early on a Sunday morning and a bright shaft of sunlight shone across the attic bedroom that Robbie and Mhairi shared, and outside you could hear the breeze in the pines. Robbie had just been down to the kitchen and returned with some tea and toast. He got back into bed and balanced the tray on the duvet between them. Mhairie was still quite sleepy, but she managed to heave herself up into a sitting position. Her auburn hair was covering her face, and she kind of blew it and brushed it away in a gesture he loved so much. She smiled at him, 'Whit a lovely morning!' she said in an exaggerated Strathskean accent, 'That toast smells gud.'

He looked at her and replied in kind, 'An' hoo's yersel' Mrs.? Aye, wir like an auld married couple taking wir tea in bed of a Sunda morn.' He laughed.

'Well, why not?' she looked at him and put her arm around him, careful not to spill her tea, 'We should be, shouldn't we?'

'Well, I,' Robbie spluttered slightly taken aback. You're not pregnant are you? and cringed to avoid the expected slap. Fortunately the tea tray prevented any violence. 'Well, there's no reason why not, is there?' he said. ' I would absolutely love to be married to you. Let's dae it Hen.'

They got married on a cold and windy Tuesday in November at the registry office in Inverness, and rapidly returned to a small reception in the hall at Sionnach Lodge. One of Robbie's cousins was the best man and a couple of long standing friends from Tyneside had made the journey too. Of Mhairi's family there was her mother Morag, still living a more or less an independent life in Strathskean since Bill's death, and her sister and brother in law. Seonaid, Mhairi's daughter, now a medic in Edinburgh, was there too with her partner.

It was a lovely warm occasion, Seonaid liked Robbie and was glad that her mother had found someone to look after her, and she had also received certain assurances about future financial arrangements. Mhairi's mother, Morag ,was tearfully joyful she had always held Robbie's family in high esteem, given that they had been close neighbours and members of the Kirk as well.

Mhairi and Robbie had decided on a short honeymoon given that Sionnach Lodge needed to be looked after and couldn't be left for long even in November, a very quiet time, and so they flew off from Inverness on a short break to Berlin. On return, nothing really had changed with their relationship now that they were man and wife other than that they both felt remarkably pleased with themselves.

43

Frazer was standing in the Fishers' Bar in the Inverskean Arms in Port Skean, he'd been delivering some of his "award winning" organic beef to the hotel. There was a scowl on his face, he was reading the latest edition of the Strathskean Herald. The headline said, "Smolt farm For Caoraich." 'Would ye fuckin' look at that,' he said, holding the paper up in a huge fist to the three or four other drinkers who just happened to be the local scallop divers and two crabbers.

'Aye, Fraz, y'll noo get a' the shite from the nets coming doon yer wee burn, just like a' the shite we get on the sea bed, it's wrecked oor fishing. It's hard to mek a livin' from it noo.' Craig looked at Frazer, 'Aye, apparently some of the lads went over to their shore base a few months ago and did some damage like, but they only stepped up the security and noo the bastards hev got round the clock surveillance on the place. Y' cannae get near it.' He said all this with a look of concern on his face.

Craig knew Frazer of old. 'So if y' are thinkin' of daein' stuff, bide yer time.'

'Aye, Craig, yir right.' replied Frazer. He would bide his time. Frazer got back into his Land Rover, he had finished his deliveries for the day. He had known, of course that the smolt farm had been given planning permission, and the Estate had seen it as simply a commercial opportunity to make some money from an otherwise barren strip of moorland. However, the larger ecological issues were simply ignored. The only local landowner who had raised objections was Lord Inverskean, who had already protested at great length and expense about the original planning application for the salmon farm, and subsequently about the disastrous decline in the salmon and sea trout runs. As expected his objections were ignored.

44

Alec James was the civil engineer of Skean Construction, the firm which won the contract from Silver Salmon to put the access road in to Loch Caoraich. The first mile involved widening the existing track from the main road to Frazer's farm or Caoraich Organics as it was now known, and had been comparatively straight forward. The existing track ran through the small farmyard, and so the plan had been to re-route through two of the adjacent fields.

Unfortunately, this had not met with Frazer's approval, and he was gently putting his point of view to Alec, 'If y' think yir goin' tae put yir fuckin' road across my best fuckin' fields yiz can think again! Why in fuck's sake can't ye no put the fuckin' track round the top of the ferm where it'll no mess up ma land?'

The exchange was reminiscent of a scene from a wild west movie. The smallholder facing down the mighty railway company wanting to lay their track through his tiny shack. Only the smallholder was Frazer, six feet four of aggravated heilan' attitude, and the much slighter Alec with his yellow plastic helmet and clipboard. The whole scene was witnessed by the JCB driver, and the two guys leaning on their shovels, all had wide grins on their faces, they were enjoying the exchange. They had been to school with Frazer.

'And ah'll tell ye this fer nothin,' yiz can come back wi' a proper plan. There is no way y' can drive yer track

180

through ma fields. No fuckin' way!' Frazer fixed the unfortunate Alec with a glare from his steely blue eyes.

Alec shuffled uneasily, 'Well Mr Ross, if that's your view, then I'll have to get back to head office to consult, but I'd like to remind you that these plans have been passed by the council planning department and you are only the tenant here.' With that he turned and retreated to his pick-up which he had left down by the main road. When he got to it he found that two of the tyres were completely flat.

Of course, after a slight delay, the track was widened as per the original plans and for a couple of months a succession of trucks ground their slow way past the farm and up to the loch. There Skean Construction had made a car park, constructed a large shed and installed a Portakabin, while in the loch, several floating cages were moored each stocked with thousands of salmon smolts. The smolts would mature for twelve months or so and then, to mimic their natural life cycle, they would be transferred to the sea farm .

To the uninformed eye the Caoraich Glen had changed little, but the solitude and wildness had gone forever. Slow but significant changes were happening too with the chemical make-up of the water in the loch and in the burn. The thousands of smolts were excreting faeces and urea, and also antibiotics and other chemicals were used to keep them free from disease. The water suffered from eutrophication and algal bloom. The deleterious effluents from the smolt farm in Loch Caoraich ran all the way down from the loch itself throughout the whole of the Caoraich burn, right to its confluence with the Skean and on to the sea itself. The whole eco system was compromised.

No one was more aware of this than Frazer. He knew that his 'organic' livestock drank the now tainted water from the burn, the peacefulness of Glen Caoraich had been violated by the extra traffic on the access road and the delicate and wonderful biodiversity irretrievably lost. He was deeply moved by the change.

45

It was about two o' clock on a pitch black morning when Craig and Allan having untied the ropes to their scallop boat, The Mermaid, and with her twin diesels gently burbling at minimum revs, quietly slipped out of Port Skean harbour. The sea was flat with just a tiny swell and there was a light breeze. Usually they would be off to dive round the Eilean Dubh for their scallops but on this trip they intended to do something quite different. Their plan was to dive by the hated salmon farm and let the tidal current carry them along and below the cages so they could take a few photos to add to the physical evidence of pollution they would gather from the sea floor. They had enlisted Wullie, one of their mates, an ancient, bewhiskered crabber who had fished the Firth for over forty years, to stay with The Mermaid and then meet them down tide of the farm. They knew that night operations of this kind were dangerous but they were both ex navy divers and had done far, far riskier stuff in their time.

They guessed that for anyone watching from the floating cabin on the farm the sight of The Mermaid motoring slowly past would not cause alarm, and no one would observe the two divers slipping silently into water from the stern of the boat. And so after he had dropped them off Wullie motored round in a wide circle before anchoring up a hundred metres or so down tide of the farm. He glanced into the wheel house. He had brought along his deer rifle, an old Remington 700, he wasn't taking any chances, he had had one or two previous encounters with the gentlemen who provided the security for Silver Salmon.

Out in the blackness of the firth Craig and Allan quietly finned along on the surface with the tidal flow helping them until they were close to the first pair of sea cages. They let the air out of their BCs and swiftly descended to twenty metres before switching on their torches, they didn't want to illuminate the surface and reveal their presence to any observer, although they had considered that some of the farm's underwater cameras might pick out their whereabouts. The visibility was good and soon, after another couple of dozen metres, they were on the bottom which appeared to consist of a slimy mud unlike the gravelly sand, rock and weed they had expected. Allan put his gloved hand into it, and brought up a handful of thick black anoxic sludge which he put into a container. He grimaced inside his mask. The tide had started to pick up slightly now and they were carried gently and inexorably towards the cages. They had done 'due diligence' and they knew to avoid the predator nets, mooring cables and the acoustic deterrent devices and other hazards.

Once past the predator nets they were underneath the cages, conscious that their nitrox would only last a few minutes at that depth. It was a surreal experience, like being in some misty cathedral with strange inverted globed ceilings. Faint light filtered down from the illuminated walkways above and it was unnerving even for these two experienced divers. The visibility had deteriorated and the water was full of particles of detritus drifting down from above.

As they shone their torches upwards, to their horror, the white beams of light illuminated dead and rotting salmon lining the bottoms of the cages, and such was their number that the fabric was bulging outwards with their weight. It looked like a picture from hell, with the sickly grinning jaws of the dead salmon pressed against the netting. As they drifted under the cages they took photographs and a video. Soon they'd seen and had enough. Craig gestured to Allan. Time to head back to The Mermaid.

Down tide of the cages the water was soiled with waste material and the visibility was poor, so it was an anxious hundred metres or so before, and to their absolute relief, they saw, pulsing through the murk, the strobe light that Wullie had placed on their ascent line. They reached it and Craig consulted his dive computer for the decompression times. It would be another forty five minutes or so with stops at various levels before they could climb back on to their boat.

On board The Mermaid Wullie waited anxiously for his friends. The boat was anchored too close to the farm for his liking. He was worried that they'd been spotted and some of the security people would come out from the shore to investigate. To his left he could see the white and

185

yellow lights of Port Skean set against the black of the hillside and in front, the lights of the salmon farm shimmered on the water. He knew that it would take the lads some time to ascend given the time they needed for the decompression stops. He waited by the stern, watching the telltale bubbles from Craig and Allan who were hanging motionless on the ascent line deep down in the blackness, the only sound he could hear was the lapping of the waves against the hull.

Suddenly, Wullie jumped. Incongruously, the notes of "Flower o' Scotland" emanated from the wheelhouse breaking the near silence. His phone. It was Neil, one of the local crabbers and a good friend, 'Hey Wullie, I've jist seen they security boys from Silver Salmon get into their workboat, ah'm sure they're headed your way mate.'

'Cheers Neil, ah'll keep ma peepers skinned for they bastards.' Wullie looked apprehensively at the bubbles rising near the stern. How much longer would they be?

There was nothing he could do to speed up the process, he just had to wait it out. Craig and Allan would get back into the boat at the stern which had been specifically modified for this purpose. He got out his binoculars, sure enough he could see through the early morning dimness the white bow wave of some sort of craft heading in his direction. Fortunately it wasn't a RIB, something slower.

Just at that point there was an eruption of water and a hiss of air and the glistening figure of a diver bobbed up at the stern of the boat. Wullie sighed with relief and then hurried over and helped first Craig and then Allan up and on to the deck where they manfully pulled off their fins and began to divest themselves of various bits of kit. The water poured off them and sluiced its way down through the scuppers.

'Christ, whit a fuckin' experience that was Wullie,' said Craig who was still recovering his breath. 'Ah've nivver seen anything like that in all ma years divin, man, it's... y'cannae describe it.'

The sound of a big diesel engine impinged on their collective consciousness, and the large shape of the Silver Salmon feed barge heaved up, it came perilously close to The Mermaid which rocked violently in its wash. A blinding white spotlight illuminated the deck and wheelhouse of The Mermaid. Craig and Allan shielded their eyes with their hands.

The workboat edged nearer and nearer, its intimidating bulk looming large over them, its engine thudding loudly, the sea between the two vessels being pushed up into angry waves which splashed over their deck. It seemed inevitable they would be rammed and sunk. Suddenly, there was a loud shot followed instantly by the spotlight going out and the tinkle of breaking glass falling onto the deck of the workboat.

Wullie was at the door of the wheelhouse, his Remington in hand. 'Fuck aff ye bastards,' he screamed, furiously working the bolt, 'afore y' get another wan o' these!'

The barge instantly put its engines in reverse and slowly backed off, only just managing to avoid The Mermaid which rocked dangerously in its wake. Craig and Allan had been pitched onto the deck and were rolling about along with bits of diving kit. Slowly the violent rocking stopped and they picked themselves up and set about retrieving their equipment. They were speechless with the shock of it all, it had not quite registered how close to disaster they had been.

They winched in the anchor and in silence started back to Port Skean. The dark shape of the workboat headed off in the greyness in the opposite direction.

Allan broke the silence, 'Wullie' y'd better gie Neil a bell and tell him to meet y' ootside the harbour, then y' can get on yer ain boat and pretend yir going to lift yer creels. Y' can tek yir rifle with ye. When w' get in w' ll jist say it was only us on The Mermaid.' Wullie nodded in agreement. He did have a licence for his rifle but he was pretty sure it did not include shooting out spotlights on barges.

Dawn was breaking as they got back to the harbour. The shapes of the other craft were beginning to take form and there was the incessant clink, clink in the rising breeze of steel lanyards hitting the aluminium masts of visiting yachts. They tied up The Mermaid at its usual buoy and got in their skiff and rowed to shore. They'd get their tanks and kit later. Craig wanted to digest the events of their early morning dive in the security of his own home.

Later that day in the homely setting of his farmhouse kitchen, with his wife bustling about the range making a fry up, the three of them and Neil went through the images one by one. They were truly appalling, clearly something had gone very wrong to cause such mortality. Had they been a day later presumably the Silver Salmon support barge would have hoovered up all the dead fish to be disposed of in some local landfill site. Outside on the patio they decanted the stinking black sludge Allan had gathered from underneath the cages into plastic containers ready to be posted off for analysis.

They decided to send the images with a little write up to 'The Ferret,' an online journal and a fearless publisher of inconvenient stories, and also one of Craig's daughters volunteered to post the video on You Tube. They also sent the pictures to the Strathskean Herald, their local paper. Craig knew that something had to be done because the alternative would be to acquiesce to the ongoing destruction of their sea and their way of life.

A couple of mornings later Craig and Allan, off on their daily scallop diving, climbed down the harbour wall, got into their skiff and rowed over to where The Mermaid was bobbing gently at her moorings. As soon as they got on board it was obvious that something wasn't right. The wheel house door was swinging in the breeze and the lock was smashed. Inside, someone had taken a hammer or similar and smashed their radio, GPS, radar and the depth finder, all the kit the brothers had painstakingly and expensively installed over the last few years. The wheelhouse floor was littered with broken bits of electronics.

Craig looked at his brother, his weather beaten face was stone. 'Well, w' ken who did this, don't we? And we ken exactly what we need to dae noo.'

46

Kurt J Prentiss was excited, in fact he was beyond excited, he was about to realise the number one item on his bucket list: he was going to fish the iconic Skean river, Scotland. He was a lifelong fly fisherman who had fished most of the major rivers and lakes in America. Fly fishing was his life and passion, and now he had retired from his professional life as a lawyer in Atlanta he had decided to take his wife and himself on a four week trip to Europe. His wife, Jane, long suffering as she was, was more than happy to spend a couple of days walking around the beautiful Sionnach Estate, and catching up with her reading. After the Sionnach stay Kurt had arranged a few days for them in Edinburgh before they flew off to Dublin. She had plenty to look forward to.

Kurt switched off the engine and got out of the hired Range Rover in the lay-by by the little wood at the top of the Sionnach water. It was just about five thirty in the morning, he stood for a moment, a liquid and dull light was gradually bringing colour to the birch leaves stirring gently in a light breeze, a thin drizzle fell, gently glossing the grass and vegetation. There was a scent of earth and pine. He gently removed his fourteen foot carbon salmon fly rod from its magnetic holders, shoved a small box of carefully selected flies into a pocket in his breathable chest waders, checked his mobile phone was on, donned his lifejacket, picked up the rod and wading stick in his right hand and, thus equipped, locked the car with the remote and headed off along a little path through the trees.

He came to a clearing, it was bisected by a small burn which tumbled noisily towards the river. He splashed across, walked under an old railway bridge and soon arrived at a wooden fishing hut with a red corrugated iron roof and ancient, faded timbers. He opened the door, placed his bag containing his flask and lunch inside, and turned to look at the river.

In front of him a narrow neck of fast water gushed untidily into a larger glide which in turn slowed into a pool of perhaps fifty yards in length before disappearing downstream round a bracken bound bank. The water, the colour of strong tea plopped and gurgled over and around the stones until, becoming deeper, swelled into a powerful and inviting run under the far bank. Several goosanders clapped away in panic.

Holding his rod high, and steadying himself with his stick he gingerly slid down the bank through the browning vegetation and arrived at a tiny beach of coarse sand at the edge of the water. Looking at the ripple marks on the sand he could see that the water level had been dropping steadily. Ideal conditions. He felt excited, he had arrived at exactly the right time.

He waded out towards the narrow neck of fast water at the head of the run. Although the water was a rich brown colour it was translucent and he could see his boots quite clearly. Behind each rock there was a little triangle of sand. If he stood in this his footing was much more secure. The current pressed against his thighs, pushing him downstream and he steadied himself with his wading stick.

He was a highly experienced fisher and his tackle was the very best that American technology could provide. His carbon rod, incredibly light, was quite stiff in the Scandi style and his line a slick floating shooting head. To this he had added a medium sinking poly leader and a metre of fluorocarbon tippet. A size 12 Snaelda tube fly completed the outfit. Robbie, the affable guy who organised the fishing had assured him this was exactly the right fly for the time of year. He pulled some line from the reel. It made a well engineered clicking sound.

He began to work his way methodically down the pool. His casting was effortless: the line flew out and landed inches away from the far bank. With each cast he made an upstream mend and watched the light green of the head swing round followed by the orange running line. At the end of each cast he drew in yards of the orange line and using a double spey cast sent the fly whizzing out again on its mission.

Over the next few hours he worked his way carefully down the pools. Each one looked perfect, real fly fisherman's water. Not a single fish showed in any. At about eleven o' clock he was joined by Robbie and they had a coffee. They chatted about the declining runs and the state of salmon fishing worldwide. They both agreed that the conditions were perfect. He had a chance. Maybe there was one there for him. He wouldn't give up hope just yet. He had another day and a half left, but he couldn't shake off that feeling that experienced fishermen get when fishing over empty water, the feeling of hopelessness that is.

47

The desk in the office at Sionnach was strewn with spreadsheets and papers and on the computer screen multi coloured graphs flickered. Mhairi was sitting in an office chair, swinging about, pen in mouth, her face a picture of troubled concentration. She picked up her phone, 'Robbie where are you? Can you come to the office, we need to talk about something.'

A couple of minutes later the office door opened and a dishevelled Robbie came through. As one of the economies they had been making he had been doing much more work in the gardens and in the general maintenance of the lodge and grounds. It was obvious he had been cutting hedges, bits of greenery stuck out of his hair and his jumper. Mhairi laughed at the sight of him, 'My God y' look like y've fallen through the hedge, I thought you were supposed to be cutting it not diving about in it!'

'Well, it's ma new technique, total hedge cutting, y've got to get in and show it who's boss!' he laughed and came across and gave her a big kiss, 'Whit's the matter hen, yir looking awfy troubled,' he said in his mock Scottish accent.

'Well, looking at the advance bookings for next year we are really going to struggle to keep this place afloat, even with the economies we've already made. As you know, we don't really have to make much of a profit to keep going , but we definitely can't make a loss.' Mhairi had bought Sionnach outright, so there was no mortgage on it but the overheads on such a large property were steep, what with the business rates, staffing, heating and the endless maintenance costs.

'It's the bloody fishing, isn't it?' said Robbie, not only did the fishermen pay handsomely for their beat, they stayed at the lodge and brought their wives and friends with them too. Recently several large groups had failed to rebook, citing the lack of salmon in the river as the only reason. It made perfect sense, for the cost of a week at Sionnach you could fly to either Iceland or Alaska where you would at least have a better chance of a fish.

'We've talked about this endlessly, and even Lord Inverskean, with all his connections can't get anywhere, our situation is no different to all those hotels and guest houses on the West Coast that have already gone under. I'm not sure what if anything, we can do.'

'Well, you might just have to close down, which would be a hell of a thing to do,' said Robbie, 'and that would be devastating to everyone who works here, they love the place, never mind that it gives them a living. And what about all the suppliers, another nail in the local economy.'

Mhairi looked at him, 'Well my darling husband, we might just have to sell up here and live in yir wee hoose in Strathskean. The mighty fallen, eh?'

'Aye, there are worse fates than living with you in a wee house,' said Robbie and gave her a huge hug. Bits of hedge fell on to her desk.

'Away and sort oot that hedge,' she said, brushing a tear from her eye, 'wir not done yet, I'll have a word with Alasdair and see if he's got any bright ideas.' with that she pulled the chair up to the desk, tapped on the key board and brought up a new screen.

48

Rory MacLennan, one of the Silver Salmon employees looking after the smolt cages on Loch Caoraich was worried. On this windy afternoon he had rowed out to check that the feeding system was working properly. Looking into the cages that contained the youngest smolts he could see that a number of them had white patches of what seemed like fungus, mostly on the head and gill areas.

He rang his immediate boss, 'Roddy, we seem to have a problem here, that fungus stuff has come back again, a much bigger percentage of the smolts is covered wi' it.'

'Ah, Christ, that's no so good. Y'd better get some more o' that formalin, and treat all the cages. Ring the lab at head office and see how much y' need. In fact don't bother, I'll ring them, collect it from the stores and bring it up ma sel'.'

Early the next morning Frazer was at the gate in the field nearest the track up to Loch Caoraich. He was looking at his cattle and wondering if any were ready to calve yet. The fact that the track had cut through two of his best fields had continued to annoy him intensely. As he looked over the strath he became aware of a Silver Salmon pick-up towing a sturdy trailer loaded with large blue plastic drums slowly winding its way up towards him. It was obviously headed to the loch. Frazer regarded it with interest. He was genuinely worried about the huge deterioration in the water quality since the fucking fish farm had started, seeing as how his animals drank the water that came from the loch. He drank it too, but at least his was, in theory anyway, filtered.

The pick-up drew level with him, it was going slowly because of the rutted track and the trailer was bouncing around quite a bit. Frazer glowered at the driver, he knew who it was, it was Roddy, the manager. Roddy was actually quite scared of Frazer, he'd come second in all their previous encounters. Nevertheless, he was still prepared to observe the niceties. 'Morning,' he said with a cheerfulness he didn't exactly feel. 'It's going to be a fine day.'

Frazer looked at Roddy with contempt. Fixing him with his piercing blue eyes, he nodded at the blue drums in the trailer, 'Whit's that shite y' hev there? I hope yir no going to be pouring a that into the loch are y'?' squinting his eyes he read out loud, 'Eastern Scottish Chemicals, Formalin. Christ, man, y' must have tons o' that stuff there. Nae fuckin' wonder that ma drinkin' watter tastes like...'

Roddy didn't wait to hear what Frazer's drinking water tasted like and hurriedly pressed the button on the door and the window wound itself up shutting off Frazer's torrent of outrage. Roddy knew that the stuff he had on the back of his trailer was pretty toxic and a known carcinogen, but it was still the industry standard treatment for a range of parasitic problems. He knew too, that there had been quite a bit of adverse coverage in the more radical press about this very topic, so he was quite sensitive to Frazer's delicately expressed concerns. Still, he had a smolt farm to run, kids to feed and unsympathetic employers to placate.

A few days later Frazer, having sniffed and tasted the water in his house yet again with all the care of a man sampling a fine whisky, decided that he would examine the water supply from source to tap in order to reassure himself as to its purity. It did taste a tad off, but he thought to himself that that might be due to his own imaginings rather than any actual deterioration.

The water that was piped into the fields for the livestock was gravity fed and came straight from the loch via the burn. He had recently noticed a kind of browny tinge to it, but then it was contained in rusty enamel baths that had been there for decades so it was difficult to assess. His own water supply to the house came from a separate filtered feed from a spring up on the braes below the loch. This water was clearer having been filtered, but he still thought it had changed in taste. Frazer's partner and her daughters had reassured him, 'the watter's fine in the hoose, y' old goat,' so he accepted that temporarily but, nevertheless, he made a mental note to wander up to the loch to check on the water his beasts were drinking.

A couple of days went by. The weather had been dry and warm for weeks, the Caoraich burn was low and whenever a vehicle went up the track it was followed by a pall of dust. The blue plastic pipes feeding the enamel baths in the fields were only supplying dribbles of brown water. Frazer had to manually fill the baths with the water he hauled from the farm. His beasts weren't doing very well, he thought they looked sickly, he had his suspicions as to why.

The next morning Frazer got up early. The sky was a cloudless blue, and the air was laden with the scent of the honeysuckle growing round the farmhouse door. His mood, sadly, didn't match the existing meteorological conditions, being altogether more stormy. He had not slept well, and as usual, his midnight thoughts had been occupied by the desecration of the Glen Caoraich eco system at the hands of Silver Salmon, the bastards. Moving swiftly he went into one of the outhouses where he kept his quad bike, he jumped on, viciously kickstarted it into life and roared up the track in a cloud of blue smoke and dust in the direction of Loch Caoraich.

Things had altered slightly at the loch. Across the new access track there was a steel gate which bore the legend: "Private Property. Keep Out. Caoraich Smolt Farm. Silver Salmon Ocean Farms," plus a whole load of warnings on yellow triangles about this and that which Frazer ignored. He simply drove the quad bike around the gate and after a few minutes he was near the point of the loch where the Caoraich burn flowed out.

He switched off the ignition, dismounted and walked through the heather and myrtle to the bank. Here there was a marshy bay where the wide shallow outflow deepened into one channel to form the Caoraich burn and then, after about fifty yards or so it tumbled over a series of waterfalls and down through the birch trees and heather and into the narrowness of the Glen. He inspected the loch water. Usually it was the colour of weak tea, completely clear, but with that wonderful peaty hue, a bit like a fine single malt. Now it was a darker colour and opaque, it didn't smell right either. Then he noticed the greeny brown scum which sat on top of the water gently undulating in the wavelets like an oil slick. Sickeningly, floating belly up, trapped in the scum along with some detritus from the smolt farm, plastic bottles, oil cans and the like, were a few small native brown trout.

He looked at the scene in disgust. Thanks to his daughter showing him similar examples of desecration on the internet he had very recently become aware of this kind of pollution caused by smolt farms in other parts of the North East, how the osprey, otters and native brown trout had disappeared and how entire eco systems that had existed since the ice age had crashed, but he never thought he'd have to live to witness it himself in his own back yard. He got back on his quad bike and returned to his farm.

49

They had started drinking a while before, and with much swearing and guffawing they had managed to erect the cheap tent they had bought from 'Real Camping', the outdoors shop in Greenock. And there it was pitched in amongst the birches right on the shore next to the small beach. From the van they had parked at the top of the wood they brought folding chairs, blankets, pillows, a small mattress, several plastic bags of food and of course the booze. Soon they had gathered enough logs and sticks to get a substantial fire going, set their chairs around it and cranked up their sound system. Their campsite was complete. Around the loch as the light faded the flickering of a couple of other shoreline fires could been seen and the thudding sound of bass and drum carried for miles over the calm waters. Party time.

The magazine article that Robbie read with interest had been about the cracking shore fishing for brown trout that could be had in Loch Tay. There wasn't too much doing on the Skean at the moment as none of the beats were booked and, in any case, he fancied a change of scenery.

It was an hour or two's slow drive down from Strathskean but at last Robbie pulled his car into a lay-by on the Ardeonaig to Ardtainaig road and extracted his fishing tackle from the boot. Holding his rod case in his hand and slinging his holdall over his shoulder he vaulted the stone wall and walked through the green of the early summer birch wood to the shores of Loch Tay. There was a nice steady breeze blowing up the loch and decent cloud cover. Clouds of flies hung under the birches and there was the small sound of the waves washing gently over the gravel in the margins. It was idyllic. Sitting on a stone at the top of a wee beach he pulled on his waders and assembled his rod.

He walked westwards along the shoreline and soon came to a promising looking bay. If he went to the point, using the breeze, he could get out a long line and drift the flies round. Perfect. He left his holdall and net on the gravel and, wading gently into the amber water, began to cast.

Robbie used to fish the big reservoirs from the bank and so was able to get his flies a good way out on his weight seven rod and floating line. He had wondered if the outfit would be too heavy but he told himself he needed the distance.

He had put up a long leader with a Dark Olive Emerger on the top dropper, a Hare's Ear in the middle and a weighted Black Pennel on the point. He had cast out across the wind and, after a second or two to let the point fly sink, started to twitch the flies back at a medium pace. Soon he was casting in a smooth and easy rhythm, he was feeling relaxed and at one with his surroundings. He methodically moved along the shoreline. Across the loch a couple of boats were trolling for salmon, behind them the north shore and beyond that in the far distance the Grampians and Ben Lawers.

Several casts later the bow in his line straightened and he was playing his first Tay trout. After a spirited fight he pulled it into margins where it lay on its side in an inch or so of water. It was a beautifully marked fish, dark in colour with a butter yellow belly and nearly a pound in weight. It had taken the Pennel. Without removing it from the water he slipped the hook out and watched it swim strongly away. He sat on the bank with his feet in the water and had a cup of coffee from his thermos. The early summer sun warmed his face. The air was soft and scented. He closed his eyes in contentment.

After a little while he stood up, stretched and picked up his tackle. He walked past the point and round into the next bay. It too looked perfect. He was just about to step into the water when, at the far end of the little beach, a blue fluttering of cloth caught his eye. Puzzled, he retraced his steps carefully propped his rod against a tree, and walked over to see what it was.

Caught in the branches of a broken birch tree was the remains of what had recently been a tent. Around it, in the grass, on the beach and in the water was scattered bedding, bottles, Tesco bags, tin foil fast food containers, and dozens of empty beer cans. A semi-submerged mattress gently lifted and fell in the small waves. There was the remains of a large fire and above that the birch trees had been scorched. There were a couple of syringes lying on the gravelly sand and further along on the beach he found two piles of what looked like human excrement.

He picked up his holdall, net and rod and went back to his car. Driving back to Strathskean up the A9 he reflected on what he'd just experienced. He felt quite sick, what had started off as a beautiful day had been ruined by the criminal selfishness of others. Some people nowadays just had no respect for, or understanding of their environment.

50

To those arriving by yacht, or the frequent day trippers and summer visitors Port Skean was idyllic. The Inverskean Arms was welcoming and served excellent bar food, there were tea rooms, bed and breakfasts, and a casual summer population mainly staying in bed and breakfasts and rented holiday houses. But there was also a permanent close knit local population and it didn't take more than a day or so for them to hear about the damage to The Mermaid. Craig and Allan Mackinnon had wasted no time in spreading the word. As far as Port Skean was concerned the employees of Silver Salmon were now, if they hadn't been before, persona non grata in the pub and shops. Fortunately, Craig had had the foresight to insure the boat and this paid for replacement kit, but it took them the best part of a fortnight to refit it and return The Mermaid to its previous condition.

Meanwhile the dead salmon had been quietly hoovered up by one of the support barges and buried in landfill somewhere down the coast. The management of the farm had stepped up security at the shore base, although, to be fair to them, they had had nothing to do with the damage to The Mermaid, that had been done by a couple of the lads from the security firm, disgruntled at being shot at by Wullie. These two operated under a different set of rules and they were also quite miffed about being barred from the local pub.

51

The bar door to the Fishers' Bar at the Inverskean Arms opened spilling a warm light into the darkness of the side alley. Craig Mackinnon and Wullie Grant stepped out into the night, they'd had a good evening and now they were going to wend their way home. They didn't notice two figures slide out of the shadows further down and follow the pair of them to the road corner. They bid each other good night, and went their separate ways.

Wullie lived in a small development of bungalows at the top of a fairly steep lane. He always found the last one hundred yards or so quite difficult and he was puffing a bit as he paused by a wall to catch his breath. He was not as young as he was and the several pints he had consumed didn't help either. He looked down the brae and became aware of two large figures rapidly approaching him. 'Evenin' lads, steep brae eh? ah'm fair peched.' Neither replied but they came right up to him.

Wullie was completely taken by surprise when the larger of the two punched him viciously in the face and knocked him to the ground. Mercifully he was unconscious for the subsequent thorough kicking he received. 'That'll teach y' to fire a shot at us y'old bastard,' said the smaller, looking round to check that they'd not been observed, before the pair of them made their way back down the brae and off into the darkness.

It wasn't until late the following morning the Craig heard the news that Wullie Grant had been attacked and left for dead the previous night and was now in Raigmore fighting for his life. As with the damage to The Mermaid he knew exactly who was responsible. He would have to carefully consider his next move. Meantime he was off to Inverness to see Wullie.

Craig Mackinnon left his pick-up in the car park at Raigmore and went across to the A and E building. After making enquiries at the main desk he discovered that Wullie was in the ICU and that only close relatives were allowed to see him. He went up there anyway but was met at the door by a doctor who told him that Wullie had regained consciousness but was still very poorly. He noticed that there was a uniformed policeman at the desk drinking tea and chatting to a nurse. He didn't want to talk to the police at the moment. On the way out he met Wullie's son Jim, who promised to keep him informed. Craig himself, felt quite responsible about what had happened to Wullie, seeing as how he had asked him to look after The Mermaid while they dived under the salmon farm. On the other hand Wullie had been more than keen to participate, because his own livelihood had been put at risk by the pollution. The whole situation needed some more serious thought.

52

Macbeath Security Ltd was accessed via a long dark staircase that led from a grimy door in a back alley off

Ardconnel Street, Inverness. Moving between the light and civilization of Ardconnel Street and the dimness of the nether world in which their office was located was a bit like arriving unexpectedly on the set of some nineteen forties noir detective film, complete with humourless secretary and hard boiled private eye. It was quite an intimidating environment. Inside the rear office three extremely large, rough looking individuals were seated round a table. On the table was a half empty bottle of The Macallan, an overflowing ashtray and some whisky glasses. The air was hazy blue with cigarette smoke. A board meeting was in full swing.

Raymond Macbeath, the owner of Macbeath Security Ltd., was an ex police inspector from central Scotland who had taken early retirement. His reputation amongst his erstwhile colleagues had not been good, and it was widely thought that he had crossed the line on several occasions in the past but never been held to account owing to his connections. The other two partners, Malc and Jim, were ex military. They were reviewing their contract with Silver Salmon and in particular the actions of two of their casual employees, Kevin Falkener and Ricky Smith.

Raymond shuffled in his chair, sucked in his gut, pulled his trousers over his roll of fat, took a sip of the Macallan and cleared his throat, 'So, let's see if ah hev this right. These two scallop divers, the Mackinnons, and their mate

Wullie Grant went oot tae the cages to take some photies of a' the deid fish. And a couple of lads from the ferm along w' Kevin and Ricky went oot tae warn them off. But they nearly ran them ower instead, so Wullie shot at them and smashed their light. Then oor twa bright sparks trashed the scallop lads' boat and beat up Wullie. And noo the polis is asking some really awkward questions.'

'Ah'm not sure how much Wullie'll be able to tell the polis,' said Jim, ' He's pretty confused seemingly and, in any case, he'll no want tae admit to shooting at the work boat.'

'Aye, Ray,' said Malc, 'W've already told Kev and Ricky to mek themselves scarce, they've gone back tae Glasgae. Mind, if the auld man snuffs it, w've a massive problem.'

'Well, w' don't want tae lose the contract wi Silver Salmon, we're lookin' efter ten o' their sites over on the West. So, what we'll dae is this. We'll see the MacKinnons , they're both ex navy special forces by the way, and tell them that what happened at the ferm and to their boat was nuthin' to dae w' us, it was Ricky and Kevin acting by themselves and that they've fucked off back to Glasgae or Embra. We don't know where they are. We'll tell them tae steer clear of the ferm and the buildings on shore and ther'll be nae further problems.'

'Aye, that's a plan fer noo, but ah don't believe we've heard the last of the Mackinnons.' said Malc. Both Jim and Ray nodded in agreement, filled their glasses and turned their attention to the next item on the agenda.

53

High tide and mid morning on the quayside at Port Skean harbour saw the MacKinnon brothers unloading that morning's catch from The Mermaid. The harbour was quite shallow and they were taking advantage of the high water to unload directly onto the quay rather than having to fill their wee skiff and row everything to the stone steps. They had already heaved up a few boxes of scallops and were now in the hold sorting out their tanks and one or two other bits of kit when they heard the sound of a diesel motor which they assumed to be that of their wholesaler's van. Craig popped his head out of the hatch, to his surprise it was not the rusty white Transit he expected but a black BMW X5 with tinted windows. He turned and looked down, 'Hey Al, y'd better get yersel' up here, we've some visitors.'

Malc and Jim, the two partners in Macbeath Security simultaneously got out of the BMW and took a few steps to the edge of the quay where The Mermaid was moored. They were not dressed for a harbour visit and already Malc could feel the seeping of fishy water through the seams of his expensive shiny black leather shoes. There was a moment or two where neither party spoke but sized each other up. The two on the quayside dressed in dark suits with open necked white shirts were both large individuals, but since leaving the army their physique had been softened and rounded by the good life, whereas the two standing on the deck of The Mermaid, about the same height and age, were a muscular testament to the hard physical life they led.

Malc was slightly disconcerted, he was used to being able to intimidate people by his sheer physical bulk, but the two on the deck did not look in the slightest way intimidated, in fact they both looked pretty handy and then he remembered that Ray had said they were both ex special forces. Shit. He had met a few from his army days. They all had that same faraway look in their eyes. Nutters to a man. He shifted uneasily, both feet were now wet through. He spoke, 'We' was hopin' for a word or two with ye, yir the MacKinnons right?'

'Aye, that's right, if it's scallops yir efter, yir too late, a' them is sold.' Allan grinned, nodding at the boxes on the quay, 'but y' can get a few for yer tea in the fish shop in the village.'

'Nah, w've come to talk aboot your mate Wullie Grant.'

'Aye, I thought ye might hev something to say aboot that. Thank God, he's oot o' hospital, otherwise yis would be facing a murder charge. What the fuck were y' thinkin' of? he's seventy years old if he's a day.' The expression on Craig's face left no room for misinterpretation as to how he felt about the whole situation.

'Aye, well, that's the thing,' replied Malc,' it wisnae us. They boys was just casuals we hired to cover for a few weeks, and they was well oot of order daen' whit they did. They were livid aboot being shot at and they took matters into their own hands. Noo they've fucked off to Embra and naebody kens where they are. The polis is still efter them. If they've any sense, they'll lie low for some time. We want nuthin' tae do wi' em. So, if y' can keep yer noses oot o' Silver Salmon's business we can draw a line under it, eh?'

'Well, there's nae promises there, mate, Silver Salmon has wrecked the sea round here, some lads has had to give up the fishing and are on the dole as a result. Silver Salmon,' Craig pointedly spat over the side of The Mermaid, 'there's naebody roond here has a good word for them. We're not done yet, and ye can tell that directly to that big Norweigan twat, Anders, or whatever his name is. So y'd better get yersels' back to Inverness, afore yir shiny shoes is ruined and yir way off the quay is blocked by the fish vans. There's another of the boys coming in now' and he nodded to the harbour entrance where a trawler was just coming through.

Wordlessly, Malc and Jim turned on their heels and got back into their BMW. With some difficulty they reversed back along the keyside which was now becoming cluttered with creels and the like, turned at the end and disappeared up the Inverness road. After a while, Jim spoke, 'Ah thought that went really well.'

Malc's answer was as short as it was obscene.

54

One fine September morning in the city of Inverness a slim, grey haired and well groomed figure strode purposefully along Huntly Street, it was Sir Richard Gillanders and the bounce in his step as he entered his offices was explained by the fact that he had just acquired a rather large estate just a few miles down the coast. Sir Richard, Dicky, to his acquaintances, was the sole owner of Gillanders Properties and had spent his early professional years as a trader in the City of London. After amassing a considerable fortune by one means or another, he had recently returned to his native Scotland, with one specific aim in mind: he'd always wanted to own a traditional hunting estate. It was the culmination of all that he'd planned and worked single mindedly towards: first the money, then the model wife, then the peerage and now the land. He didn't really need to work but he set up this property business anyway which he regarded as a kind of useful hobby.

He was as smart as he was ruthless. He had, over the short time he had been back in Inverness, made some very shrewd investments. But this was "The Biggie," the one he had waited for, The South Skean Estate, complete with a hunting lodge up in the hills, grouse moors, deerstalking and some salmon fishing on the Lower Skean above the town stretch. Additional assets included Loch Caoraich, currently rented to Silver Salmon, and four farms with attached holiday cottages.

In all honesty, there were many estates that would have done almost as well, but this one ticked all the boxes. Inefficient management, and a ridiculously low income from the assets, had meant that the aged owner, Archibald Lennox, had been forced to put it on the market at a bargain price. None of Archie's relatives had shown the slightest interest in it and his accountants told him at his age and mounting debts made a sale unavoidable.

So, there he was, Sir Richard Gillanders, now the owner of a large slice of land close to the very strath where his great, great grandfather had been an estate factor or some such. It was his destiny. He knew that his Russian wife, Yelena, at present sunning herself on their yacht in Monaco, would approve as her brothers both liked the grouse shooting and stalking. He wasn't bothered about the salmon fishing, by all accounts that was fucked anyway. He turned to his young manager, 'Steve, South Skean, the rental incomes from the farms, we should be getting at least thirty a hectare from the upland ones, and much more from the fertile ones in the strath itself. Say at least fifty. Get some letters out, oh, and don't forget to ask for a big rental on the farmhouses themselves. In fact, we should look to price them out of the farmhouses and and convert them into holiday rentals. That's where the money is now. These folks have had it far too easy for far too long.' With that he turned briskly on his expensively shoed heel and swept out of the office. He had a date with his attractive female accountant.

55

Mhairi and Robbie had been invited for "coffee and a chat" with Lord Inverskean in Skean Castle. Mhairi was on first name terms with him, having met him a few times before. Robbie had met him once, the occasion being the annual Strathskean show. He had been introduced as a Dr. Ingram, and he'd had to explain to much laughter that he wasn't a real doctor and so would be absolutely useless in the event of anyone present having a medical emergency.

They left the Sionnach Lodge Land Rover on the wide gravelled drive and were met on the steps by Lord Inverskean, 'Call me Alasdair,' he said to Robbie, 'I know we've met once before. Come in, come in, we'll take our coffee in the Library.'

They went in through the main hall which was everything you would expect of a Scottish castle, with a huge staircase at one end and various stags' heads and oil paintings of ancient ancestors adorning the oak panelled walls. At the base of the staircase a full suit of armour, a huge sword clutched in its mailed fist stood guard. Alasdair shepherded them into another room to the left, the library. 'I'll spare you the indignity of the full tour,' he said, 'I'll just go and fetch the coffee.' When he returned, putting the tray down carefully on the table he said, 'I'm really anxious to talk about what's happening to our river, because we have a shared interest, don't we?'

'Aye, we do indeed Alasdair,' said Mhairi, Robbie and I were just talking about it the other day.'

'Well, the runs have really crashed these last couple of seasons, there's been a downward trend for years according to the counter but something has gone seriously wrong now. Even this time of the year when the Sionnach Lodge water should be crammed with fish it's pretty obvious that the river is almost empty. The sea trout run has collapsed too. I've only caught a couple this year, plus a whole lot of those damned farmed salmon.' Robbie sighed in resignation.

'I agree, if you remember those three weeks in August when the river was really low, even two years ago our beats would have been stuffed with grilse and some bigger fish too. Now there were so few fish that it was hardly worth wetting a line. The trouble is that, like yourselves, we have regular guests, and over the years they have become friends as well as clients. Now they are not renewing their bookings because there are no fish for them to catch.' Alasdair looked forlorn. 'Actually it's more serious than just losing the fishing isn't it? I'm having to lay off the ghillies, there's no money coming in to pay them. That's a whole way of life gone. Not to mention the local shops and hotels, it's not all of their business, but it's a big part.'

He continued, 'I've tried explaining this to the Minister at Holyrood but all you get is their counter argument that salmon farming is essential to the Scottish economy and they have plans to double the capacity over the next few years. The inference I take from that is that a degree of environmental degradation is a small price to pay.'

'Well, there's some other issues too, ' replied Robbie. 'The seas around Scotland are being absolutely netted to death by the continentals with their bloody super trawlers. They have even been in the Marine Protected Areas. Apparently there's a Dutch one called the Margiris with nets the size of a football field. It can take and process up to two hundred and fifty tonnes of fish a day! No wonder we're catching grilse that look like they've been on a starvation diet,' his voice rose slightly with the unfairness of it all.

'I'm seriously worried about the economic situation in the strath at the moment,' said Mhairi. 'It's all very fragile, jobs are scarce, we need more visitors and the collapse of the fishing has hit us hard. The town water in Strathskean used to attract dozens of salmon fishers from all over Britain and from all over the world come to that. I should know, because my father was the president of the

Association, as you well remember, Alasdair. It's seen as an elitist sport but these fishers all stayed at local B and B's and hotels, or the caravan park, ate in the local cafes and drank in the bars.'

She continued, 'It's no better on the coast at Port Skean either. Craig Mackinnon was telling me only the other day that his scallop business is struggling because of all the filth on the sea bed and other pollution from the salmon farm, he had some samples analysed, and you would not believe how toxic they were. The crab and lobster fishers are struggling too.'

The conversation continued along similar lines but they agreed there was no easy solution but they had to keep up the pressure on the politicians.

Mhairi had a mischievous look on her face, 'Changing the subject, tell me Alasdair, have you met your new neighbour up at South Skean yet?'

His lordship's face was a picture. 'Well, if you mean that mountebank Gillanders, he's bought it with his funny Russian money you know. It's nothing more than a tax scam, it's probably registered in Panama or Guernsey. He'll be around for a few weeks a year with his dodgy Russian chums shooting at anything that moves. And that's it. It'll stand empty for eleven months of the year with that crook of a head keeper Donaldson, or whatever he's called looking after it. Last year I was told he shot at least fifty mountain hares and poisoned a couple of eagles and God knows what else in the name of efficient grouse moor management. Disgusting! No, I have not met him Mhairi, nor do I intend to.'

'He's got a bit of fishing on the Skean, but he's not interested,' said Robbie, 'but I did hear that he is pretty financially ruthless, so if I was a tenant of his I would be concerned.'

The conversation having petered out Alasdair courteously offered them lunch, but they declined his offer, thanked their host for his hospitality and conversation and drove slowly back to Sionnach Lodge. Mhairi said, 'You know, Robbie, the difference between his set up and ours is this: he does not have to make any income from his guests to survive, he has enough investments and of course there's the rental he gets from all the farms and holiday cottages he has. We, on the other hand, are a very small operation and we need to have a regular stream of guests so we can keep paying the few staff we have. Our situation is not nearly as secure. We talked about this before.'

'Well, mebbes you will have to advertise a bit more, what about re- emphasising the nature side of things? We could get Frazer involved, we could offer 'Wild

Caledonia, a safari into the untouched Scottish pine forest. See the magnificent crested tit and a' that.'

'Shut up, y' idiot, snorted Mhairi, 'hey, doesn't South Skean own the Caoraich land? I'll bet Frazer's worried that the new owner will want to increase his rent.'

'Oh, my God,' laughed Robbie,' I'd pay good money to see Frazer's face if he got a letter from Sir Richard Gillanders telling him his rent had doubled. Can you imagine his reaction? he'd be straight into his Land Rover and up to South Skean Lodge.' He imitated Frazer's gruff accent, 'Whit the fuck's a' this shite aboot a rent rise ya jumpt up wee bastart...' They dissolved into fits of laughter.

'Actually, seriously Robbie, he probably will put the rents up because it was a well known fact that old Lennox was pretty lax in his running of his affairs. Ultimately that's one of the reasons why he had to sell.' Mhairi looked thoughtful, 'it would hit Frazer hard, especially after they put the smolt farm in his loch. They drove on in a thoughtful silence.

56

The little red Fiat post van bumped and rattled its way down the track from Caoraich farm. Cam, the postman, had just delivered an important looking envelope marked 'Private and Confidential' to Mr. F. Ross. Mr. F. Ross was standing in his porch holding it in his massive hands and turning it over speculatively. The expression on his face was grim. He was pretty sure he knew what was in it. It had 'Gillanders Estates' embossed on the back. He shouted, 'Hey Elsie, come and look at this, ah think it's a rent demand.'

Elsie came through to the porch. She was a small dark haired woman with a no nonsense attitude. She had supported Frazer's drive for a new eco friendly life but turned a diplomatic blind eye to his now only occasional indiscretions. She was very astute, a quality which she had passed on to her daughters both of whom were now at university, the younger studying Computer Science and the elder, Law. 'Well,' she said, 'open it y' great lummox.'

Frazer opened it and extracted a sheet of paper embossed with the Gillanders Properties logo. Slowly, he started to read, 'Dear Mr F. Ross, As you are no doubt aware...'

He got no further, Elsie snatched it from his hand. She continued reading, ' As you are no doubt aware, the South Skean Estate has recently been acquired by Gillanders Estates. As a valued tenant of long standing we

224

would like to welcome you to the Gillanders Properties family and assure you that we will take our responsibilities as your landlord very seriously and, should any problems arise, we promise that we will deal with them in a fair and courteous manner.... blah, blah blah,'

She paused and then continued, her voice shaking with incredulity. 'Christ Almighty! Listen tae this shite Frazer. 'As a result of our recent review of rents on the Estate we note that the rent for Caoraich farm house and associated lands has been far below the market standard for many years.   In order to maintain the financial integrity of the Estate a viable rental has been assessed as thirty pounds per hectare of farmland per annum, and six hundred and seventy five pounds per calendar month for the farmhouse. Please consider this letter as an official, "Landlord's Rent Increase Notice." You do have the right to appeal to..." She stopped reading and sat down on a chair to gather her thoughts.

She took out her mobile phone and accessed the calculator. 'Right, Frazer, let's keep a calm sough, and just work a' this oot.' Whit's a hectare and how many have we got?'

Frazer was also sitting. He didn't trust himself to stand, his first impulse was to get his shotgun and drive up to South Skean lodge and let Slippery Dicky Gillanders have the benefit of both barrels of no. 6 shot up his bahouchie.

'We've aboot two hundert and fifty acres including the Caoraich glen, but we've only aboot fifty acres o' fermland, and much o' that's jist moorland grazin'.'

'Jesus Christ, Fraz, wir lookin' at paying aboot twelve grand a year in rent. W' cannae afford that, no way!' and she started to cry. Frazer was stunned, he had thought that there would be an increase, they had only been paying a pittance for decades, and he knew that as soon as auld Lennox was off the scene the rent was bound to go up, but not by this massive amount.

Elsie was immediately on the phone to Jenny, her eldest daughter, who was quite sharp in the world of Tenants' Rights, being on the Students' Union Committee dealing with that very topic. After a lengthy chat, somewhat mollified, she turned to Frazer.' Jenny says there's lots we can do, for example a' that land in the Caoraich glen isnae fermland, and so w' shouldn't be peyin' rent on it. Secondly, w' can appeal to the rent officer by makin' somethin' called a 'Tenant's Referral' and nothin's goin' tae happen for a few months yet anyway . So w' can jist relax and sort this oot calmly, OK?'

'OK,' said Frazer, but inside he was seething with the injustice of it all. He had lived in Glen Caoraich all his life, save for an unhappy handful of years in Strathskean, he regarded it as his, and now his tenure of the wee but an' ben had been put at risk by outside forces beyond his control. This bit of ground was his by rights. His family had been the tenants since the middle of the nineteenth century for fuck's sake. He would, he knew, fight to keep it.

57

Mhairi, on more than one occasion, had been doing some serious thinking and financial modelling about the future of her business: Glen Sionnach Lodge. Having worked in the hotel industry for so long she had always lived in on the premises so to speak , she'd never had a place of her own. Granted, her accommodation had always been pretty luxurious, but an apartment in a hotel was kind of sterile, impersonal even. Sionnach was hers, but it wasn't really a home, was it, what with all the visitors. It lacked domestic intimacy. She had bought it as a project, something to keep her going and occupy her mind and time after her divorce. She enjoyed working in the hospitality sector and was good at it, but now she had Robbie, other circumstances had changed, and mebbes it was now time to sell the Lodge while it was a going concern.

She had looked at the bookings which were reasonably healthy over the Christmas and New Year period, but were a little thin for the spring and early summer. Due to the complete collapse of the salmon fishing there was only a handful of bookings for July, August and September, normally the high season, there were not enough to break even. She had to avoid making a loss at all costs, she did not want to eat into her capital, and nor did she want to get a mortgage on the place in order to keep things going. She needed to talk things through again with Robbie.

She found him in the sun lounge reading a copy of the Guardian, his favourite paper. He was always banging on about some social injustice or other and she would gently rib him about his politics bearing in mind his present situation. 'Aye Hen,' he'd said to her on a number of occasions, 'y' can be a member of the landed gentry and still hev a social conscience!' And then he would dissolve into fits of laughter.

'Robbie,' she said sitting next to him on the sofa, 'I've been doing some thinking.'

'More thinking! that sounds ominous, whit's on yer mind?'

'Well, I've finished reviewing the finances yet again, and I know we've been over this before and the only conclusion I can come to is that we'll start making a loss from about next summer onwards. So, we've a couple of options. We could close down the whole operation and just live here the two of us, in decaying splendour, for the rest of our days. Truly the ancient ruins! Of course we would still have to pay enormous heating bills, rates and upkeep of house and gardens. Even your gold plated teachers' pension couldn't cope with that! And, my love, strong and fit as y'are now I'm sure y' wouldn't want to be spending all yer declining years sorting out the grounds. Another option would be to sell this as a going concern, but, whichever firm took it on they would do due diligence on the finances and most likely come to the same conclusion as me about its future viability.'

'Mind you there are two further options, we could sell it as just a big hoose for some wealthy person, or to some developer for apartments.'

'That sounds like a good idea, ''Glen Sionnach Lodge, Eco Apartments in the Heart of the Ancient Caledonian Pine Forest.'' Wake up to the sound of pine martins calling you out to play,'

'Shut up 'y'idiot. Robbie, w' need to make a decision soon, by early next year at the latest anyway. Otherwise we might be in trouble.'

'Ok, being serious, we could sell my house as well and buy something near Strathskean that would be big enough for us and to accommodate family, I'm sure Seonaid will want to visit from time to time, especially now she's got a job up at Raigmore. And then there's your sister and her kids. My wee hoose is great but it's a bit small for having folks to stay.'

'Well, all that sounds like a plan, I'll put some feelers out about the current state of the market and we can get some idea of how things are. Chances are it might take some time to sell. When I first bought it, I could only see its potential for development, I thought it would be a great project and it was, but now circumstances have changed and I don't want it to become a liability.

58

In fact, it was Elsie and her daughter and not Frazer, who had, using their accumulated legal skills, tried really hard first to dispute and then to delay the egregious rent increase, but without much success and it seemed unavoidable that they would have to pay a lesser but still exorbitant rate for the land and farmhouse. They had, however, managed to renegotiate what exactly was farmland and what was not, and this reduced the land rent somewhat. Even so the family would be still be hard pressed to find the money, given the seasonal and random nature of their income. Frazer thought he might have to resort to some of his old tricks in order to keep afloat although he didn't tell Elsie. He had been told that the new rental would start from January the first. ' Some fuckin' New Year present that is,' he thought to himself. He was left with an even stronger simmering resentment to add to his inbuilt sense of injustice.

All this came to light in a conversation between Robbie, Mhairi, Frazer and Elsie in the Strathy Bar one early evening in late autumn. They'd met up there because Frazer had asked Mhairi if she knew anything about Sir Richard Gillanders. Robbie and Mhairi had already heard about the rent increases demanded by Gillanders Properties because it wasn't just the Rosses that were affected, there were other tenants in the strath too and the increases were common knowledge.

'OK,' said Mhairi putting her glass of Savignon Blanc on the table, 'I've rung up my ex brother in law, Mark, the one who's running MacLune Hotels now, and he says that "Slippery Dicky," as he is known in the finance world is bad news. Firstly, he's up to his neck in funny Russian money, secondly, he is completely ruthless, and if you cross him he has some very unpleasant friends. He's smart, impossible to pin down, hence his nickname. He has his fingers in many pies, including, you'll be alarmed to know, Silver Salmon. Word has it that the aquaculture industry is on the up in Scotland despite the huge

231

environmental cost. It's totally supported by the government. Now, Frazer and Elsie, here's the thing, and it's a real bummer: the rent you will pay as a sitting tenant for Caoraich farmhouse is, I imagine, around about six to seven thou. a year. However, if your farmhouse was rented out as a holiday house it could generate as much as three times that. For someone like Gillanders it's a no brainer. So if you times that by all the properties he could potentially convert on South Skean then you're looking at serious cash. He's trying to force you out by making the rent as steep as he possibly can.'

'Fucking hell,' growled Frazer, 'it's the fuckin' clearances all over again! Ma family, the Rosses, were cleared oot aff Glen Calvie in eighteen forty five, and that's how we ended up in Glen Caoraich. And noo wir being moved on again. Well, Mr Slippery Dicky, you can think again!' He took a long pull of his Deuchars, his face a picture of defiance and hatred.

'If yer thinking of doin' owt stupid Fraz,' Robbie said, 'Don't. For the simple reason they'll know it was you. Anyways, what, short of shooting the bastard, could you do that would actually make any difference?'

Frazer didn't say anything but 'shooting the bastard' sounded good to him.

Later, Mhairi back in their sitting room at Sionnach, was talking over the whole situation with Robbie. 'Frazer will definitely do something, won't he Robbie, if only to make a point. He's not the only one who is affected is he though? There's all the young folk up and down the strath who can't afford to buy houses, they have to rent if they can. More likely they can't afford to and so they have to go off to the cities to earn a crust and we become like some massive holiday park with no permanent local population.'

'Aye well, that's what's happening all over the UK. I know there's some places have limited the sale of holiday houses, and they have a locals first policy. Mind you, Frazer's situation is slightly more complex what with the smolt farm and the massive pollution that's brought to his wee glen. That probably needs to be called out somehow.'

'Well if he can't pay the rent come the new year he'll be in trouble. It would kill him to be evicted. In fact, I'd be worried that he might do something incredibly stupid and end up in gaol.'

'Well, I think he could easily get violent. He used to be on a very short fuse when he was a kid, no self control. So maybe it would be better to think of some way for him to protest without him taking his rifle up to South Skean and letting Slippery Dicky know what a heilan' man can do when his way of life is threatened. Mebbes I'll have a word with him and I could suggest a course of action that doesn't involve him killing anybody.'

'Right, Robbie, but y've got to make sure y' don't get yerself involved in some harebrained scheme that puts you at risk as well. Remember what Mark said about his Russian contacts.'

'Look Mhairi, it's probably time to get off the fence. Think of the damage that Silver Salmon has done to us and our way of life. Maybe I'll speak to Craig and Allan down at Port Skean and see what they think. After all they had that trouble with the security guys beating up poor old Wullie Boyd, I'm sure they wouldn't want to let that go unanswered.' He yawned, anyways it's best not to act in haste, what do they say? 'Revenge is a dish best served cold.''

'Ok, bed now and think some more in the morning,' said Mhairi before heading off towards the bathroom.

Robbie had a fitful sleep. His mind was too active, his thoughts occupied by the situation that Frazer found himself in, and also the larger picture, the destruction of the environment as evidenced by his earlier trip to Loch Tay and the disastrous collapse of the salmon on the Skean. He had been looking on the internet for the other fish counts on East Coast rivers, they were all down, but the Skean's was not even ten percent of what it had been even a few years ago, not since the advent of that bloody fish farm anyway.

Half asleep and half awake he fantasised about all sorts of wild schemes to destroy the farm, but couldn't think of one that was practical. None were legal. All were impossible, the stuff of Holywood films. However, he had one thought that wouldn't go away: the day he came back from school to find his mother had sprayed the kitchen with insecticide and all his fish in his aquarium had died. Mebbes there was a solution after all. He'd give Frazer a ring in the morning. He wouldn't tell Mhairi, not yet anyway.

59

Frazer and Robbie met near the top end of the Town Water on The Skean. At the end of a narrow winding road through the woods there was a car park next to an old cemetery. Over the gate hung the branches of an ancient beech tree and now, in late November, the ground about was carpeted with golden brown leaves. In fact, the adjacent pool was called "The Cladh," the graveyard in Gaelic, and was a slow deep bend which in better times held big concentrations of salmon at the back end of the season. Now, the water slid silently and slowly by, greyly reflecting the clouds. There was a bench on the bank overlooking the pool , one of many such up and down the water, donated by the family of some ancient fisher, "He loved this place."

Frazer was leaning against the bonnet of his pick-up. He was smoking a roll up and a cloud of blue tobacco smoke drifted slowly away. His face was stone. Typically he did not turn to greet Robbie when the latter stepped out of his Land Rover. 'Aye, aye, it's yerself,' he muttered, whit can ah dae for you?'

'Well, Frazer, me and Mhairi were thinking that, knowing you as we do, there is no way that you would actually take that ridiculous rent increase lying down, and we were worried that you might do something incredibly stupid like going up to South Skean with your shotgun. So, I thought mebbes there's a way to get your own back without putting yourself at too much risk of criminal prosecution.

So, I had an idea, Frazer. There has been a bit in the press recently about the use of formalin in smolt farms and how dangerous it is, and how much damage it does to the ecosystem. There's several lochs in the north that have been ruined by it, just like yours. The smolt farm in Caoraich isn't protected is it, no one actually looks after it twenty four seven do they? It's vulnerable, and if it were to have an accidental overdose of something it would really fuck them up wouldn't it? And, Frazer, if it was something, say formalin, that they already use, well who's to say it's not their own stupid fault. Loch Caoraich is completely destroyed anyway as long as they have their smolts there.

Secondly, I can't imagine, with respect to you and Elsie, that Caoraich Farmhouse is in the best state of repairs is it? Well, if the estate is demanding a huge increase in rent, them mebbes you could demand a huge amount of repairs and modernisations. Also, your water supply, it's essentially from the loch isn't it? You were saying it tasted funny, that would make a good headline: "Drinking Water Contaminated by Salmon Farm." They would have to sort that out , and it would cost them. Imagine having to fund a new water supply. Craig Mackinnon sent samples of the mud he collected to a lab to be analysed, you should do the same. In fact, I'd be pleased to do that for you. Also Mhairi's got access to a really sharp lawyer so it might be a good idea to channel all your stuff through him.'

Frazer nodded slowly, Like Craig's, Robbie's advice was sound. Play the long game. It wasn't in his nature, but he could see the sense of it.

'And I'll help with the other too. But not yet, w' have to box clever on this. Wait for a bit till things are quiet, say early next year or, better still just before Christmas say, then with a bit of luck they won't discover it for days. Or, if w' pick our time, we'll do it just before a hard frost, or a storm and then they'd think it was a natural disaster. "Hard Frost Kills Thousands of Young Salmon."

'Aye,' growled Frazer, 'they keep the formalin in their shed up there. I've looked through the window and seen it. There's all kinds of other stuff there too. That numpty o' a worker Lachie, he's forgotten to close it afore now, he left the combination lock open once so ah hev the code. There's nae security camera there neither. It would be better if w' could jist let the smolts go, they might be able get doon to the sea at some point, but they'd they'd ken it wis me. Yer right Robbie, we'll dae it quietly.'

'Ok, good, we'll start by getting your drinking water analysed, and then y' should get one of yer dodgy builder mates to look at the house and say what's in need of urgent repair. The wiring must be a hundred years old at least, that is if y'even got electricity up there, y' savage.' Robbie laughed at the look on Frazer's face.

'Fuck aff, w' don't all live in the lap o' luxury wi' wealthy women,' Frazer replied, but at least there was the semblance of a smile on his face. He felt better now there was a plan.

60

A few days after Robbie and Frazer's meeting at the Cladh Pool Frazer was in his farmyard loading some bales of hay onto his pick-up when a little white van drove in and pulled to a stop outside the farmhouse. A youngish looking guy stepped out. He had round spectacles, a baseball cap and a wispy beard. He gave Frazer a wave and went straight to the rear doors of his van , opened them and took out a holdall, a couple of boxes, a bright yellow hazmat suit and welly boots which he duly donned and thus attired went across to Frazer who had stopped loading his hay to watch the performance.

'Hi,' said the guy, ' you must be Mr Ross, I'm Matt from Aquasay. I'm here to get some samples of your drinking water, and some from the burn as well if that's OK. Am I right in thinking that yer water comes from the loch on the moor.'

'Aye that's right, who sent ye again?'

'Well, we got a call from a Dr. Ingram, er Robbie, he said his name was, and he said he thought the drinking water at Caoiraich farm and the water in the burn was contaminated and he was acting on your behalf. He's paid for a survey.'

Frazer was a tad non-plussed, Robbie hadn't actually said when he was going to get a survey done but he went with it, 'Aye, aye, ah remember noo, he said,' y'd better come in and get yer samples.'

Matt went into the house, he ran the kitchen tap for some time and then filled about three beakers. He went outside and held up one of the beakers to the light. 'I can tell you now, Mr Ross, that this water will not meet current UK drinking water standards. It has a slight smell, I'm not sure what of but something's not right. Also, it's quite coloured isn't it? I would strongly advise you to boil it before you drink it for now and I'll get it analysed this afternoon. Now, if you'll point me in the direction of the burn, I'll get some samples from there too. Do your cattle drink from it?'

'Aye, they do,' said Frazer,' and they've not been daein' so well either. I'm worried, I'm tryin' tae run an organic ferm here for Christ's sake!'

'Ok, well, that's not so good. I'll get the samples and shoot off back to Inverness. If you give me your email I'll

240

send the results straight back to you and Dr. Ingram as soon as possible, by tomorrow lunchtime with any luck. Cheers now,' and with that he disappeared in the general direction of the Caoraich burn.

Frazer decided that he'd better ring Robbie, he'd only recently got a mobile phone since everyone he did business with seemed to have one these days. He hated it, and it took him three goes before he found Robbie's number, his big fingers were not designed for the delicate operation of electronic equipment. He was brief, 'Y' might've said y' wis sending some bairn up tae sample the watter.'

'Well, I talked it over with Mhairi, and we thought the sooner the better. They said they were going to email the results straight through as soon as they got them. If it's as expected we're going try to get it in Friday's Strathskean Herald. While yer on, y' need to get that builder yer pally with to survey yer house. Mhairi's lawyer friend says he'll send a letter demanding repairs before any rent increase. When we've done all that we can think about the other.'

'Ok, Robbie, at least we hev a plan, and we'll see what the survey says, ring me with the results will ye as soon as y' get them.'

'Sure Frazer, it's about time these people thought about what they're doing. They have got to consider other folks. Speak soon.' As he terminated the call he looked at his phone for a few minutes and wondered what he was getting himself into. He'd come to Strathskean to live a rural life, to fish and to write. The fishing, brown trout excepted, had mostly collapsed but he'd miraculously rediscovered the love of his life and he didn't want to compromise that under any circumstances, but even she was affected by the degradation of the river. As he'd said to her earlier: 'Sitting on the fence was no longer an option.'

61

Later, that evening, after their dinner Robbie and Mhairi were sitting in the sun room, there were no guests so they had it to themselves. They had wee drams and were discussing events. Robbie looked at Mhairi, 'OK so, assuming that the water survey shows some degree of pollution, both in the drinking water and in the burn what next, we get on to the paper?'

'Well, hopefully, Frazer will be able to use the information as leverage against a reduction in his rent. Also, if it becomes public knowledge that the Caoraich burn is contaminated then the environmental lot might impose restrictions as to what they can tip into the loch, but, as Lord Inverskean pointed out SEPA are, er, "less than effective."' They both laughed, what Inverskean had actually said had been expressed in unexpectedly forthright language for a peer of the realm. 'There's the other houses on the estate too, some of them must get their water from the same source.'

'Well, I think that might help Frazer a bit, but his real beef is with the continued presence of the smolt operation. It's a constant reminder to him that his world has been destroyed, and that, actually, he is as powerless as his ancestors were back up in Glen Wherever.'

'Glen Calvie,' laughed Mhairi, 'I hope that Frazer gets some sort of rent reduction, otherwise he will do something daft.'

'I agree, Mhairi, speaking of that, we did have an idea about what could be done to mess them up. Firstly, they've had real problems with disease and fungal infections, hence all the formalin in the water. Secondly, the Firth of Skean farm lost thousands of fish earlier this year in that storm Karin, or whatever it was called. They are such a global operation they might just shut down here because the East Coast of Scotland is not profitable for them. I have been reading that they have been developing a huge deep sea farm off the coast of Norway, also they have salmon farms in Chile and British Columbia. And, people with nothing to lose have nothing to fear. You can't make it any worse for Frazer than it is at the moment. So, I thought I'd just help him, if needs be, and keep whatever he does within reasonable limits, at least. I know it's a risk for me, but a slight one and I do think, seeing as how these people have been flouting the environmental laws for long enough, it's about time w' had a bit of direct action.'

'Oh Robbie, I agree that something effective needs to be done, but you will promise me that you will keep yourself safe, won't you? I couldn't bear it if something happened to you. Also you don't want to end up being prosecuted do you? Visiting my husband in jail is not on my list of preferred retirement activities!'

'Well, it's safe enough for us, and they won't know anything about it until well after it's happened, it'll be like a sly stab with a dirk, a Skean Dhu! Appropriate or what.' He smiled grimly, ' You won't have any part in it, or even know if and when we do it. You have my word.'

Mhairi was unhappy, but she knew his mind was made up, he had decided to get off the fence, and she could only admire him for that.

62

'Hey, hev y' seen this lads?' it was Neil, Wullie's mate and he had just come in to The Fisher's Bar at the Inverskean Arms. It was blowing a hoolie outside and the rain spattered against the windows. It was late Friday afternoon and, it being autumn, the light had already faded outside, but inside the bar was bright, cosy and full of the usual harbour crowd enjoying their first weekend pints. 'This' was a copy of the Strathskean Herald. Craig, Allan, a still recovering Wullie and a couple of other fishers, shuffled along to make room for him at their table and someone pushed a pint in his general direction. He plonked the paper down in the middle of the table, 'Frazer Ross is on the front page!'

Everyone crowded round to see. On the front page the headline read: "South Skean Estates: Drinking Water Contaminated" and then a large picture of Frazer holding up a glass of water, he had a disgusted expression on his face. It wasn't a flattering image, he looked every inch the wild highlander he was. The article went on to say that in an independent survey a large quantity of organic and inorganic contaminants had been found in the drinking water supply at Caoraich farm. There was a quote from Frazer which said that the water had tasted funny ever since the smolt farm had started. He went on to say that not only was his own drinking water unfit, the water in the Caoraich Burn was also full of contaminants and, as the owner of an organic farm it had made his cattle sick and compromised his business. Actually, when interviewed, Frazer hadn't used the words 'contaminants' or 'compromised' but, as Andy the reporter said to his editor, you couldn't ever print what he actually said.

Frazer, in language civilised by Andy, went on to point out that it was a bit rich of the Estate to demand swingeing rent increases when they couldn't even provide their tenants with clean drinking water and, not only that, the ancient wiring in his farmhouse made it into a death trap, not to mention the damp and dry rot. He further said that he felt the real motive behind the huge rent increases was to drive out local folk because holiday rentals were more profitable. He claimed it was "the clearances" all over again. The article ended with a statement that the Estate had been contacted for their views but they had declined to respond. In fact, they were in a state of "heightened alert" as they had faxed Sir Richard a copy of the front page and were awaiting the inevitable explosive reaction.

'Fuckin' hell,' said Allan. 'Well done Frazer. This is gonnae stir up some shite. Frazer's gonnae hev to watch his back.'

Craig agreed, 'Aye, yer no wrong there Al. Robbie Ingram was telling me that Dicky Gillanders is a major shareholder in Silver Salmon and, according to what he's heard, he's a really nasty piece o' work. We've all seen what Silver Salmon hev done tae oor fishing, and there's still the small matter of Wullie here and whit they bastards did. So, ah think at some point soon w' need a plan. Just damagin' their stuff on shore is a waste o' fuckin' time. It jist makes them mair watchful, mair aggressive. I say w' back aff fer a bit and then, tae mis-quote the words o' Biffy Clyro, "When w' hit 'em, w' hit 'em hard!"' He took a long slurp of his Deuchers and re-read the front page.

63

The motor yacht Lucky Lassie moved imperceptibly, not enough to make the coffee splash out of her cup but enough to make Yelena look up from her magazine. Like Frazer Ross she too was the subject of a front page spread. Unlike the unkempt wildness of Frazer, the image she presented to the world was six feet of an immaculately toned, blonde, bikini clad model posing seductively on the white sands of a tropical beach. The caption read: 'Is Your Body Beach Ready?' Hers certainly was.

To her intense irritation, her husband had unexpectedly arrived a couple of days ago and was now sitting opposite her in the upper lounge. He was not in a good mood. She was not in a good mood. She had been enjoying the athleticism of one of the Russian security guys and now all that was on hold while she had to enjoy the softer and wrinkly delights of Sir Richard. She looked out of the windows. Nickoli, the aforementioned security guy, wandered past, giving her a cheeky wink. Beyond his retreating muscular physique, she could see Port Hercule with its serried ranks of motor yachts and behind them, the world famous Monte Carlo harbour front glistened opulently in the bright sunlight. She yawned. Maybe she would take a stroll around the front later.

Evidently things were not going smoothly for her husband. That morning he had printed off a newspaper article which had annoyed him. He had been on the phone for at least an hour. First, it was his lawyers: "tossers all" apparently, then it was to that nice Scottish boy who ran his Estate offices in Inverness: "useless twat" apparently. Now he was speaking to her brother. She knew what that meant.

Eventually, South Skean Estate, at the prompting of "the useless twat" in Inverness, issued a carefully worded statement to the press. It said something along the lines of that they regretted the water supply to the properties on the Western side of the estate had been temporarily contaminated but this was entirely due to exceptional meteorological conditions and the matter had now been fully investigated and remedied. As for the rent increase, well, there was no rent increase was there? Rents had merely been readjusted to conform to the current market standard. South Skean Estate was proud of its exemplary record of looking after its tenants and its wider support of community projects. As for the charge about the Estate enacting "The New Clearances," categorically not.

'Well, whit the fizzin' hell did y' expect, Fraz?' snorted Elsie, 'They wis always gonnae lie through their teeth aboot it. There wisnae a single chance o' they bastarts admittin' liability.' She showed him another page in the paper. 'Here's some shite from Silver Salmon. It's all aboot how eco friendly their salmon is and how they are reared, blah blah. Oh, and get this, she read in a la -di-dah voice: "From their birth in the high mountain streams and early life in the pristine waters of inland lochs to their adult life swimming freely in the crystal clear waters of the Firth, our salmon are carefully nurtured to bring to your plate the ultimate in responsibly managed health food, rich in omega 3 and protein." Fuck's sake!' Elsie threw the paper away in disgust.

"Crystal clear, pristine waters," growled Frazer, 'They were before Silver fuckin' Salmon put their dirty ferms there!' Still shaking with indignation he got up and went out into the mid-afternoon gloom.

64

The new owner of South Skean Estate liked to communicate directly to his staff via text and the head keeper Donaldson had learned very quickly to turn up the volume for the notifications on his phone. Dicky always wanted an immediate response. Donaldson was taking a leak behind a birch tree when his phone boinged loudly. He jumped involuntarily and warm urine splashed on his hand and trousers. 'Fuck' he shouted, and further down the field two pheasants whirred away in fright. As expected it was a text from his boss. It said: Tito and Dimitri arriving Flight EZ239, pick-up from airport 16.45. Staying two days for stalking.

'Stalking, my erse,' thought Donaldson. 'They'll be efter wanting to sort somethin' oot. I'd better get onto hersel' at the big hoose tae mek sure the've got the rooms ready.'

The weather had deteriorated somewhat by the time he got to Dalcross, the light had gone and the mist had settled. To his relief however, the easyjet flight was more or less on time and it wasn't long before he had met Tito and Dimitri in the arrivals hall, and escorted the stony faced pair to his pick-up. They sat in an unfriendly silence for the entire journey back to South Skean. Donaldson didn't even try to make any small talk. They were obviously less than happy to be up in the Highlands and he was less than happy to see them there.

As they got out of his pick-up on the drive at South Skean the larger, Dimitri, said, 'Be here at nine tomorrow morning, and we need this pick-up, a map and two rifles.' His English was heavily accented. They picked up their cases from the back of the pick-up and without a backward glance strode into the lodge.

Donaldson gunned the engine and swept out of the drive. He needed a drink. what a pair of tossers he thought, not so much as a thank you. Auld Lennox would have thanked him profusely and given him a tip as well, he thought. This new lot, well the more they stayed away the better he liked it. Still you wouldn't want to mess w' them wid ye?

Still irritated he went into the Strath Bar and ordered a pint of Deuchers and a whisky. He took a long swig of his beer and followed it up with most of his dram. God, he needed that. Donaldson was not the most popular of the bar's regulars but he was a local, and his views on gamekeeping and so forth were respected if not always agreed with. He was definitely old school. He had a clear idea about the relationship between the landowner and the professional who ran the shooting on the estate. In his mind there was no doubt as to who was in charge. Slippery Dicky didn't understand that, did he? The twat.

Now on his third pint he had lightened up a bit, and had entertained a couple of the other drinkers with a less than flattering description of the Russian stalkers, what the hell were they doing he wondered out loud, why would you go to the expense of coming up now when the stag season was well past and all you could shoot was hinds.

One of the company excused himself saying he was going outside for a fag. In the car park he lit up and took out his mobile.

65

A quite seriously hung over Donaldson was waiting on the drive at nine the next morning. He had got the other, older pick -up from the garage and on the back seat there were two Ruger M77 hunting rifles, a few rounds of ammunition, a packed lunch and a map of the estate. The weather wasn't brilliant, the rain hefted in from the north and the tops of the hills were covered with a sprinkling of snow. A raw day in the East of Scotland. The two sportsmen emerged from the lodge, they weren't really well dressed for a day on the hill, they had blue anoraks with furry fringes on the hoods and their footwear was far too flimsy. Donaldson would have provided them with some decent boots had they been civil or even if he'd been asked, but their silence of yesterday was obviously going to continue today.

'Morning, gentlemen, a grand day fer it.' Donaldson said without a hint of irony. Ah've given y' the two Rugers with ten rounds each, a packed lunch from the excellent Mrs Carmichael, and the map y' asked for. Jist return everything to the front here when y've finished an' ah'll sort it all oot.'

Tito looked at him, 'Show me where is Kayrick on map,' he demanded. Donaldson, assuming he meant Caoraich, took the map from the back seat, opened it in the shelter of the pick-up door and pointed to the general area of the loch.

'Mind ye, maist o' the deer wull be in the glen, noo,' he said, 'there's nuthin' on the tops this time o' the season.' He wasn't sure how much Tito understood, he was conscious that he'd made his Scottish accent deliberately obscure, a technique he had used in the past with arsey English clients. He gave them thirty minutes tops before they would be soaked through he thought. 'That's you then,' he said, and as an afterthought, 'enjoy yer day!' He got into his pick-up and drove off.

In fact, Dimitri and Tito did have a plan of sorts. They had been told by their boss Artem to get up to Caoraich and communicate in an unequivocal way how disappointed Artem's brother in law, the owner of South Skean Estate, was at the recent actions of one Frazer Ross. In short, they were Artem's muscle, and intimidation and violence was their profession, albeit usually in an urban setting. So they had thought, breeze in, shoot a couple of the guy's cows from distance as an anonymous warning to behave himself. Then get back to London as soon as. They hadn't thought the weather would be this shit, or that Caoraich farm would be as inaccessible as it was.

Dimitri and Tito had studied the OS map and realised, that short of driving up to the farm itself and shooting a couple of Frazer's beasts in the actual farmyard, they would have to park up somewhere and walk over the hill to a position above the farm which would give them a view over the surrounding fields. Perhaps they would encounter some of the cattle en route and they could dispatch them then and there without having to walk too far.

Having located a suitable area in which to park up near Caoraich, they set off down the stony track towards the turn off. The rain had now increased in intensity and little rivulets of water were coursing down the ruts in the road. Visibility was poor. They were slowing down so as not to miss the turn off up to Frazer's when there was a loud bang from the front and the pick-up lurched off the track and slid into a ditch at the side. Neither Dimitri nor Tito had bothered to put on their seat belts so both were thrown in an untidy and painful way onto the dashboard and steering wheel respectively. Tito had cut his head and blood flowed freely over his face. He was clearly concussed. Dimitri was shaken and bruised, his shoulder hurt like hell, but after a few minutes he was able to struggle out of the front door and get his phone out.

Donaldson got the call as he was sitting in the warmth of the lodge kitchen enjoying one of Mrs Carmichael's legendary fry-ups. 'What the f...' he said, 'slow doon man I cannae unnerstan' ye. Y've what? crashed? Where are ye, haud oan, I'll be with ye directly.'

Pausing only to finish his tea and jamming a large piece of toast in his mouth he hurried out of the back of the lodge to where he had parked. It only took him five minutes or so to arrive at the scene. The pick-up was a skewed at an angle, its nose in a ditch and both back wheels about a foot off the ground. Dimitri had been trying to staunch the flow of blood from Tito's head. Tito was moaning softly, but was conscious.

'How in fuck's name did y' drive aff the road? Are ye all right lads?' he enquired with feigned solicitousness. 'If yez jist haud oan a wee bit ah'll get ye intae my truck and back up tae the lodge. Y'must be shaken.'

Dimitri helped Donaldson to get the still groggy Tito out of their pick-up and into Donaldson's. On the way back to South Skean Lodge, Donaldson tried to get some sort of idea what had happened, obviously there had been some reason for them ending up in the ditch. When asked Dimitri mumbled, 'There was a bang at the front, like the tyre went or something.'

Donaldson speculated , 'Well mebbes it was the tyre or mebbes wan o' the steering rods. I'll get the tractor and pull it oot later an' I'll hev a look at her.'

'OK, we are going back to London now, Tito needs to be looked at. I have damaged collarbone where it hit dashboard.'

'W' can take y' both tae casualty at Raigmore, it's only an hour or so away along the coast.'

'No, no hospital.' Dimitri was clear. 'No hospital. Private doctor in London.'

'Well, if that's what y' want, it's OK w' me. I'll get Ally tae run y' to Dalcross. I'm sure y'll make the afternoon flight. And,' he added with total insincerity, ' I'm sorry yer stalking was spoiled, y'll hev tae come back and see us soon.'

He left them in the hall at the lodge with the no-nonsense Mrs Carmichael clucking around after them. He was keen to get the tractor down to the pick-up. He'd remembered about the two rifles in the back and he wanted to secure them.

He got the ancient Massey Ferguson tractor out of its garage and, making sure he had a decent amount of tow rope on board, jolted his way noisily down the track towards the accident site. The pick-up was exactly at the same angle of lean as when he'd left it. Luckily it hadn't slid further into the ditch. He put his rope around the tow bar and attached it to the back of the tractor. A couple of seconds later and he'd dragged the pick-up out of the ditch and back on to the level verge. The front was muddy and dented and there was all sorts of vegetation sticking out of the radiator at odd angles. Fortunately, there didn't seem to be too much damage, just the dents, broken headlights and the driver's side front tyre which had come off the rim.

He opened the rear and checked that both rifles were still there. They had slid off the rear seat and, together with the packed lunch and ammunition box were in the foot well. They were still in their cases, he would check them later.

With a bit of an effort he managed to get the jack and the spare wheel out of the pick-up, and after loosening the wheel nuts and making sure that the jack was securely grounded on a flat stone, raised the front of the vehicle until he could extricate the tyre and rim. It took him all of his not inconsiderable strength to get the tyre and rim out. It was kind of jammed in the wheel arch. Once that was done, it was a considerably easier job to bolt on the spare.

Blowing hard and covered in mud from his exertions, he examined the tyre closely. There was a neat hole through the outside wall and a more jagged hole on the inside. He nodded to himself, he knew exactly what had caused them to crash.

Back at the lodge he was relieved to find that Ally had already left for Dalcross with the two sportsmen. Mrs Carmichael was wearing her "I am not amused" face. He thought he should send a text to Sir Richard. In it he said that while out hunting due to a failure with one of the steering rods on their pick-up Tito and Dimitri had lost control of the vehicle and ended up in a ditch. They weren't wearing seat belts, luckily they had only suffered minor injuries and had returned to London for private treatment.

Later he rang Frazer. 'Hey Frazer it's Donaldson here. There was a wee bit of an accident up at the lodge this morning. Two of ma guests from London were oot fer a bit of late deer stalking, and they had an accident w' their pick-up. They went off the track intae a ditch near yours. Did y' happen to see anything?'

Frazer, was in his workshop and had just finished oiling and cleaning his hunting rifle, that old, unlicensed Remington he'd come by all those years ago. 'Nah,' he said, 'I wis daein stuff in the byre, nae fucker in their right mind wid be oot huntin' in such weather wid they? See y' Don, thanks for the info.'

He ended the call and put the phone back into his pocket. He hung up his NATO issue goretex camo jacket and trousers. They were soaking wet and would take at least a day to dry out. He turned off the light and locked the door. There was a slight smile on his face.

The next morning Donaldson drew up at Caoraich Farm. He parped the horn and Frazer came out, holding a cup of tea and looking dishevelled as usual. Donaldson got out and gestured to Frazer to come and look in the back of his pick-up in which was a large muddy tyre. 'See that tyre,' he said, 'that's the wan that came aff the Ford they two guests o' mine were driving. It's got an interesting couple o' holes in it. Any wan w'd think it had been hit by a bullet.'

Frazer shrugged, 'Aye, mebbes, whit are y' showin' me this fer Don?'

'Well, Frazer, I also found this aboot fifty metres away up the brae.' "This" turned out to be a .308 brass cartridge, which he lobbed in Frazer's direction.

'If ah wis a Russian security guy and ah found that ma tyre had been shot aff It widnae take me long tae figure oot who'd want tae do something like that. So that's why y' can get rid o' that tyre. Luckily for the baith o' us they think it wis the steering that went bang and because they soft bastarts wisnae wearing seat belts, they got pretty shaken up. I telt Sir Richard yesterday that it wis the steering that went, but if he found oot the truth we'd all be in the deep shite. So, I'll fit a new rod and tyre but you get rid of this wan. I don't want anyone on the Estate looking at this, puttin' two and two togither and blabbin'.'

Frazer looked at Donaldson speculatively, Dicky must have really upset you he thought, mebbes Donaldson was the same as him, he'd had his little world and its old certainties shaken up. Things weren't the same any more.

'OK, right y'are, thanks, I'll buy yis a dram when ah see y' next.'

Donaldson nodded and drove off without a backward glance.

66

Craig Mackinnon was round at his daughter's house along the coast from Port Skean. He and his wife were looking after the grandchildren while their parents were out at some function or other. The youngest, Kirstie, was fast asleep upstairs but Eddie, the nine year old, needed some help with his end of term project which was about the Ancient Greeks. Together they were looking on the internet at some of the sea battles that had been fought at the time of the Persian invasion. In particular they looked at the triremes, their crews and the tactics they used. Being ex navy Craig found all this stuff really interesting and Eddie and he speculated about what life must have been like for the crews of these craft, and how dangerous and uncomfortable life would have been.

Craig's wife Susan, looked at her husband and grandson sitting on the sofa and smiled, Craig had not been so happy these days, he was often preoccupied with his struggling scallop fishing business. Also that nasty business with Wullie, who was still poorly, was troubling him greatly. At least they could take some solace from their lovely grandchildren.

Later, driving back to Port Skean, Craig was lost in thought. His mind was still full of the Greek triremes and the major tactic the Athenian ones used; they had a spike fixed to the bow at or just under the waterline and they used it to ram the enemy ships.

67

'So, Fraz, it was Donaldson who tipped y' off about the two Russians. What do think they were up to?' Robbie and Frazer were sitting on the veranda of the Glen Sionnach fishing hut. Both were looking at the water sliding past. They were drinking tea.

'Nah, it wisnae Donaldson, it was Ian. He was in the bar when Donaldson was shooting his mooth aff aboot how rude the Russians were and what the fuck were they uptae anyway and not even a tip! But it was Donaldson who worked oot what had happened to the pick-up and kept his mooth shut. He brought me the tyre tae lose. He must hate his boss as much as I dae.'

'What d' y' think they would have done had not 'someone' shot off their tyre. Jesus, the country side's a dangerous place what with Russians and people with guns running round all over the place.' Robbie laughed.

'Well, my guess is that they wanted to shoot a couple of ma beasts as kind o' warning to masel. But noo, as long as they think it wis jist an accident, they won't be back. But, man, that shot was somethin' else. Bang! That pick - up just disappeared intae the ditch. Fuckin' brilliant!' Frazer laughed, it was clear he felt that there had been some slight re-alignment of the local power dynamic.

'Right, Frazer, we need to think about the best time for our little plan. Mhairi's going away for a few days before Christmas to stay with her daughter and do some shopping, it would be good if we could do it then. I'll look at the weather and give ye a call. OK?'

'Right y'are, pal. Ah'll wait fer yer call,' and with that he stood up, stretched his large frame, got into his pick-up and drove off. Robbie looked after the disappearing Frazer and wondered, not for the first time, what he was letting himself in for.

68

Mhairi was quite excited about spending a bit of time with Seonaid, her daughter. Seonaid was working as a surgeon in the A and E Department at Raigmore. She was enjoying the work but after months of twelve hour shifts was looking forwards to some down time. Also, her boyfriend Peter, another doctor, had just proposed and so there was some serious planning to be done. Seonaid lived at North Kessock just over the bridge from Inverness and although it was only an hour and a half or so away Mhairi would be staying over for a few days.

Before she left she had given Robbie a set of instructions about looking after the couple of undemanding guests that were staying at Sionnach enjoying a quiet time before returning to the States for Christmas. As she got into her car she fixed him with that knowing look of hers and said, 'Mind what y' do English, take care, love you,' and she was off up the road to Inverness without a backward glance.

As soon as he got back inside Robbie looked at the met office weather forecast for early December. Up to then the weather had been fairly mild, with a mixture of light rain and low cloud, but now the wind was swinging round to the north and dragging with it much colder arctic air and snow. "If it were done when 'tis done, then t'well it were done quickly." For some reason the Macbeth quote intruded upon Robbie's consciousness. He agreed with himself. He took out his phone. 'OK Frazer, the weather's going to close in tomorrow. Tonight would be good. I'll see you where we agreed. Seven.'

'Aye, right y'are.' came the succinct reply.

By four o' clock most of the light had gone and Lachie, one of two Silver Salmon employees who spent most of their time looking after the smolt farm on Loch Caoraich had switched the lights off in the storage hut, made sure the door was shut, and the boat tied up securely to the jetty. He'd spent the afternoon filling the feed hoppers on the smolt cages and generally pottering about. It was Friday, and he was knackered. Roy, his mate was off sick, and he'd had to do more than usual that week and he was anxious to get off. On the whole, it was a good and easy job for him, he didn't live more than ten miles away, and Loch Caoraich was so far off the beaten track there were never any security issues. His manager, Roddy, was a pleasant enough guy, and was only around when something technical needed to be done, like transferring some of the fish, or maybe overseeing their treatment for this or that. He took a casual glance around, everything seemed ok, jumped in his pick-up and drove off.

As he drove past Caoraich Farm his headlights shone across the farm buildings, and briefly illuminated some of Frazer's cattle in the adjacent fields.   In the darkened byre Frazer, noting the sweeping headlights, thought to himself: 'that'll be Lachie away home then.' There was a grim smile on his face.

Robbie wasn't worried about leaving the old American couple, the Doves, the only guests at Sionnach. The two remaining staff would look after them. Besides which he planned to be back well before midnight. He'd just said he was out visiting a supplier who lived in Port Skean.

So it was an apprehensive but determined Robbie who drove up the track to Caoraich farm that early winter's evening. It was cold, with intermittent cloud cover but mercifully it was dry. He swung the Land Rover into the farm yard and parked it at the far end out of sight behind Frazer's pick-up. He took out a back pack from the passenger seat, zipped up his jacket and went over to the byre where Frazer was waiting.

Frazer seemed calm, Robbie guessed this was due to Frazer's previous nocturnal career as a poacher of some notoriety. He was used to moving silently and illegally over the dark terrain. Their plan was to walk to the loch, even though it was highly unlikely anyone would have seen them had they taken the pick-up, but as Frazer had pointed out, car headlights can be seen from miles away.

Without speaking they walked up the track, their boots scrunching on the gravel. As they climbed higher and

266

reached the plateau a freezing wind whipped across the moor and made their eyes water. Frazer held up his hand for them to stop. He swung his back pack off and took out what turned out to be the night vision scope from his rifle. He spent a good few minutes surveying the area. 'There's nivver any one here at this time o' night. They've nae security at all. not even a camera, I've been up here quite a few times. But w'll tek nae chances.'

After a few more minutes he was satisfied that there was no other human presence in the area and they moved to the yard on which was a Portakabin office and behind that, the dark shape of a large wooden shed with double garage doors. A silhouette of a fork lift truck and an angular pile of pallets completed the scene. Frazer motioned to Robbie and they went up to the garage doors which were secured by a large combination lock. Lachie had evidently remembered to lock up this time. Frazer took out a small torch from one of his pockets and switched it on. It had a faint red beam, 'Of course,' thought Robbie, ' Frazer's done this kind of stuff loads of times.' Two seconds later they were in the shed.

In the black interior Frazer's dim red light illuminated faintly the shadowy outlines of bulk bags of feed pellets. There was a pile or two of empty bags and some netting, and a stack of tins with hazard warning signs. At the back of the shed there was a line of blue cylindrical containers all with the big hazard pictograms. On the side of each was written "Tyne Chemicals" and "Danger Formalin" and "Corrosive" and other information. 'Them's the boys,' muttered Frazer.

Robbie took off his back pack and took out two pairs of black rubber gloves, two masks and two pairs of goggles. He had read up on handling Formalin and what he had read frightened him. He whispered to Frazer, 'Put the gloves on now, and when we open containers, w' must wear the masks and goggles.'

'Right y'are, pal.' How many d' y' think w' need?' asked Frazer, nodding at the line. 'Ah've counted twenty.'

'It's what we can manage to get to the cages, we probably need as much as possible. I've been trying to work it out, but I think each of these containers has five gallons or twenty litres, that's about fifty pounds of weight each. Two per cage should do it. Let's get the fuckers to the boat.' In truth Robbie didn' t know how much was needed to give a fatal dose or to provide 'treatment losses' in the industry jargon. He had done some rudimentary research on the internet but still was no wiser. But he guessed forty litres of this shite per cage might do something.

Frazer's red light picked out a trolley lurking in a corner of the shed and it wasn't long before they had loaded on twelve containers and pulled it over the yard to the tiny jetty where a solid looking, wide beamed fibre glass rowing boat was tied up. Frazer was relieved to note that the oars had been left in the rowlocks. There was also a small electric outboard attached to the transom. It was still connected to a sizeable battery with crocodile clips. 'Jesus,' thought Frazer, 'wir lucky it's Lachie that's workin' here.'

Transferring the line of containers from the jetty to the boat wasn't as difficult as they had envisioned, Robbie handing them down carefully, one by one, to Frazer who stacked them securely, and soon they had begun the fifty metre voyage to the cages. Frazer was in the front of the boat with the formalin containers and Robbie at the stern operating the motor. The jetty had been sheltered by a bit of a headland and as they left its lee the waters of the loch became choppy, whipped up by the cold wind. Freezing spray splashed over the bow. Momentarily, the clouds parted and a shaft of silver moonlight illuminated the loch with the little boat heading silently to the smolt farm with its six circular floating cages arranged around a T shaped walkway.

Robbie managed to bring the rocking boat broadside on to the docking area. He scrambled out in an ungainly fashion, the non slip surface of the walkway hard on his knees. He was quite wet now, and beginning to get cold.

He had been sweating quite a bit, with both the stress and physical effort, and now it was cooling on his body. Still, now for the important part.

Frazer passed up the containers, one by one, and soon all twelve of them were on the walkway. Frazer heaved himself out of the boat picked up a container in each hand and was about to disappear into the dark when Robbie shouted, 'Don't forget your mask and goggles Fraz.' Frazer nodded. Taking a couple of containers himself, Robbie was only just able to stagger along the undulating walkway to the furthest cage. He left the containers there and repeated the process twice more.

It was surreal, he had to focus on what he was doing and not let his mind wander. He returned to the furthermost cage, donned his mask and goggles and unscrewed the lid on the first container. Trying to hold it as far away from his face as possible he held his breath and tipped it into the dark water. It sort of glugged out, and it took a little longer to empty than he expected. He repeated the action and then moved to the second and third cages.

When he had finished, he returned to the boat and loaded the empty containers. He was just finishing the loading when a bemasked and goggled Frazer lurched out of the dark like some zombie in a horror film, he was carrying three of the containers and then he vanished again before returning with the remainder.

Soon they were back on the shore. Robbie knew he had to concentrate. Every fibre of his being was screaming at him to get out, job done, but he knew that the last bit was vital to the whole enterprise. They arranged the containers on the little jetty, carefully unscrewed the lids and refilled them with the water from the loch. Then, manfully now, because they were knackered, loaded the trolley, and repositioned them carefully at the back of the shed.

Frazer snapped the padlock back on the shed door and made sure that it was secure. Robbie had brought a black bag with him and into that they put their goggles, masks and gloves. Robbie looked at his watch. It was nine fifteen, they'd been on site less than two hours. Frazer took out his scope and scanned the whole area. 'Naebody, nuthin, let's go. Ah need a dram.'

They strode purposefully away, Robbie didn't dare let himself relax. His main emotion was one of relief. They got back to the warmth of Caoraich farm house, where Elsie was waiting anxiously with drams. 'Well,' she demanded in her usual forthright way, 'How wis yer feckin' S.A.S. raid, did yis no fall in?'

'Nah,' said Frazer, warming his big frame in front of the log fire, 'it wis a piece o' piss. Slàinte,' and he took a good swallow of his dram.

Robbie didn't think it had been a "piece o' piss," but he felt they'd acquitted themselves well, they had kept to their game plan, they hadn't panicked. He was anxious to get back to Sionnach. He said cheerio to Frazer and Elsie. As he was just about to walk out of the door Frazer said, 'Here, English, this is for you. Thanks.' "This" was a bottle of The Strathskean, a non chill-filtered twenty five year old malt.

Robbie looked at it in shock, a bottle of twenty five year old year old Strathskean was worth a small fortune. 'God, Fraz, y' shouldn't... This must have cost y' loads.'

Frazer winked, 'Nah, not really. It's fer you to drink, but ah widnae be flashing that bottle aboot if yer drinkin' wi the polis!' and he laughed uproariously.

As Robbie got out of the Land Rover at Sionnach Lodge the wind had got up and there was snow in the air. He was feeling chilled and damp. He needed a hot bath, a whisky and some food in that order. He was massively relieved that their little adventure bad gone to plan. He could dispose of the black bag with the goggles etc. in the morning. Holding his bottle of whisky in one hand he locked the Land Rover with the other and went inside.

There was no sign of the American couple, he presumed they had gone to bed and Jane, one of the staff, was just about to leave, said that nothing of note had happened during his brief absence. Wishing her goodnight he went upstairs and ran a hot bath. He put on the TV in the bedroom. The weather forecast was not good for the East Coast. Snow and wind. Some drifting. Freezing temperatures. Excellent, thought Robbie, and sipped his illegally sourced, stunningly flavoursome Strathskean.

69

When the alarm on his mobile phone went off Roy Mackie, Lachie's co-worker at the Caoraich smolt farm, rolled over in bed and switched it off. It was about seven o' clock Saturday morning and it was his turn to go up to check if everything was ok. He had missed the whole week through illness, genuine at first, but extended for a couple of days while he lounged about at home in his pyjamas, drinking tea, and improving his very personal international relationship by cuddling up with his Estonian girlfriend Eva, who worked at a care home in the strath. Now, she was off doing a twelve hour shift and he had to check them fuckin' smolts. He pulled the curtain back. The weather was atrocious, outside a vicious wind propelled horizontal snow against every surface still visible. It was a whiteoot. Excellent. He couldn't get to work even if he'd wanted tae.

Similar sentiments were being expressed in two other locations. Frazer was genuinely snowed in, and Robbie was thinking he'd have to spend quite a bit of time clearing the long drive and looking after the charming old Americans, the Lonesome Doves, as he called them. Mhairi was less affected, North Kessock being on the coast. In any case she was not due back until the Tuesday.

The upside was that it would be some time before anyone would be checking the smolts in Loch Caoraich. Robbie and Frazer heaved a joint sigh of relief. It was as if the advent of the snow had pushed their little adventure into a different time zone: 'Before the snow,' and who could tell what went on back then?

As often happened with early cold snaps, by Monday the weather had turned slightly milder. The A9 had been cleared by and also the local main roads. Only the higher tracks remained snowbound. Frazer was able to get down the to the main road in his pick-up but, above his farm, the snow fields stretched in an unbroken blinding white blanket right to the Cairngorms.

Tuesday, after lunch Mhairi returned to Sionnach Lodge. She was laden with Christmas presents, clothes and all kinds of other stuff that she had bought while shopping in Inverness with Seonaid. She and Robbie were up in their sitting room and he sat on the settee while she tried on various blouses and skirts for him to see. ' I can take this one back if y' don't think it suits me!' she said, striking an exaggerated pose like a model on the catwalk.

'Aye, champion, they aal suit ye, Hinny,' said Robbie reverting to his native Geordie, ' Ah've nivvor seen owt so stylish!' He was pleased because she was obviously so happy. Because of her slimness she always looked good he thought.

She laughed, folded the jacket she and placed it carefully over the back of a chair, and then sat down next to him, put her arm around him. 'Now, tell,' she said.

'What?' but he knew damn fine what she meant.

70

Tuesday turned out to be an interesting day for the Caoraich smolt farm team. Roddy had insisted that they should at least try to get up there to check on the fish. So they met at the layby on the main road to Strathskean and got into Roddy's big pick-up, that vehicle being adjudged to have the best heavy duty capability.

The track up to Caoraich Farm was fine, Frazer had been up and down it a couple of times anyway. But as soon as they left the farmhouse to begin the climb up to the loch, the snow was unbroken and the track more or less obscured. Very slowly they edged along. In some places, where the wind had drifted the snow, there were indications as to where the track was. Mostly, they had to proceed by guess work. Lachie said, 'There's the gate, y' can just see it up ahead.'

They reached the gate, and after a few minutes of energetic shovelling managed to get it open. Before them was the undulating white of the hills, the grey sky and the choppy grey waters of the loch. A stiff, viciously cold wind cut through their jackets. Round the shore the track led to the porta cabin, jetty and shed.

'Y' ken,' said Roy, 'they Eskimos, they dinnae get a sweat oan, because, if y' sweat, it freezes oan yir body and y' freeze tae death.'

'Well, y've nae danger o' freezin' tae death, Roy. Y've nivver got a sweat oan in yir fuckin' life!' laughed Lachie.

They got back into the warmth of the pick-up and edged their way along to the yard. Once there, they discovered that the snow cover was patchy, the wind had swirled the snow about and the Portakabin had a large drift in front of it. However, the shed with the feed and life jackets and suchlike was accessible with only a moderate amount of shovelling and it wasn't long before they'd unlocked the combination lock and walked into the gloom. Roddy switched on the light and the generator outside hummed into action. Lachie got three life jackets and three yellow waterproofs from the rack near the door. They loaded the trolley with some sacks of feed pellets and went out into the cold. They had not noticed that the trolley had been left in a slightly different place nor did they spare a glance for the slightly rearranged line of formalin containers at the rear of the shed.

The boat was in exactly the same place as Lachie had left it. Roddy was less than impressed: 'Y've left the fuckin' battery attached to the motor, y' numpty. Whit the fuck are y' paid for?' Roddy was usually a mild mannered person but he knew if anything went wrong he would ultimately be responsible. For some reason he felt tense. They cleared the snow and ice from the boat, loaded the feed and set off. Luckily, for the hapless Lachie, there was still some juice in the battery.

After a searingly cold two minute transfer they tied up at the floating walkway. It was icy and a bit of a scramble to get on to it. Unusually, some of the surface water in the cages was frozen. It had obviously been a really hard frost. Roddy looked into the first cage. His degree in Aquaculture [Hons] had not prepared him for the what he saw in the first cage. Hundreds of smolts were floating belly up, some frozen into the ice at the edge of the netting. He checked the other cages. His face was white. He took out his phone.

A few days later when most of the snow had melted, two covered lorries bumped their way up past Frazer's, and then down again a few hours later. 'There's quite a bit of activity up there,' he thought, 'I wonder what they're doing. Mebbes I'll wander up later and hev a wee looky.'

In fact he didn't need to go up for "a wee looky." He got a phone call from a mate of his called Jack who had been in a bar and had overheard Lachie and his mate Roy moaning about their jobs. Apparently, there had been a "treatment loss" or some such up at Caoraich and most of their smolts had died. They'd all gone to landfill seemingly and Lachie and his mate were bemoaning the fact they had been moved down to Port Skean where they'd have to do some real work for a change. The smolt farm operation had been closed down while the owners worked out what to do. Later that week Silver Salmon issued the briefest of press statements which said that due to operational difficulties their smolt farm in Loch Caoraich had been closed and their workers redeployed. No further explanation was given.

As Robbie had explained to Mhairi, he felt really bad about killing the smolts but then it was not as if they were wild fish. They would have faced an existence where thousands were crammed in a cage being fed on pellets containing all sorts of stuff: soya, fishmeal, colorants and ground up chicken feathers. The irony of it: chicken were fed on fish meal and their feathers were fed to salmon in a food chain of sheer madness. Their other option would have been to release the smolts, but that might have had profound genetic consequences had some of them survived and returned to spawn. There were enough problems already with salmon escapes. Anyway, it would have been impossible to release them without cutting the nets, and then the crime would have been obvious.

At least, this way, their activity stood a good chance of remaining undiscovered. A swift stab with a Skean Dhu. And if the Caoraich burn recovered after the pollution, well, on balance that was a great result. Silver Salmon were legally entitled to have a smolt farm in the loch but they weren't entitled to pollute the whole system were they? The real crime was not the farming of salmon in the loch per se, but Silver Salmon being able to walk away from the pollution and environmental degradation they caused.

Mhairi listened to all this, she'd been worried sick about Robbie getting involved but now she knew he'd done it she was proud that he'd had the guts to stick up for something he believed in. She knew, also, that Strathskean being Strathskean whatever had happened up at Caoraich would come out at some point, in a quiet way, and people would know the Robbie had had something to do with it all. He was the outsider no longer.

Frazer went about his winter farming and supply activities as normal. He felt better about things and it gave him a quiet satisfaction that he'd managed to get one over on "The Bastards" as he called them. He was still worried about the rent increase which would come into effect at some point in the New Year, but that was still under review. Until then he was a happier man.

71

In Port Skean Wullie Grant had taken a turn for the worse. His wife and friends had thought he was on the mend after the attack, but now he seemed to be going downhill. He'd had a bit of a dodgy ticker anyway due to an unbeatable combination of fags, poor diet and genetics, but now he was frail, and the doctor had prescribed him some antibiotics to clear a chest infection. He took to his bed and although he said to his wife he'd be up and about for Christmas, she had her doubts. Craig and Allan had popped round to see him a couple of times but he didn't want to chat for long. He was very tired.

72

At Glen Sionnach Lodge preparations were well in hand for the Christmas and New Year celebrations. The entrance hall was lovely, all sparkly and glittery, there were quite a few guests booked in. Robbie had worked really hard with the decorations inside, and outside he'd put lights on the ornamental fir trees that lined the drive. From time to time he stood by the front doors and admired his handiwork.

And incrementally, the guests arrived. Without exception, they were wealthy older citizens enjoying a quiet and luxurious decline, shuffling around the world from one exclusive destination to another. The atmosphere was restrained, genteel, cordial. The ambience that of an up market home for the aged. Christmas came and went, it had been a great success.

There was some changeover of the clientele between Christmas and New Year, and Robbie was slightly relieved to see that there were some younger guests, "younger" being a relative term. Less risk of us having to deal with sudden cardiac arrest he thought. The Hogmanay celebrations were lively without being too excessive, some of company having gone to the excellent firework display and street party in Strathskean and returning more or less intact in an expensively hired minibus. Then, on New Year's Day itself, and indeed for the next day or two as well, there was the usual round of visits to and from friends and relatives.

Optimism was temporarily in the air. The spring bookings were just about OK now and Mhairi had thought that she might possibly be able to sell Sionnach as a going concern. That plan had firmed up and they both accepted that a move to a more modern, and manageable, property was the way to go.

And then January and February, the dead months. Up at Caoraich Frazer had his work cut out looking after his beasts. In years gone by there would have been endless snow and ice but now the changing climate meant that sometimes there was snow, then a thaw and sometimes there would be a few days of milder damp or wet weather. However you looked at it, it was dreich. Frazer was looking forward to the spring, and to the resumption of his guiding career. To his immense satisfaction not a single vehicle had passed his farm en route to the loch.

73

In Port Skean, January and February meant usually meant days of rough seas powered by bitter winds from the North East smashing against the breakwater. For the fisherfolk it was a time for routine maintenance and such like activities. However, for the Mackinnon and Grant families this year was also a time of great sadness. Wullie Grant had been failing fast and half way through February he passed at home. The death certificate said that he died from Coronary Heart Disease and Pneumonia but everyone in the village knew that his death had been caused by the savage beating he'd received in November. The culprits for that were still at large and Macbeath security had washed their hands of it. Northern Constabulary said that Wullie's case was still open, but the crime remained assault and battery rather than manslaughter, which disappointingly would be difficult to prove given that he had apparently died of heart failure.

Wullie's funeral was a sombre affair with the interment at the local Kirk and then the wake at the Inverskean Arms. It was rammed, the whole village was there. Craig had said a few words for his friend at the Kirk, but he'd been very emotional. That was partly because he felt an overwhelming sense of guilt that it was he who'd got Wullie involved with the dive under the salmon farm.

When Craig had expressed his feelings to Jim, Wullie's son and a fisherman, Jim was unequivocal in his answer,' Dinna fash yersel' man. Wullie would have been gutted if y' hadn't asked him tae be with y.' There's not wan man or woman in Port Skean who blames you for Wullie's death. Nah, not wan. The question is, whit are w' goin t' dae aboot it?'

Craig did have a plan. Wullie would not go unavenged. Of that he was sure.

74

One evening, a couple of days after the funeral, Craig, Allan, Neil and Jim, Wullie's eldest, were sitting in the corner of the Fishers' Bar in the Inverskean Arms. They had been deep in conversation for an hour or so, and were on their third pint. Craig had outlined his plan to them and they all agreed that it was feasible and they should just get on with it, the sooner the better. They knew they were about to do was illegal, but, "people who have naethin to lose, have naething tae fear," was the general consensus. Actually, they all had plenty to lose, what they really meant was if they did nothing to avenge Wullie then they would count themselves less than men.

75

Around about the beginning of March the Coronavirus Pandemic was just beginning to impact on Scotland which had its first recorded deaths about that time. Within a short period of time bars, restaurants and hotels were closed, staff sent home, the country locked down and life as folk had known it changed completely. Mhairi and Robbie were sitting in their empty sun lounge discussing the situation, outside, a warm spell hinted at Spring and everything looked normal, inside, the opposite. Glen Sionnach Lodge was closed for the foreseeable and the furlough scheme had just been announced by the

Chancellor. Mhairi had been working hard to find out exactly what support was available for her staff. There was also the not inconsiderable problem of cancelling bookings , returning deposits and emailing suppliers.

Robbie helped where he could with the paperwork, but his main contribution was looking after the building, but as he had said on more than one occasion to Mhairi, 'If you're going to be locked down then Sionnach is the place to be.' Mhairi , however, was preoccupied with the business and she was worried sick about Seonaid and Peter who, as medics, were on the front line. Through Seonaid, Mhairi was kept up to date with the situation, and she probably realised sooner than most that it would be a long time before normality would return.

For Frazer, up in his newly "rewilded" Glen Caoraich, life had changed little, he still had to make sure his beasts were fed, milked etc. but he was yet to pay the increase in rent owing to the ongoing dispute with South Skean Estate, his landlord. In any case January, February and most of March were always a slow time for hill farmers, even organic ones. He did wonder, however, when guesthouses and restaurants would be opening again. Until then he wouldn't be selling his "Award Winning" produce any time soon, according to Robbie, who seemed to know about these things.

Things hadn't changed all that much down at the coast either. Port Skean was locked down, along with the rest of the country but, outside the holiday season, it was a dead and alive place anyway. The Inverskean Arms was closed of course but the fisher folk still met here and there, they had to check their boats, didn't they? and a certain amount of fishing was going on anyway. It was easy to socially distance if you were the only person on the boat. Some of the bigger boats had furloughed their crew, their catch usually going to fish processing plants for continental consumption anyway. Smaller boats were still fishing, several couldn't get Government support anyway because they'd somehow missed sending in their tax returns. People had to eat. Meanwhile, out in the firth, and looked after by a substantially reduced workforce, hundreds of thousands of salmon still swam round and round in their cages.

76

Craig and Allan were busy "progressing" their plan. They had enlisted the help of two other friends of Wullie's; Colin, who ran a small agricultural repair business and Gregor who had a farm down the coast. For their own part, they had been busy working on The Mermaid which they had relocated to a small pier three miles down the coast. The Mermaid was a sturdy broad beamed wooden boat of about twenty metres length. It was powered by twin Perkins diesel engines. Craig and Allan had bought it from a ship repairing company on Tyneside who had used it as a heavy duty work boat. Because of its solidity, seaworthiness, and all round flexibility they had thought it would be an ideal craft for their scallop business. They were right. Now, below decks they had reinforced the bow area and bolted four metal hooks on the foredeck and two on the hull below the waterline.

Colin's agricultural repair shop was reminiscent of an industrial revolution era farming museum: ancient implements were stacked untidily in the shadowy rear premises and outside, a herd of old tractors and harvesters grazed like angular metal cattle amongst scrubby wasteland bushes. Colin could repair any piece of broken farm equipment no matter how old. If he couldn't get the part, he'd just make it. He was excellent at his job, and well liked. He'd never overcharged a soul in his life.

And so it was to Colin that Craig had brought his design. Craig had drawn up a rough sketch of what he wanted and Colin had cast about his premises for some bits of half inch steel that would do. And there it was, standing on its own in the front, a V shaped piece of metal, approximately ten feet tall and weighing a not inconsiderable five hundred pounds or more. Craig had told Colin if, in the highly unlikely event of anyone seeing it, it was a "garden sculpture" that he'd commissioned, but it was hush hush and for single use only. They'd had a great laugh about that, 'Aye that's the best fuckin' garden statue ah've made, in fact it's the only wan ah've made!' wheezed Colin who had refused absolutely to take a penny for his expenses. 'Dinnae insult me Craig. Ah wis at school wi' the man. They bastarts deserve a' they've got coming. Gud luck. Nae doot, ah'll hear whit's happened.'

'Thanks, Colin, if y' can pull that oot to the front, when I tell ye, and Gregor will be aroond wi his tractor tae pick it up. It'll be at night though. Ah've got tae work oot the tides.' With that he left on his bike. During lock down he didn't want to be seen driving about the countryside in his car.

77

A couple of nights later Craig and Allan were in Craig's kitchen. On the table Craig had spread out the Admiralty chart of the Firth of Skean. Allan had the tide table up on his laptop. They were going through the plan. 'OK,' said Craig, 'low tide is at five past six, and The Mermaid will be high and dry at five. W' hev less two hours tae get organised. Gregor's goin' tae be on the beach at aboot five fifteen. So thirty minutes tae fit it and then w'should have enough watter at aboot eight. Forty five minutes oot, and say wan hour for it and forty five minutes back. Back home and safely in wir beds by midnight!'

'We'll tell Neil and Jim they need tae be afloat by nine then.' said Allan. 'They need to make sure the fuckin' support boats cannae get oot of the harbour, that's if they get a call which is unlikely.'

'Ok, that's it then. The weather forecast tomorrow is good for us, lightish winds and a clear sky. It's better if w' can see what wir up tae.' With that he folded up the chart, and poured out two generous drams of the Strathskean. He handed one to his brother. 'Allan, here's tae us, wha's like us?'

'Gey few and they're aw deid!' Allan finished the toast with an Ironic laugh.

78

At about six o' clock on the following evening a well used JCB Fastrac tractor with a forklift on the front rattled up outside Colin's workshop. Craig stepped out of the shadows, 'Evening Gregor,' are y' ready tae pick up ma piece o' garden sculpture?'

'Aye, how heavy is it, onyway's? enquired the ancient farmer, who had arthritically climbed out of the cab and was casting an eye over the "artwork."

'W' think it's aboot five hundred poonds, Gregor. Nae bad eh?' Gregor shook his head in disbelief and laughing, climbed back into his cab. He restarted the engine and drove his JCB over to where the V shaped construction was standing vertically in the yard like some sort of monolith. He raised the fork lift on the tractor till it was level with the top of the metal. Craig had already attached two loops of heavy duty polypropylene rope through holes at the top of the V. Gregor skilfully manoeuvred the tines of the fork lift through the loops and raised the forks higher still until the metal V was swinging about a foot off the ground. Craig tied the bottom of the V to the front of the tractor to secure it, and, having made sure it wouldn't break free gave Gregor the thumbs up. The JCB turned round, and pitching slightly like a boat in a rough sea, slowly began its journey down the lane towards the beach.

It was on the sheltered stretch of sand next to the same small stone pier at which The Mermaid had been moored for the past few weeks where Craig and Allan had positioned The Mermaid. Now the tide was out she was beached high and dry on the hard sand. She was kept upright by wooden timbers chocked underneath the hull, the positioning of which had been, in fact, the hardest part of the whole operation, so far. All that remained to do was to attach the V shaped metal to the bow.

The tractor lurched down the slipway and onto the sand. Gregor wasn't worried about getting stuck. He'd had to pull boats off the beach before, mostly when they'd needed repair or had to be laid up for the winter. Slowly the JCB approached The Mermaid. Carefully Gregor, guided by Allan who was on the foredeck, edged the metal V shaped plate up to the bow. Allan looped more polypropylene rope round the newly installed hooks in the deck and through the top of the metal V, then he passed the rope to Craig who secured it in the same way at the bottom on each side. Then, finally he pulled the whole thing tight.

The JCB reversed away, Gregor climbed out and the three of them stood on the silver beach in the moonlight and admired their handiwork. The Mermaid now had a new prow, a ram, ten feet of sharpened V shaped steel which fitted perfectly.

'Fuckin' hell,' wheezed Gregor,' I'd love tae see that boy in action!'

'Aye, looks bloody impressive, even if ah say so masel.' Craig was running his hand over the point of the V. 'We shud call her Wullie's Revenge!'

Gregor climbed back into his JCB and they waved him off. He looked back at the two men on the beach and their boat. He hoped they'd be OK. He'd not wanted to know any details about what they were going to do but he could guess. Allan looked at his brother. 'We've pulled some mad stuff in wir time bro, he said, but this beats it aw.'

'Apart from the navy stuff, Al,' said Craig, 'apart from the navy stuff.'

'Yir not wrong Craig. OK, all w' need noo is the tide and we'll be awa. Ah cannae wait.' And with that the brothers climbed up the ladder into The Mermaid to await the flooding tide.

79

Since the Covid 19 lock down the salmon farm had been operating with a reduced number of shore based employees. At least half the work force had been furloughed, but the remaining ones were on a call out system, so that in the event of a problem arising, there would be some staff available to deal with it. They weren't actually paid any more for this privilege and, of course, it was pretty bloody inconvenient, especially if they liked a drink or two of an evening. They might get a phone call and have to drive to the shore base, hop into one of the fast work boats and get out to the farm. On this evening the two unlucky operatives on call were the redeployed Lachie, and a heavy from Macbeath Security called Tam.

Neil and Jim were already afloat. They were in Neil's crabber and had motored quietly out of Port Skean harbour and were approaching the salmon farm's shore base. They had a particular brief that would require some criminal damage, and then a long period of waiting. Essentially they were the back up if anything should go awry. The Port Skean salmon farm had two fast response work boats, as well as the massive feed barge that had so nearly sunk The Mermaid the previous year. The work boats were robust RIBs each powered by a huge Yamaha outboard. They were certainly fast and if the sea was calm the workers could get out to the farm in a few minutes.

Neil cut the engine on his boat and it drifted up to the reconstructed wooden jetty. He noted that the work boats were secured with chains and locks, even though the petty vandalism had stopped, they were obviously taking no more chances. He hopped aboard the first, it rocked gently with his weight. Moving swiftly to the stern he took a pair of heavy duty snippers and a spanner from the pocket of his waterproof. A couple of minutes later he was done, and had moved on to the next boat where he repeated the operation. Soon he was back in his crabber and away back down the coast. CCTV protected the yard on the shore side but it didn't cover the jetty, or anyone arriving by sea. Neil had known that from a previous visit. They moored up in Port Skean harbour just near the mouth. Hopefully, their part was now done. They would just have to sit it out until it was over. Neil poured Jim a cup of coffee from a flask. It was liberally laced with whisky. They pulled their hoods closer round their heads. It would be a long, cold night.

80

Slowly the tide rose around The Mermaid and she began to move imperceptibly as the water deepened. The beach upon which she was stranded was sheltered and so, there being little wind, the waves were slight. Craig knew that he would have to wait until he had a reasonable depth of water under his keel before he should start the engines. He had put out a small anchor called a kedge twenty metres from the stern and, when he felt the boat lifting, using the electric winch, slowly pulled The Mermaid into deeper water. The supporting timbers floated off, Allan fired up the twin Perkins and soon The Mermaid had turned her modified bow seawards and under a bright moon and calm seas, Wullie's Revenge was finally under way.

The Mermaid was now quite bow heavy thought Craig as he looked at the foaming white wave pushed up by the ram. Fortunately, The Mermaid being such a sturdy craft, the stern was still low enough for the twin screws to bite into solid water. Craig had been worried that if the bow was too low The Mermaid would lose power because of cavitation. Still, that was only one of many potential problems they might face. Soon they were well out into the firth. On the left were the harbour and street lights of Port Skean, up ahead were the lights of the salmon farm and on the horizon he could just about make out the dark mass of the Black Isle. Time to get his dry suit on. He'd anticipated there might be a little underwater disentangling to do.

Craig had thought long and hard about how he could effectively disable the salmon farm. His training with the navy had taught him to analyse the enemy's weaknesses and strike accordingly. He had downloaded the original construction plans for the farm. Silver Salmon had sought to get planning permission on the basis that the farm had a 'revolutionary design' and could withstand the "strongest seas" and a "once in a hundred year event" well, Storm Karin had proved the invalidity of their claims, they'd lost thousands of fish because the tubular floats supporting the nets had buckled.

The nets or cages were supported by rectangular plastic tubular floats made by Aquaplaz, a Norwegian firm well established in the industry, and were meant to offer a degree of flexibility to withstand heavy seas. The whole system was anchored to the seabed with cables that were attached to the bottom of the cages in the complex geometric patterns that Craig and Allan had encountered during their previous dive. Underwater cameras, acoustic devices, predator nets and GPS movement sensors completed the assemblage. Above water there was a docking area for the feed barges and cabin cum store for the farm employees. At present, because of Covid 19, none were on the farm overnight. There was an alarm system linked to the movement sensors which was meant to alert those on the shore who were on stand-by . On this night, it was the aforementioned Lachie and Tam.

Actually, thought Craig, the whole million pound caboodle was massively sophisticated and ingenious, a real feat of technology. It was such a shame it was so fuckin' destructive, it was the ultimate example of making money while leaving others to pick up your shite.

The Mermaid was now adjacent to the farm. Craig slowed her right down till she was wallowing slightly in the small swell. He nodded to Allan, it was time to begin. Slowly he turned The Mermaid towards the first of the cages. When was about twenty five metres away, he opened the throttles wide. The Mermaid surged forward, the water white at her sharpened bow. Just like the fuckin' ancient Greeks, thought Craig as he braced himself for the impact.

81

Tam was in a deep, alcohol induced sleep when his mobile went off. It was a voice he didn't recognise, but it knew him. The message was as unwelcome as it was clear. He had to get his large self down to the jetty asap and get out to the farm. The sensors were going mad. Something bad was happening. Lachie was already on his way. Tam had only just got himself dressed when there was a ring at his doorbell. It was Lachie, for once he'd been alert and sober. Tam, still mumbling and rubbing the sleep out of his eyes heaved himself into Lachie's pick-up.

'Whit the fuck's goin' on,' mumbled Tam, who was only just conscious and still fastening buttons.

'Christ!' said Lachie, 'y' stink o' booze, yir supposed tae be on call!'

'Aye, so ah am, but fuck all ever happens, so it wis a night on the pish, even though w' cannae drink at a bar. A couple o' mates came roond.' And that was the end of the conversation.

Soon they were at the shore base, and had opened up the Portakabin, located a key for one of the workboats, donned their waterproofs and life jackets and made their way to the jetty. Lachie had brought a torch, and made sure he had his phone. He jumped into the first workboat, and telling Tam to unlock it, put the key in the console. Tam was fiddling with the combination lock.'Whit's the bastardin' number?' he swore, 'ah cannae remember it.'

'It's wan, two, three, four, five, y' ...' Lachie was going to add a suitable insult but given Tam's size, and what he was employed for he held his tongue.

He turned the ignition key and the big outboard roared into life. Tam had managed to unlock the boat and pull in the mooring rope. Lachie engaged gear and the boat surged out from the jetty and out towards the farm. It had no sooner got up onto plane when, suddenly, inexplicably, the motor cut out; there was a complete loss of power. The RIB stopped absolutely dead in the water. Tam, who hadn't been holding on to anything, was flung onto the deck, and Lachie only just managed to stay in his seat.

'Whit the fuck,' moaned Tam, 'Whit happened?' He was trying to lever himself into a sitting position. The RIB bobbed about gently in the light swell.

'Christ knows.' Lachie was already looking at the outboard with his torch. He couldn't see anything, but there was a strong smell of petrol. 'Shit, ah think it's a fuel problem Tam. It stinks o' petrol back here, so do not, repeat do not, light wan o' yir ciggies!'

'Well, said Tam, ah guess w'll jist hev tae get oot the paddles.'

'There isnae ony fuckin' paddles,' came the forlorn reply.

82

It was a strange collision. Both Craig and Allan were braced for a solid impact, but in fact it was more like a car braking hard. The Mermaid stopped, but not instantly. The black plastic tube along the side of the first cage had buckled and then folded inwards with the weight and force of The Mermaid's ram. Salmon leapt. Walkways and tubes bobbed about in the waves created by the collision. Craig engaged reverse and The Mermaid disengaged. Craig looked at the damage. The rectangular tube had collapsed where they had hit it. Good, now on to the next cage.

Methodically, they repeated the operation moving down the line of cages, with more or less the same result. The tubes were not strong enough to withstand The Mermaid and her ram. In a few instances both Allan and Craig thought that their boat had got entangled with ropes and other wreckage, but The Mermaid's twin engines were powerful, and on each occasion they managed to pull free. When they got to the end of the right hand line they started on the left. They did not look at the time, but kept their nerve, moving from one cage to the next in a steady and methodical way trusting that Neil and Jim would have done their job.

As they reached the final cage Craig looked at Allan, he knew what he was thinking. 'Lets go,' he said, 'we've certainly given Silver Salmon something to remember Wullie by!'

'Aye, whit a great job! Whit a buzz as well, I love it when yir plan works oot. Now let's away home and get a dram.' Allan was relieved that they'd managed to do what they said they'd do and get out unscathed. Craig turned the wheel and The Mermaid headed towards their little harbour. He took out his phone, and texted Neil, 'OK,' he typed, 'see you for a dram.' A relieved Neil replied with a thumbs up emoji.

After a couple of minutes Allan took over, and Craig went forward up to the bow, and took out his diver's knife. This was the final part of the operation, and one that could potentially cause a problem. He had attached the steel ram onto the boat in such a way that if he cut the polypropylene rope on both sides at the hooks on the foredeck the whole construction would disappear into the firth, hopefully never to appear again. ''Single use,' he thought, and sliced through the ropes. The ram detached itself from one side and then swung round to the other with a shuddering clunk before disappearing silently into the black water underneath the boat. The Mermaid rose up at the bow, the water sighing as if a burden had been lifted and, with normal trim restored, they motored back to their pier.

The tide was still flooding, and the breeze being onshore the salmon farm workboat drifted slowly towards the long beach between the shore base and Port Skean harbour. Lachie had been at a complete loss as to what to do and Tam was worse than useless. They weren't in any danger as far as he could tell, and although it was bloody cold, the wind was light and the sea calm. It was just a question of bobbing about, mebbies they'd get near enough to the shore for him to jump out and wade ashore. As a crew member of the local inshore rescue boat he did not want to call out the RNLI just yet. He could imagine the decades of piss taking. 'Lifeboatman Rescued by his own Lifeboat,' would run the headline in the Strathskean Herald. He'd tried phoning the manager and Rory but there was no reply from either. He decided the safest thing to do was to chuck the anchor over and make a few more calls.

On shore, mission accomplished, and all operatives returned safely to base, a small celebration was in order. In the warmth of Craig's kitchen, social distancing temporarily abandoned, they shook each other's hands, embraced , toasted Wullie with the Strathskean, and collectively sighed with relief. Sure, they had broken the law, caused thousands of pounds worth of damage, but, morally they felt they were in the right. Silver Salmon had all the might and power of a huge industry, but it was they, with their gross pollution, gratuitous abuse of antibiotics and pesticides which lead to a wanton destruction of the environment, who were the real criminals. In any case, it was Silver Salmon who had started the law breaking with their attempt to sink The Mermaid. They got what they deserved, the bastards. Slàinte!

83

Early Thursday morning, late March and a weak spring sun shone through the kitchen window at Craig's. He was making himself a fry-up. Radio Scotland was on and the discussion was all about lockdown and who could go to work, and who had to stay at home. Craig was nursing a slight hangover, but he had stuff to take care of, so he was off down to the little pier along the coast as soon as he'd had his bacon and eggs. According to the local news the inshore lifeboat had assisted in the rescue of a workboat believed to belong to Port Skean salmon farm. Engine failure apparently.

At the Port Skean salmon farm's shore base, there was a distanced meeting. Anders, the manager was quizzing an exhausted Lachie, Tam, having long since returned to his bed. 'So, you got the call about nine, you say, and you were here soon after. Yes? and then what?'

'Well, me and Tam got intae the boat and w'd nae sooner got away when w' had a loss o' power. The engine wis deid. I couldnae start it. It stunk o' petrol. In the end ah had tae ring the coastguard. We was heading for the rocks near the Port.' He was still suffering from the indignity and mental trauma of having being towed back to base by his mates on the inshore rescue boat.

The mechanic, who was in the work boat looking at the motor in question shouted over, 'Hey, Anders, come and see this, wid ye,' and he held up the fuel lead. 'It's bin cut,' he said.

'Fuck's sake, not more vandalism, Eric, fix it now. And you need to check the other boat as well.' he added as an afterthought. 'We need to get out to the farm.' And with that, he turned on his heel and strode off to the Portakabin to put on his water proofs. He had a very bad feeling.

84

It was the GPS sensors which had detected unusual and erratic movement of the cages and that was what had triggered the alert in the first place. In the cabin the CCTV footage proved to be worse than useless because it only showed the blurry and indistinct outline of a boat. It was likely some sort of collision, Anders thought, as the newly repaired RIB sped over the grey choppy waters towards the farm.

Before tying up at the docking area Anders steered the RIB in a wide circle around the cages. The wind had picked up somewhat, and In the grey light of the morning he could the cages were moving rhythmically up and down with the swell, each cage appeared to have the seaward side deformed or collapsed, each black plastic tube was bent, one sticking incongruously out of the water like some sort of strange sea creature. As he motored closer he saw that some tubes had what looked like a long vertical cut. It did not take a genius to work out that this had been a deliberate attack on a large scale. Nils, his deputy, was almost speechless, it was really the thoroughness and systematic nature of the damage that amazed him. It was almost like it had been done with military precision.

They tied up the RIB at the docking area and inspected the farm from the walkways, looking at each cage in turn and assessing the damage. It appeared that while there was absolutely no possibility of the farm sinking or drifting away with the tide, the outer side of all of the cages had been breached to a greater or lesser extent, with the ensuing and inevitable mass exit of salmon.

There being nothing more he could do at the present, and having satisfied himself that the farm was safe, he got back into the RIB and returned to the base. By the time he got back to shore, a couple of the other farm workers had arrived, plus Malc and Jim from Macbeath Security. They had another impromptu and non socially distanced meeting in the Portakabin.

Later that afternoon Anders was on the phone to Gunnar Hendriksson. 'Well, Boss, it's bad, we will have to wait for a full assessment by Aquaplaz, they're coming tomorrow, to work out exactly what the damage is, but I have never seen anything like it myself. It's much worse than Storm Karin. Every cage has been damaged, and we don't know how much damage has been caused to the cables on the sea bed. It's going to cost thousands to repair if, in fact, it can be repaired. What's for sure is that it won't be operational for a few months at least.'

'Do we know who did this?' enquired Gunnar, 'Was it anything to do with the last troubles we had there?'

'Well, I'm sure the Mackinnon brothers had a hand in it, they certainly have a grievance, what with their boat being trashed and then their fisherman mate dying. But the whole village is locked down with the Covid and no one will say anything anyway. We're hated there now. Obviously, we're going to have to get the police involved, but unfortunately our own hands aren't clean, and if the whole story came out it wouldn't do Silver Salmon any good. I've told our lot not to speak to the press but it's impossible to keep that quiet. The lads who were in the workboat were rescued by the locals anyway so we're fucked as far as keeping it out of the papers is concerned.'

'So, Aquaplaz will tell us what the score is, so we'll wait until they report back, and in the meantime I'm going to get Macbeath to ask around to see if we can find out how it was done, we can guess the who and why of it,' and with that Gunnar rang off.

Anders was exhausted with the whole Port Skean business. First there had been the petty vandalism, then the Storm Karin damage and all the fuss from the fucking environmentalists and those bastard salmon fishing

308

landowners, and then the inexplicable deaths up at the smolt farm, probably treatment issues, but who knew? and now this latest, and potentially terminal disaster. Fuck. Time for a stiff drink.

Later that afternoon a chartered helicopter flew over the farm and on the six o' clock TV news a report about the "Mysterious Damage" to the farm, along with aerial shots of the mangled tubes and a whole lot of comment about how the farm was supposed to be of a "revolutionary design etc. etc." BBC Scotland North East had even sent a reporter down to scan the deserted village for some local comment. On the pier they came across a crab fisherman called Neil who was unloading a few creels from his boat.

'Have you seen the damage to the farm, and what do you think caused it?' they enquired.

'Aye' ah wis oot ther this efternoon gettin' ma creels. There wis a bit o' damage ah could see right enough,' he said, 'I dinnae ken whit caused it, but there's always dolphins and the like oot there, ye ken. Dolphins love salmon and a ferm like that must be like a supermarket tae them. Aye, likely it was a big pod o' dolphins done it. They're gey intelligent like!'

And so that explanation, unlikely as it was, gained credence, and the next day the papers ran a story about salmon loving dolphins helping themselves to a free meal at the Port Skean Salmon farm. "Dolphin Drive Thru." read one of the headlines. There was also a stock picture of a dolphin with a salmon in its mouth and a grin on its face.

The police promised they'd make enquiries but manpower was short because of Covid and they'd got plenty on their plates hadn't they? Besides no one had been injured, it was probably the dolphins anyway, and what rudimentary enquiries they'd made drew blank looks from the very few Port Skean locals they could find down by the harbour.

Two days later, Craig was working in The Mermaid's engine compartment when he heard the scrunch of tyres and the quiet burble of a diesel exhaust on the pier to which The Mermaid was tied. Rubbing the oil from his hands with a rag he popped his head out of the hatch. It was Malc and Jim from Macbeath Security. This time they were wearing wellington boots.

They stood on the pier side and looked down at Craig. 'Mr Mackinnon,' said Malc, we wis wonderin' if w' could have a wee chat?

'Well, it'll certainly will be a wee chat,' said Craig, because ah've naething tae say to yis. But, y'd better mind the engine there, its covered in oil and ah widnae want yis tae dirty yer fancy suits now.' He pointed at the diesel engine which was on the pier side ready to be lifted back into The Mermaid. ' Aye, she's bin oot of action for the past week, and ah'm desperate tae get that engine back in tae ma boat and back oot fishin'.'

Malc and Jim looked at each other, it was an interesting tableau, the two from Macbeath Security, standing on that remote pier, their suits flapping in the stiff breeze, now sort of lost for words, their yet to be asked question answered, and the solid figure Craig on the deck of The Mermaid looking intently at them with his piercing far away eyes. 'Well,' he said,' if that's all, gentlemen, next time gie's a call and ah'll bake a cake fer yis.' And he smiled a contemptuous smile.

Jim clenched his fist and took a step forward, but there was a cough from behind. He turned round, and there was Allan. He was smiling too. Without another word the Macbeath boys got back into their BMW. As they were driving off Malc looked at Jim. 'Jist dinnae say a fuckin' word.' he hissed.

Those salmon farm workers who had not been furloughed had their work cut out making temporary repairs to the cages, and feeding the remaining salmon. They had lost at least fifty percent of their stock. Aquaplaz sent a team of with an engineer and two divers who spent a day or two carefully examining the farm both from above and below. They left, promising a detailed a report.

As the Covid crisis deepened on shore everything remained closed and Port Skean was deserted, no Easter visitors, no shops apart from food shops, no cafes. People walked their dogs and the local fishing industry continued in a restricted way. When people met while out taking their allowed exercise, the talk about the dolphins, and the salmon farm faded away after a few days. Most locals were glad about what happened and, if they thought they knew who was responsible, they kept it to themselves. Gradually, life settled into the "New Normal" that Covid 19 had brought to Port Skean, Scotland and the rest of the world.

Back at their Head Office, Silver Salmon were reviewing their East Coast operation in the light of recent events, future trends and their global strategy. A policy announcement was expected any day soon.

85

By mid April the Covid 19 lockdown was in full swing. No leaving your home unless for exercise and essential shopping. No travel unless you were classed as an essential worker. Mhairi was working flat out to make sure all the bookings for Glen Sionnach Lodge had been cancelled, deposits returned and that all the would be guests were fully aware of the situation. Robbie had spoken to Frazer when he appeared one day with some beef he'd not been able to sell. Robbie took it, it would freeze. Over a coffee and a dram they had talked about the carry on at Port Skean and had a good laugh about the dolphin story and Lachie being rescued by his mates. Frazer told him that there had been not one single visit by the Silver Salmon people to Loch Caoraich, the empty smolt pens were still floating around, the shed and office locked, still full of all the gear. 'So, they didn't change the combination then?' laughed Robbie.

'Ah widnae ken,' replied Frazer, 'ah've no been up there, and neither have you!' They both fell about. 'Ah'm taking a leaf oot o' the President Trump playbook, deny everything, it's fake news!'

'So yer wee burn is clear again, Frazer, and when aal this shite has passed y' can get back tae being organic once more.'

'Aye, that's the plan, if ah dinnae get kicked oot o' ma ferm for not peyin' the rent,' he said, suddenly serious.

'W' hev protection at the moment but ah'm not sure how lang that'll last. We'll see.' And on that solemn note he made his farewells and drove off.

Robbie was having a busy lockdown, Spring had arrived in the glen and he had quite a bit of gardening to do. Temporarily he'd shelved his writing and was spending the bulk of his time either outdoors or inside helping Mhairi with some redecorations and cleaning. They were happy in each other's company and it was a sweet time for them. Mhairi was naturally worried about Seonaid and Peter who were up at Raigmore dealing with the Covid crisis, but they seemed to be OK and Mhairi was able to have a WhatsApp video chat with them most evenings.

At lunch time on dull days he'd wander down through the gardens and along the river bank. As that part of the river ran through the estate if he were to fish, he wouldn't feel like he was breaking any of the lockdown regulations. As far as he knew there was no fishing going on at all anywhere else. He was worried about poachers who might take advantage of the empty river banks so he'd phoned up the two ancient ghillies, Davy and Tam, and said if they wanted to have a cast or two on the Sionnach Water they were welcome, and to give him a ring if they saw anything untoward. A few days later Davy had said that he'd had a couple of farmed fish, and they both wondered how many would now be in the river after the latest escapes from the Port Skean farm.

On a dull and humid lunchtime at the beginning of May Robbie thought he might try the Home Pool, he'd fish down it with the big rod, and then see if he could pick up a trout or two on the dry fly, should there be a hatch.

He started at the top of the pool, the river was at a nice height, and the air was soft. The gentle downstream wind would make his casting seem good he thought. He was fishing with a fifteen foot scandi type rod, a shooting head and a medium to fast sink tip. To the leader he tied on a big black and yellow tube. Not the most sophisticated of outfits, but pretty efficient at getting down and covering the water which was still quite cold, there being some snow left on the mountain tops.

sing his favourite Snap T cast which he'd learned from Youtube, much to Davy the ghillie's disgust, he sent the fly across the river and let it swim round in a wide arc. Halfway down the pool he got the tug tug of a fish and soon he had beached a farmed salmon of seven pounds or so. It lay on its side on the gravel in about three inches of water. After a few second's deliberation he thought he might let it go. It might not have been anything like a spring salmon, but it's spawn might produce a spring salmon. Who knew? Then he remembered recent study he'd read which suggested that hybrids had a much slimmer chance of success than native wild fish. He hit it on the head. It would make a meal he supposed, despite his reservations about what it had been fed in its caged life.

About half past twelve he noticed a few Large Olives floating down the river, looking for all the world like little sailboats, now and again there would be a splash and a trout would take one from the surface. And so he returned to the hut and assembled his little trout rod and tied on a CDC dry. This time, wading carefully, he started in the deeper water in the middle of the pool and drifted his fly along the centre crease where the current slid past the slower water of the bend. Now the rises were more frequent as the trout switched on to the hatch and it wasn't long before his fly disappeared and he was playing a lively fish about the pound mark, another soon followed. Towards the end of the pool in the deep water under the far bank he had spied a couple of solid rises and he thought there might be a bigger trout lurking there. He had to wade out quite a way to cover it, but he managed a decent cast and he held his breath while the fly floated, drag free, over the spot. There was the solid rise again and he tightened into a much heavier fish. It ran strongly upstream and jumped in a shower of silver spray. 'Bloody hell' thought Robbie, 'it's a sea trout.' He didn't get to find out though, because as often happens, for no apparent reason, the line went slack. The hook had pulled out. He felt that temporary extreme feeling of disappointment felt by fishermen the world over when they lose a good fish. 'That's the appeal of the sport, the uncertainty of it,' Robbie told himself, by way of compensation, although he was really annoyed not to have landed such a fine fish.

He fished on with the dry fly for another half an hour and took another two decent trout. Then the hatch petered out and with it the rise. He went down the pool again with the big rod but he didn't get a touch.

Walking back to the lodge, through the scented woods and gardens just beginning to come to life, he thought to himself how lucky he was to be locked down in this environment. One of the few. He shouldn't ever take all this for granted. Imagine being stuck for days on end in a high rise flat in a city with two or three kids. Christ Almighty! That was the reality for most urban dwellers. Still thinking about lockdown, he put his rods in the garage and ran up the steps to the front door. He needed a cup of tea.

86

Sir Richard Gillanders had not been in Scotland during lockdown, but, if his body was at present in a leather chair aboard MV Lucky Lassie which was presently anchored in The Rubicon Marina in Lanzarote, his heart was in the Highlands, not chasing the deer but thinking about South Skean Estate. His associates and employees were still able to take business flights around the globe, and so Sir Richard, even in these challenging times, and even though he was supposedly retired, was able to have his meetings and keep his financial empire ticking over. Also aboard were Sir Richard's wife, Yelena, and his chief accountant and his architect. The former had flown in from Guernsey, the latter from Edinburgh. Not aboard was the muscular Russian security guy, Nickoli, who had previously been helping Yelena with her exercise regime. Strangely, he had left for 'another opening back home.' Sir Richard was having a planning meeting. He was particularly keen to develop certain areas of his highland estate. He had a scheme in mind that, in time, and given a little investment and planning permissions, would maximise revenue, and also clear any unwanted tenants from his land. As usual his accountant and architect were in complete agreement: it was an excellent project.

87

Mhairi and Robbie were in their favourite place, sitting cuddled up together on a leather settee in the sun lounge. Apart from themselves there were was no one else in the lodge. Mhairi had closed it for the foreseeable. It was six o' clockish, on a sunny late afternoon towards the end of July, and there was a gin and tonic and a beer on the coffee table in front of them. Robbie was noisily eating crisps and Mhairi was scolding him for the mess on the floor.

'So, Ah think ah've become institutionalised, he said. 'This is the future: me sittin' here all day eatin' crisps and drinkin' beer, while wor lass, that's you by the way, gets on with cleaning the hoose and cookin' my dinner.'

'Well, if it is the future,' Mhairi laughed, 'it's a future that doesn't include me! Yer on yer own with that pal.' They both laughed. 'Right, on a serious note, I've got Andy Tulloch coming round tomorrow and he's going to give me a quote as to what it would cost to convert the existing suites into fully self contained apartments as we discussed. If the quote is reasonable, I'm going to give him the go ahead because I'm pretty sure he can actually start soon, and I know he's a good lad.'

'Right, that's great, the sooner we get started the better. As we've discussed on a number of occasions I'm sure there's a market for luxury apartments in a such a fantastic setting, especially as we're offering the salmon fishing as well. Older folks are going to be reluctant to travel internationally these days with Covid, and having a place to staycation in the Highlands is a great alternative I think. You could probably make more money in the long term by renting the apartments as holiday lets rather than selling them outright , but it's all regular extra hassle with organising the cleaning them etc. and frankly, w' need to enjoy life. Also, at some point, you would have to sell anyway. I suppose the service charge will cover the upkeep of the grounds and so forth. We can probably employ one or two of your existing staff for that. And, looking to our own situation, we can live in one of the apartments here if we want and if not, then we can sell it and with my house together, buy something else nearer Strathskean.'

'It's been a surreal time. You're right, this way, I'll recoup the initial investment, and we'll still have somewhere nice to live. Renting them out as holiday lets would mean a lot of work, as you say plus we don't know what the future might bring. Actually, it's the sensible thing to do, I couldn't keep on running this as a luxury country retreat forever, could I sweetheart?'

'Aye sure you could, in a few decades you'd be the only centenarian hotelier in Scotland, and I'd still be here, incontinent, demented, but still eating crisps and drinking beer!' They laughed and settled down in the settee.

88

A few days later, the weather having held up, they decided to take a run down to the coast and have a walk along the beach near Port Skean. There were a few cars parked up near the dunes, with their windscreens shining in the sun, their occupants encamped on the sand surrounded by wind breaks, picnic baskets and the like.

The tide was out and little kids ran madly on the flat wet sand, their reflections mirrored on the surface like a Jack Vettriano painting. 'Wid yiz just look at that,' said Mhairi,' her hair blowing in the breeze. 'The kids are having a great time on the beach. Mebbes things are slowly returning to normal.'

'Aye, ah hope so,' replied Robbie,'It's been the weirdest of times.' They walked on and soon they came to the small headland at the end of the beach. Next to that there was a small stone jetty, a couple of huts, and beyond that a small sandy bay. As they walked over they could see that there were a few boats tied up at there and some beached nearby, it being low water. A couple of cars were parked by the huts. They recognised the biggest boat, The Mermaid, and ambled along the jetty to see if anyone was on board.

'Aye, it's yersels,' smiled Craig, 'come aboard and ah'll make y' a cup of tea.'

So they climbed down the iron ladder on the stonework and Craig helped them aboard. Soon there was the whistle of a kettle from the wheelhouse and he brought out three mugs. They sat on the deck rails in the sunlight and sipped their tea. 'I'd gie yis a dram but it's still pretty early,' he laughed. 'How have y' been keepin' anyways?'

'We've been really good, thanks, life's simple now we don't have guests to look after.' Actually, Craig, we've decided to shut the Lodge and convert it into apartments. It was struggling anyway because of the salmon fishing, and this Covid thing has finished it off. So, we won't be consuming any of your wonderful seafood, unfortunately.' Mhairi smiled an apologetic smile.

'Ah nae worries, me and Allan are jist aboot retired anyways, w' used tae sell most of the scallops tae the local restaurants and hotels, but noo a van comes from the wholesalers along the coast and they take it all. It's much easier fer us, but a bit less satisfying like.' There was a small moment while they all looked into the distance and reflected on times past.

'So, how's yer local salmon farm doin,' Robbie said by way of breaking the silence. 'Have they got it back up and running again, what was it? Dolphins?' and he burst out laughing.

Craig looked around as if to check that there was no one within a mile radius to hear what he was saying. 'Well, ah did hear that they managed to repair some o' the cages, but some were damaged beyond repair. So the farm is less than half the size it used to be. No one here talks aboot it any mair, but the word is they ken it was us that damaged it, but they hav'nae a clue as tae how it was done. There's not a single shred of evidence. A bit like the smolt farm up at Caoraich eh? And he gave Robbie a massive wink and grin. Also, ah hev it on good authority that the polis is no interested either, they don't like the Macbeath lot, and their hands is full with other stuff as well. So, wir all just hunky dory eh.'

'Well, ah hope they continue to struggle, the bastards, but I don't think things will ever be the same again. We had the best of it, and now, mebbes, it's gone.'

'Well, y' won't believe this, but Allan's son Michael told us that he had seen a press report on the internet saying that the Silver Salmon lot had had a massive sea lice problem, and so they brought in one o' them barges which has a thing called a 'thermolicer' on board. They suck the salmon oot o' the cages and put them in a tank o' watter heated up to aboot 30 odd degrees plus. This kills the lice, but it also kills quite a few fish as well. Apparently the fish are in agony wi' it. Aye, it's true, Michael showed us the drone footage someone took o' it. It's disgustin'.'

'Well I hope that the RSPCA do something about.' replied Robbie, ' That's outrageous.'

After a few more minutes, Robbie and Mhairi said their goodbyes and climbed back on to the jetty. As they walked away Mhairi said that she thought Craig was fine. He seemed to have got beyond Wullie's death. Maybe the damage to the farm had proved something of a catharsis for him. Craig had obviously been behind the damage, but God alone knew how they'd managed it. Robbie doubted if anyone would ever find out.

They got back to the Land Rover and drove slowly back to the Glen Sionnach Lodge. Each lost in their own thoughts. Mhairi, was only just getting used to the new emptiness of the place. Her adult life had been spent in hotels with many other people living in the same building, and now she would have to adjust to a life less populated. Thank God for Robbie, had it not been for him she would have been facing all this by herself, distanced by circumstance from the real world, a bit like the Lady of

Shalott, alone in a huge tower and looking out, hoping to join in. As he drove along Robbie was thinking darker thoughts about the massive and unfeeling power of big companies like Silver Salmon, where all ethical considerations were sacrificed at the altar of profit. He looked at Mhairi and smiled, his mood lifted, he swung into the drive for Sionnach. Time for a beer and something nice to eat.

89

Late August's edition of the Strathskean Herald caused a bit of a stir, containing as it did a front page article with the headline: "Forest Park for Caoraich Glen." It started, "In an exclusive interview with the Herald Sir Richard Gillanders, the owner of South Skean Estate, reveals his multi-million pound plan for the development of the Glen." And it continued, each sentence revealing yet another outrage. There were to be dozens of "Lodges" nestling on terraces up the sides of the glen. These would be like static caravans but different, as they would be painted to blend in with the "unspoilt" wilderness of Caoraich. There was going to be a bar, shop and club area, and lots of attractions like zip wires and treetop walkways. A cycle track was to be created right around the periphery of the site taking in the loch which would itself provide opportunities for water sports. In the future there might also be a caravan and motor-home park. Dozens of jobs would be created for local people and the strath's economy would benefit hugely by the increased footfall. What was not to like? It was an ecologically sensitive development with massive advantages for the area. It was certain to go ahead, everything had been arranged. Sir Richard would be cutting the first sod in a starting ceremony in October.

'Not if I can fuckin' help it, he won't.' snarled Frazer as he read the article in the newly created beer garden at The Strath Bar.

In the town opinion was divided about the scheme. Some, mostly the young, welcomed the investment where as the older population just saw it as more disruption in an ever changing world. The talk in The Strath Bar was mostly about 'mair fuckin' low paid jobs,' and the work being outsourced to firms from the South. But a couple of local contractors were hoping to get some kind of employment out of it. They would wait and see.

Up at Caoraich Organic Farm, the mood was sombre. Frazer, already seriously worried about how he was going to pay the increased rent was stunned by the news. He was in a state of shock. With Elsie's help he'd got the complete planning proposal from the internet. The buildings that were at present Caoraich Farm, the actual buildings that were his home now, were going to be converted into the Forest Park Centre. Elsie was in tears, life as she knew it was about to come to come to an end. Thank God her kids were all elsewhere and it was just the two of them to consider. She was worried sick, too, that Frazer would do something deranged by way of retaliation. She was right, he would.

As in times past, Frazer went down to the Caoraich burn to think things through. There was a pool down there in the green shaded coolness of the glen that was quite special to him. The water tumbled down over a short set of rapids into a deep dark glide which undercut the bank and on top of that was an ancient Scots pine with monstrous roots like twisted limbs. There was a little bank on which he sat, and he could see the whole of the pool. Often, he'd be lulled into a kind of reverie by the soothing noise of the water over the stones and the hum of insects around. He'd like to think that he was the only human ever to have sat by that pool, such was its seclusion. On one occasion when he had been sitting in his usual silence and stillness, an otter with her three kits in tow swam up the length of the pool, and they slipped past him like brown sinuous water snakes, not realising he was there. And now this world, his world, this tiny unchanged world, would soon be gone forever.

As he sat there, a thought came to him, and now he knew exactly what he was going to do.

A couple of days later the little red post van rattled up to the farmhouse and delivered an important looking package to the door. Frazer picked it up and, noticing the South Skean Estates embossment, with a contemptuous curl of his lip, tore it open. Elsie as usual, was on hand to decipher the contents. 'Well, in short, Fraz, it says that wiv got tae get oot by the end o' October. That's when they're starting tae build. They're offerin' us anither hoose way up on the ither side o' the estate up at Fasach. It's that wan on the moor at the end o' the track. It's at the back o' beyond. And, there's nae grazing or buildings for wir beasts. Wir done for!' And she put her head against his chest, her body racked with sobs and he felt the wetness of her tears through his shirt.

Frazer was quite calm, his decision made, there was, in his mind, no going back. 'Well, wir not movin' darlin',' ' he said, 'they will hev to pull oor bodies oot o' the rubble.' Ah'm steyin' put!' '

Over the next day or two, he had two phone calls that were not from his immediate family. The first, predictably, was from Robbie worried that he might do something deranged. How right he was, thought Frazer. But, it was his fight now, so he just told Robbie that he had accepted the inevitable and would probably be moving out of

Caoraich soon. Robbie didn't believe a word of it, but decided to hold his tongue. The second call was from Craig and he was offering his support, but again Frazer said that he had accepted that things didn't always work out the way you wanted them to. Craig said that if ever he changed his mind and wanted to take some kind of action that was more active than passive, if Frazer got his drift, then he would be more than willing to help. Frazer thanked him and said that he'd be in touch if he ever decided to move in that direction. Craig didn't believe a word of it either.

90

The late summer sun warmed the beautiful, red,yellow and blue waterfront apartments and houses of Alesund in Norway's fjord region. The days were still quite long and the winter darkness was at least a couple of months off. This same sun shone into the board room of the Silver Salmon company where a long and, at times, painful meeting was going on. The polished table was littered with trays of coffee cups, water glasses and sheaves of papers while around the table the executives were seated, their individual body language betraying their feelings: resignation, anger for one, and in the case of the rest, excitement and relief.

Dr. Gunnar Hendriksson, the C.E.O., the company's chief accountant, and all of the major stake holders had backed a complete restructuring of their whole operation. To be closed down with immediate effect was the damaged and loss making Scottish East Coast farm at Port Skean, the smolt farm up at Caoraich, [where the fuck was that anyway?] and a couple of smaller processing installations along that coast. All the redundant kit, including the work boats and feed barge, was to be moved round to support the West Coast where the operation was still well in profit despite the usual losses caused by lice and disease. The thermolicer idea had been quietly dumped. It was unfortunate that the operation had been filmed. But good news was on the horizon.

Huge amounts of finance had been raised to develop three new initiatives. The first was an on land system where the water was recycled known as a Recirculating Aquaculture System or RAS. This would be used to bring on millions of smolts which would then go to one of the Deep Ocean Farms, now being developed by Aquaplaz, or the brand new five hundred metre ocean going vessel, The Silver Leaper, that could grow ten thousand tonnes of salmon at a time. This was nearing completion in a Chinese shipyard as they spoke and would be ready to take the first salmon early in the Spring. This was all excellent news for the company but not for Anders or his deputy Roddy , the unlucky managers of the East Coast Port Skean salmon operation, who now, apparently, didn't have jobs. Whether it was excellent news for the environment was also a moot point.

The meeting broke up and most repaired to a local hotel for a drink and a meal. Gunnar had stayed behind to prepare a press release and arrange a TV interview. He'd had to listen to Anders who was understandably pissed off at the closure of the East Coast operation. 'You've let those Scottish bastards get away with destroying thousands and thousands Krones' worth of equipment , not to mention my job and the jobs of the shore workers.'

Gunnar shrugged his huge shoulders. Privately, he, Gunnar, didn't give a fuck. He was only interested in the money. Sorry, he'd said to Anders, that was how it worked. Big business. Anders should have realised that. Nothing personal. Why should he worry anyway? He'd get a decent payout and a good reference. See you mate.

The news about the closure of the Port Skean salmon farm took a while to filter through to the local press, and there was a fairly even-handed article in the Strathskean Herald about the economic loss to the area, balanced against the environmental gain. Privately the fisher folk of Port Skean were delighted, they'd already detected an improvement in water quality and were hoping that their fishing grounds would recover soon. Apart from moving the equipment there weren't any immediate plans to dismantle the onshore base, and there was still some discussion as to who was going to remove the farm. In the interim, plastic waste washed loose from the cages and piled up along the beaches of the Firth.

Further up the Strath, the river fishers were pleased that the hated fish farm was no more, but less optimistic about a recovery. It would take years, they thought, for the run of salmon to re-establish itself. But you never knew, did you? Meanwhile they would continue to fish their favourite pools in a Proustian remembrance of times past.

91

Late summer, early autumn, and Sir Richard Gillanders was pre occupied with his next "Big Thing," which was, of course, his ongoing plans for a Forest Park at Glen

Caoraich. He'd flown back to Inverness from Funchal, Madeira, where he'd thought he'd left his lovely wife Yelena happily aboard The Lucky Lassie. Actually, she had barely spoken to him for several days. Not that he'd noticed.   She had been bored shitless. The restrictions imposed on her by Covid were inconvenient, "For the little people, Darling," and although she would not have told him to his face, he was extremely disappointing in the bedroom. She was missing her physical work outs with her Russian security guy Nikoli. So it was entirely predicable that within a day of his departure to Scotland she had taken herself off to Moscow to visit her relatives, so she said, and do some shopping. When he heard that she had gone, he wasn't unduly worried. Fuck her, she could go, he thought, he was sick of her moaning, she was getting to be hard work. He'd ask one of his Russian guys to keep an eye on what she was doing.

For a few days then, he was in residence up at South Skean Lodge all by himself, the redoubtable Mrs Carmichael now only being there during the day, because of her needing to look after her ailing father. Then there was Donaldson, who was hardly around any more and who had grown increasingly surly since the stalking and grouse shooting this year had not been organised to his exacting standards. He was going to meet with a couple of contractors, but the manager of his property company, Steve, was handling most of that. The plans were well advanced. He'd heard nothing from Steve about when that mad farmer chappie was going to move out of the farmhouse. He might need a reminder. He was interested in moving forward with his plans. He would be back on his yacht soon enough.

That evening alone in the Lodge, he finished the meal that Mrs Carmichael had left for him in the oven, and very good it was too, if you liked traditional Scottish cooking. The rhubarb crumble was to die for, and mince and tatties were not on the menu at the kind of restaurants he usually frequented. He piled the dishes on a tray and took them through to the kitchen. He carefully scraped the plates and put them in the dishwasher. Moving to the cupboard above the long granite work top he took out a bottle of twenty five year old, non chill-filtered, cask strength Strathskean. He poured a generous amount into a cut glass whisky tumbler and added a tiny drop of water. He took a sip and rolled the exquisite liquid round his mouth.

He opened the back door of the kitchen and moved on to the rear south facing lawn. The air was still and cool, the light fading as the sun dipped behind the mountains, leaving a pinky cobalt sky. He stood at the edge of the lawn enjoying the view, the stillness, the scent of heather and myrtle, and the taste of the whisky in his mouth.

The next morning, a little later than her usual nine o' clock start, Mrs Carmichael parked her old Ford Focus at the front of South Skean Lodge. Sir Richard's Range Rover was nowhere in sight. He must be out, she thought to herself. It was odd, but not particularly surprising that he hadn't mentioned it. In fact there was little communication between herself and Sir Richard. As far as he was concerned she was the ideal servant, reliable, anonymous, deferential. Not like Donaldson. She unlocked the front door, went through to the kitchen to start her daily routine of hoovering and generally tiding up. She was pleased to see that he'd put the dishes in the dishwasher, but tutted at the bottle of whisky left out on the work top. Upstairs, she was surprised to see that his bed had not been slept in. However, as Sir Richard had made abundantly clear, the comings and goings of her employer were absolutely no concern of hers. She made sure everything was clean, neat and tidy, and later that afternoon locked the front door and returned to her own house in Strathskean, where her father was noisily demanding his tea. He was a bit of a handful now his dementia had worsened.

92

Steve, the manager of Gillanders Properties, was getting concerned. He had tried to contact his employer, there were a few pressing issues: contracts to sign, decisions on details required. It was very difficult to know what to do now. He didn't know who to contact. Sir Richard had compartmentalised his businesses very successfully. He was the only one with the overview. None of his businesses were interlinked. They didn't really know who was in the extended family so to speak.

So it was a few days later that some one finally managed to reach Yelena. Where was her husband? As far as she knew he was in Scotland, at that barn of a shooting lodge, Strath something or other. She was having a nice time in Moscow. She had seen her family, caught up with some friends of her own age, and been to a nightclub or two. She had not been able to track down Nicoli, but she had a new personal trainer called Alex. She enjoyed exercising with him. Life was not so boring now. Having to sort out her crustacean husband was irritating and damned inconvenient. Then one of her brothers arrived from London. He said that Sir Richard had apparently disappeared, no one knew of his whereabouts, he had not been seen for days now. What was she thinking of? She had to get her arse into gear. Those bank

accounts needed to be secured. Their family's future
wealth depended on it.

93

Two days earlier...

As Frazer saw it circumstance had handed him an
opportunity. He'd been in the beer garden of the Strath
Bar when Donaldson had arrived needing a pint and a
chaser. He bought him both, a nod to a past blind eye.
Donaldson needed to unload. Frazer was an ideal listener.
He understood, he agreed. He, Donaldson, was very proud
of what he did, that is, he managed the grouse shooting
and the stalking on the South Skean Estate. It was a short
enough season anyway, wasn't it? and now the new
owner, Sir Richard, who was there by himself in that huge
lodge, seemingly hadn't the slightest interest in the
shooting, the estate or anything other than developing
his proposed Forest Park in Caoraich, and what would
that do to the stalking and grouse shooting? In
Donaldson's opinion the whole nature of the strath would
be changed. More visitors, more disturbance, all those
people previously flying off to Spain, now coming up here

for camping holidays. He went on with his rant. Frazer bought him another dram.

At about nine thirty pm the next evening, with the sun having dipped below the Cairgorms, and the sky a light cobalt blue and pink hued, the back door to South Skean Lodge opened, and a rectangle of yellow light illuminated the lawn. The smallish, slim, middle aged figure of Sir Richard Gillanders stepped out onto the grass, a whisky glass in his hand. He walked to the edge of the lawn and stood for a moment, completely still as if in a pose, semi silhouetted in the gloaming.

In the night sight of Frazer's Remington .308, every detail was clear. It would be a longish shot, but he didn't have to make any allowances for the wind. Emotionless, calm, certain, he held his breath and squeezed the trigger. Boof! The figure threw its hands in the air and collapsed in an untidy sprawl at the edge of the lawn. Silence. And then a pigeon clapped away from a nearby tree, and somewhere in the dusk a pheasant called.

Frazer waited for a few minutes. He had to execute his plan exactly. He replaced the Remington in its case, first of all making sure he had the spent cartridge. Then, shouldering the case and his bag, he walked carefully down the brae towards the back of the lodge. The remoteness of the location made it highly unlikely that anyone would have witnessed the collapse of Sir Richard, but, you never knew. Besides, Frazer had learned over the years, if you are doing a bit of poaching and you rush things, that's when you make a mistake. Keep a calm sough. A few minutes later he walked up to the body of Sir Richard. He was definitely dead. His eyes had glazed over already and a smear of blood seeped from his mouth.

Pulling on a pair of gloves, Frazer took a large sheet of polythene from his bag and laid it out on the grass. Without apparent effort he lifted the limp, warm body, and holding it in his arms as if he were offering some sort of sacrifice, carefully arranged it on the polythene and then wrapped it, securing the package with gaffer tape. It took him a little while to find the whisky glass which he put in his bag and then he quickly surveyed the area. The only evidence he could see was a dark stain of blood on the grass. Out of his bag he took a partially dismembered rabbit and left it on the stain. He made sure that some of its fur was entangled in the grass.

Moving swiftly now, he picked up his package and went round the side of the lodge where he left it near the front door. Then he returned to the back and went into the kitchen locking the back door behind him. Swiftly he moved through the house to the study where he picked up a set of car keys, a mobile phone, a laptop and a wallet which he had found in the desk drawer.

He locked the front door and, opening Sir Richard's Range Rover with the remote, he manhandled the polythene wrapped corpse into the boot. Taking one last long look round, he climbed into the driver's seat, pushed it back a good ten inches and started it the engine. Fifteen minutes later he was on the A9 heading South.

Frazer needed to establish the idea that Sir Richard had driven somewhere away from Strathskean, and so he had decided to drive down the A9 for a few miles at well above the speed limit, and hope that the average speed cameras would flag up the offence. It was the riskiest part of the whole thing he thought. What happens if... A myriad disaster scenarios swirled round his head. Keep focussed, keep focussed, he repeated to himself.

After a good few miles at an average speed of eighty miles an hour he felt that he had gone past enough cameras. They must be working, judging by the weekly reports in the local paper: drivers named, shamed and fined, excess speeds recorded for friends to laugh at. There were only a few other vehicles about, mostly lorries. No police. It was with considerable relief that he turned off the A9 just south of Dalwhinnie. There was a convoluted way back to Strathskean on single track roads over the hills. It would take well over an hour and a half to get back.

The Range Rover was a beautiful car to drive he thought. Fully automatic and powerful. Smooth even on these twisty roads. It seemed a shame to do what he was about to do to it. It must be worth about fifty thou, top of the range, but driven by a complete.... he didn't finish the thought. He had arrived at his first destination. Off the B road was a little turning into some birch woods, way out in the scrubby hinterland north of Deeside. He parked up and opened the tailgate, and again, effortlessly, he removed and flung over his shoulder the package containing the earthly remains of Sir Richard, as he had now started to call him in his own mind, in a sort of ironical hypocritical sham deference to the corpse. He walked up the track a little way, it was now early in the morning and the light was becoming imperceptibly stronger and he could distinguish the individual shapes of bushes and trees.

Soon he came to a nameless wee lochan, whose waters were as black and deep as sin, as he'd once found out when he'd been out on one of his expeditions and had tried to wade in to cool off on a hot summer's day. He stopped by the remnants of a dyke or stone wall. Taking a penknife and some binder twine from his pocket, he made a slit in the package into which he jammed as many of the stones as would fit and then he bound up the package with the twine so it looked like a grotesque mummy. He shoved the whole thing as far as he could out into the lochan. It sank quickly, front first, in the manner of a torpedoed tanker. The binder twine was made from polypropylene and wouldn't rot, so, with any luck, the polythene shrouded and trussed corpse of Sir Richard would lay undisturbed for aeons in the black anoxic gloop. A fitting resting place he thought. He felt no guilt, no remorse, no emotion. As a final gesture of remembrance he stamped viciously on Sir Richard's mobile phone and chucked it out into the middle.

Dawn had just about broken by the time he reached Caoraich farm. He'd have to get a move on. He drove up through the farmyard and out onto the back field behind the byre. There was a large mound of earth by his tractor which had a digger attachment, and behind the byre, out of sight in the corner of the field was a large hole. It had a sloping entrance. He drove the Range Rover in, opened all the windows and the sun roof and, having checked Sir Richard's laptop and wallet were on the backseat, climbed out. Walking over to the tractor he started it up and commenced the not inconsiderable task of refilling the hole. Satisfied with his efforts he ran the tractor over the area a few times before returning to the farmhouse where Elsie was waiting, Lady Macbeth like, for an account of the night's work.

Later that morning, mostly, but not completely, refreshed by a few hours sleep, still completely calm, and using his tractor, he shovelled a few tonnes of his 'organic' manure over the recently dug earth. And then, as a final disincentive to any potential investigations, he moved his bull into the field and made sure it had plenty of hay to munch on in that corner.

Elsie and he had agreed, that in the event of the eviction going ahead, that they were just going to sit it out, refuse to move, and if necessary barricade themselves in the house. Now that Sir Richard had "disappeared" they were hoping for, at the very least, a stay of execution, if that was an appropriate term under the circumstances. They would say nothing, deny everything, and await events.

94

A day or two later still, a reluctant and sulky Yelena, at the urging of Caspar, her elder brother, had flown back to Funchal and was now back aboard The Lucky Lassie. Specifically she was looking for any details of her husband's accounts, passwords, anything really. She knew he had accounts off shore in all the traditional places. He was clever, and he had brought a new meaning to the expression, "concealing one's assets."

At some point the British press had got hold of the story. "Billionaire in Mystery Disappearance," was the way most headlines went, plus there were lots of glamorous pictures of Yelena spread out across their front pages. Some of the more serious papers had conducted an analysis of his business affairs and concluded that he was in financial trouble and he might have had to cut and run. The tabloids had conducted an analysis of his other affairs, complete with pictures of previous female celebrity associates. The Russian connection was heavily commented on and there was speculation that he'd fallen out with his Russian relatives who had decided that his usefulness had come to an end.

Police Scotland had concluded that Sir Richard's car had sped southwards, probably down to Edinburgh , and were now asking colleagues there to progress the enquiry.

In Strathskean, for some, the concern was for the viability of the proposed Forest Park up at Caoraich. Local firms had put in tenders. Gillanders Properties manager, Steven Bain, had given an interview where he'd claimed everything was still secure, the project was fine, but he'd had to lie through his teeth. Vital contracts still hadn't been signed and there were consultancy fees owing. There was little money in the firm's accounts. Sir Richard had moved most of it. By the end of that week he was reluctantly admitting that, should Sir Richard not resurface, there was a distinct possibility that he would have to temporarily close the business, there being no money to pay the wages. He did not know that, weighed down as he was by about thirty pounds of granite stones, there was literally no immediate chance of Sir Richard resurfacing.

Back on The Lucky Lassie, Yelena, Yuri and Caspar were having a meeting. They did not yet understand what had happened to Dicky as they called him. Nobody knew anything. They had been able to locate and access some of his assets, but the whereabouts of the larger extent of his vast wealth was unknown. Like the dark side of the moon it certainly existed, but it was presently mysterious and frustratingly unattainable. It was essential that they retrieve his laptop, they knew that it was bound to contain his codes and passwords. So it was decided that Yuri and Caspar would start again at South Skean Lodge and see what they could find. Maybe they should talk to the locals as well.

95

Frazer, dispite his initial sang-froid, had become increasingly disturbed by what he had done. No matter how much he had tried to justify his actions, he couldn't escape his feelings of guilt. He was in a state of heightened vigilance, awaiting a knock on the door. He spent hours either keeping an eye on the track up to his farmhouse, or wandering alone in the Glen, reliving his childhood. Othertimes, he'd take himself off with a bottle, and achieve a temporary peace of mind that way.

If Elsie was concerned she didn't show it, and in her frequent communications with the family, all now mercifully far away and settled, she presented a calm 'everything's fine' face. She was hoping that things would settle down with time. Actually, when she thought about it, nothing had really been resolved, had it? Hadn't they just kind of delayed the inevitable? At some point the extortionate rent still had to be payed. That was what might finish them in the end.

96

The hired Discovery pulled up outside South Skean Lodge. Yuri and Caspar stepped out. It was a grey autumn day. There was a cold wind blowing off the hills, and brown leaves whirled around the around the drive. The Lodge was already showing signs of negelect. It had that empty look, with weeds poking through the gravel on the driveway and grass uncut. They had talked about putting it on the market, but until things had resolved themselves, they weren't legally able to. In the meantime it would just slowly deteriorate.

They'd arranged to meet Donaldson, they wanted to find out if he could throw any more light on the strange disappearance of their brother in law. Donaldson drew up a few minutes later in his pick up. The interview was short. Donaldson answered their questions in his nearly incomprehensible accent. They struggled manfully to decipher the stream of strange Scottish sounds but they but they got the gist. He'd not been around when Sir Richard had left. There was nothing for him to do was there? No stalking had been arranged and he was owed wages anyway. And, to the point, when might his cash be forthcoming? He hadn't a clue about what Sir Richard may or may not have done with his laptop. If it wasn't in the house then he presumably had taken it with him. He'd not been in the house himself except for the kitchen and the servants' bit. Ask Mrs Carmichael. He got back in his pickup and drove off. Fuck them. He could have told them about the previous episode with their countrymen, or the smear of blood on the back lawn he'd found, both of which might have pointed them in Frazer's direction, but, hopefully they'd sell the estate to someone who wanted to use it for what it was intended.

Yuri and Caspar made a thorough search of the Lodge, but it was clear that there was nothing there that would shed any light on the disappearance. More importantly there was nothing there that would shed any light on his finances. They went back to their hotel to think things through. Maybe all the account numbers and passwords were in Sir Richard's head. Just maybe, they would never appear.

Later that evening they went to see Mrs Carmichael. They left none the wiser, she had been distracted by the interruptions of her demented father who seemed to think that Yuri and Caspar were his long dead brothers.

The next day they decided to pay Frazer a visit. He had been the one who had kicked up all the fuss about the rent increases, he was the author of all that unfavourable publicity. Maybe he knew something.

The Discovery turned up from the main road onto the track to Caoraich Organic Farm it was if they were entering another reality. A fantasy land in a Netflix movie. Grey. Wet. Windy. They pulled into the farm yard, the far end was full of noisily moving cattle, and the ground underneath their wheels a slurry of straw and cowshit. They stepped out of the car being careful as to where they stood. In the middle of it all was Frazer, a wild, wind whipped ginger haired colossus. He was wearing boots and filthy, stained overalls. He had a long staff in his hand and was directing his cattle with it. He looked like some supernatural figure from an alien kingdom. He stopped what he was doing and fixed them with his piercing blue eyes. 'Whit can a dae fer you two fine gentlemen?' Each word pronounced succinctly, and with an unmistakable undertone of menace.

They looked at him and then each other. 'If you can spare a moment Mr Ross, we have some questions about Sir Richard Gillanders for you. He is married to our sister, Yelena and we are naturally worried about him.' Yuri's English was precise, accented.

'Aye, mebbes y'have, and ah ken yir worried, but ah'm nae sure ah can help yis. Y' see ah nivver actually met the man. Ah did hev a lot tae say aboot the rent increases like, but ah only spoke tae that wee twat Steve Bain. As far as ah ken he wis nivver up here at a'. Sorry, ah can't help you boys more.'

And he looked at them as if to say, 'Is that all gentlemen? On yir way.'

The noise and the movement of the beasts behind him grew more intense, and he turned around to control them. When he looked again the Discovery and its occupants had gone.

97

The following Spring came, and Mhairi and Robbie were in the middle of the rearrangement of Glen Sionnach Lodge. They had decided to divide it up into six apartments, each with fishing rights. They had spent quite a bit of time with their lawyers making sure that the prospective purchasers were aware of certain restrictions as to its use, they didn't want it turned into a party house for example. Robbie had been keen to have the fishing controlled, each apartment having a maximum of two rods, not transferrable , strictly fly only.

And so, it being a fine warm day towards the end of March, Robbie was minded to take a stroll down to the riverside. He took with him his fifteen foot scandi rod and his usual early season kit. Although the air was warm, nature had not quite started to burst forth yet, nevertheless, it was nice to be outside, a hint of warmth on one's face, and the prospect of wetting a line.

He stopped at the ancient fishing hut, with its grey slatted timbers and rusty red corrugated roof. He sat on the steps and pulled on hs waders, fastened his belt, and, rod in one hand and wading stick in the other, entered the water. Soon he was sending his black and yellow tube fly right across the pool, and he visualised it swinging seductively around a few inches off the bottom.

He did not really expect to catch anything, the spring run being a thing of the previous century, but one never knew. His mind was clear, absorbed in the moment, that almost trance like state of peace, of calm, that comes with the rythmic casting, the water, the riverbank.

Halfway down the pool, there was that electric tug, tug and he was into a fish of some sort. It felt heavy but slow, probably a farmed fish. Soon he had drawn it into the shallows where it lay on its side on the gravel in a couple of inches of water. It was a silvery, long, thin male kelt. It probably would have weighed in excess of twenty pounds when it came into the river, he thought. Now it's done what it came to do and it's trying to get back to sea to have another go. Hope it makes it. Think of the odds against. Carefully, and without taking it out of the water, he removed the fly and, holding it facing the current cradled it while it regained its strength. A minute later its tail began to beat and it swam slowly off and was soon lost to sight.

He sat on the bank in the weak spring sun with the river sliding by, and thought that in some way he and Mhairi were a bit like a couple of well mended kelts, not leaping about in youthful abandon like salmon fresh in from the tide, those days had long gone, but having a second go at happiness nevertheless.

National Libraries Ireland Catalog
Registers
St. Patricks

Printed in Great Britain
by Amazon